what i came to tell you

Tommy Hays

SCHOLASTIC INC.

ISBN 978-0-545-69222-9

12 11 10 9 8 7 6 5 4 3 2   14 15 16 17 18 19/0

Printed in the U.S.A.   40

First Scholastic printing, March 2014

CONTENTS

CHAPTER ONE

NOT HIM AGAIN

Before their mother became Buddhist, she would take Grover and his sister to the First Presbyterian Church downtown. The minister talked about God being everywhere—*omnipresent* was the word he liked to use. But what Grover believed more and more, if you could call it believing, was the omnipresence of absence, the everywhere of gone.

The feeling was with Grover as he and his sister, Sudie, walked out of the Bamboo Forest and headed up Edgemont Road toward the cemetery. Between them, they carried a stiff weaving that glinted with autumn leaves Grover had carefully worked between tied sections of bamboo. Biscuit, their little mutt dog, followed them. It was a chilly Saturday afternoon in October, six months and two days since the dog's leash had snapped and sent Grover's family reeling.

The cool breeze picked up, tugging on the weaving. Grover glanced at Sudie to make sure she had a good grip. Lately it had seemed that his sister, who had turned ten in September, looked more and more like their mother—with her high cheekbones and winter blue eyes. Grover, who was twelve, knew all too well that he'd been looking more and more like their father. Whenever he found himself in front of a mirror, he saw a skinny, stoop-shouldered kid weighed down by his father's caterpillar eyebrows.

A sudden gust of wind pushed on the weaving.

"Hold on," Grover said.

Sudie held her end with both hands. Grover's eyes lingered on his sister's face. The first sign of tears and he was taking her right back to the house.

"What?" she asked.

"Nothing."

The wind died the moment they entered the wrought iron cemetery gates, as if they'd stepped into a room. Riverside, the city's oldest cemetery, was where the writer Thomas Wolfe was buried. Wolfe, who some people—especially if they weren't from Asheville—hadn't heard of, had once been as famous as Ernest Hemingway or William Faulkner or F. Scott Fitzgerald. He'd written several long books, the most famous being *Look Homeward, Angel.*

Riverside was also where, twenty years ago, Grover's parents had met. Grover's father had been a tour guide for the Thomas Wolfe house before he became its director. Grover's mother had been a student in a college English class that was studying Wolfe's novels, and their father had taken them on a tour of Riverside.

If it wasn't for Thomas Wolfe, their father liked to remind Grover and Sudie, they wouldn't even exist. Grover's parents had held their wedding in Riverside and bought an old house on the edge of the cemetery. Their father had wanted to be close to Wolfe and all the other historic graves. Their mother had liked the view from their large upstairs bedroom window. More like a park with headstones, Riverside stretched across eighty-seven acres of rolling hills and thick-trunked oaks and tulip poplars. Their mother had set up her little Buddhist altar so that every morning, as she meditated, she looked out on the cemetery.

Carrying the weaving, Grover and Sudie walked over one hill, passing the Jewish section. They heard the scrape of a shovel. A man with long gray hair, a beard and a battered hat was digging a hole. A sapling rested on the ground, its root ball in a burlap sack. Grover recognized the fan-shaped gingko leaves.

"Another one?" The man set down his shovel and came over to look at Grover's weaving, which they had rested gently on the ground. He squatted down, looking it over closely. Jessie, a landscaper, did a lot of work for the cemetery and lived three doors down from Grover's family. He'd become close friends with Grover's parents long before Grover was ever born. Sometimes Grover went on jobs with Jessie, helping him weed or plant shrubs or mulch flower beds. Jessie told wild stories about growing up poor in Charleston. He had a way about him that made Grover think of Yoda, Yoda with a Southern accent.

Jessie walked around to the other side with Biscuit following him. "Some intricate work here."

— 3

Grover felt his face heat up with embarrassment. He respected Jessie's opinion.

Biscuit sniffed the weaving.

"It'll look good with the others," Jessie said. "I went to straighten up over there a little bit this morning but I saw that you beat me to it."

Grover shook his head. "I haven't straightened it."

"Me neither," Sudie said.

"Oh, I bet it was Matthew," Jessie said. "He's my new assistant. I've got him working over in that area this morning." Jessie often hired assistants from the University of North Carolina Asheville to help him part-time. "Has your daddy seen this one?" Jessie nodded at the weaving.

"He's at the office," Sudie said.

"As usual," Grover couldn't help adding. Their father had always gone over to the Thomas Wolfe house on Saturdays and sometimes Sundays to catch up on paperwork. What surprised Grover was that he'd started back working weekends only a couple of weeks after the accident. At first he thought it was his father's way of dealing with it all, throwing himself into his work. But lately, he'd kept even longer hours. From overheard conversations, Grover had gathered that the Wolfe house was in some kind of trouble. So he couldn't tell where his father's sadness stopped and his worry about the Wolfe house started.

"Your father has a big job," Jessie said. "A lot of people count on him."

It was something their mother used to say when their father

didn't show up for a soccer game or Meet Your Teacher Night or the Fall Fling. Grover picked up the weaving and walked away.

Sudie ran after Grover with Biscuit behind her. She took up her end of the weaving. They passed a worn headstone with a little statue of a lamb curled up on it. A lamb or any kind of animal meant a child's grave. *Lily Starbuck 1910–1918.* Grover'd noticed many graves of people who'd died in 1918. Their father'd said a lot of people had died then because of the Spanish flu, spread by soldiers coming back from World War I.

At the top of the hill was Thomas Wolfe's grave, surrounded by his family's graves—his mother, his father and his brothers and sisters.

Wolfe's marker read—

TOM
SON OF
W.O. AND JULIA E.
WOLFE
A BELOVED AMERICAN AUTHOR
OCT. 3, 1900—SEPT. 15, 1938
"THE LAST VOYAGE, THE LONGEST, THE BEST."
LOOK HOMEWARD ANGEL

A couple of folded notes rested on the bottom ledge of Wolfe's marker. People often left cards and even letters to Wolfe. The notes usually praised his books. Sometimes there'd be a note from someone sounding desperate—their boyfriend had just broken up with them, or their wife had cancer, or their father had died of a heart attack.

Grover and Sudie arrived at the Johnston family plot, mostly old, worn, gray markers, some newer-looking than others. Their grandparents, their father's parents, were buried here. Great-aunts and uncles. A white marble marker gleamed in one corner. Propped against the marker were all sizes of bamboo weavings with leaves and grasses and bark woven together. The first ones were the smallest. They'd faded and started to come unraveled. Not really aware he was doing it, Grover had made each weaving a little bigger. They leaned against all sides of the grave marker, covering everything but the inscription.

JEAN CAROLINE JOHNSTON

MARCH 10, 1967—APRIL 6, 2011

"WE ARE NOT WHAT WE THINK"—THE BUDDHA

More weavings covered the ground around the marker, like a gigantic quilt. Sudie helped Grover move the most recent weavings to the side and set the new one at the foot of the marker.

Several plots away, a man in a green Army jacket raked around several headstones. Grover guessed this was Matthew, Jessie's new assistant.

"She'll like your new weaving," Sudie said, resting her hand on the marker.

Grover watched his sister's face darken.

"Now you said . . ."

"I know. I won't . . ." Her lip trembled.

"We better go," Grover said, starting to take his sister's hand, but she jerked away.

"God is stupid!" Sudie said.

Grover sighed. "Not Him again."

"Well, He is!" she said louder. "If He can't think of anything better than having everybody die in the end!"

Crows lifted from a leafless dogwood, and Matthew had stopped raking and was looking in their direction. He was chubby, pale, and wore thick-lensed black-framed glasses.

"Keep your voice down," Grover said.

"Well, God *is* stupid," Sudie said, "and I don't care who hears it!" Her shoulders slumped and she sank down on the ground beside their mother's headstone. She clutched a tiny silver cylinder that hung from a necklace that she never took off. Grover had kept his in his dresser drawer.

He sat down beside his sister but didn't say anything.

Sudie wiped her nose on her coat sleeve. "It just seems so . . ." Then she said softly, "Stupid."

"You won't get any argument from me," Grover said.

"Is that how come you don't believe in God?" Sudie asked, petting Biscuit.

"Partly," Grover said. *Mostly* is what he should've said. *Mostly* he didn't believe in God because their mother was dead. Since then he'd paid closer attention in school when they'd studied the slaughter of the Indians, the horrors of slavery, the nightmare of the Holocaust, the bombing of Hiroshima, not to mention all the wars that ever were. The evidence had been there all along; he'd just been too happy to see it.

"I've been dreaming again." Sudie was looking at the headstone, her eyes rimmed in red.

"Same dream?" he asked.

"Daddy pulls over, asks Mama if she wants a ride, and she gets in the car with us and I think everything is going to be okay. She climbs into the backseat between you and me, holding our hands. Daddy drives home, turns onto Edgemont, pulls in front of the house. I turn around . . ."

". . . and she's gone," he said in an almost bored tone.

"I've had that dream a hundred times," she said. "Every time I tell myself, *this* time, *this* time, I'm going to hold her hand tighter."

"Sudie, nobody can hold that tight."

She bit her lip and for a minute Grover worried she might start sniffling again. He hated when she cried, when anybody cried, for that matter. He never knew what to do.

"My butt's getting cold," Grover said, standing up. "Let's go home."

Sudie looked up at him.

"Come on." He motioned for her to stand. "Maybe *This Old House* is on."

"That doesn't come on till three," she said, getting up. "*The New Yankee Workshop* is on right now."

The only TV channel they'd ever been able to get with their antennae was public TV. Their mother had never allowed cable.

Never allowed them to play video games. Never allowed them to have a computer in the house. She believed children were losing the ability to entertain themselves. She said it was something she'd noticed over the years at her job. But her rules went for their father too. He had to leave his laptop at the office. One of the biggest fights Grover could remember his parents ever having, and they didn't have many, happened on a night when their father had smuggled his laptop into the house, and their mother had caught him in the kitchen late at night checking his e-mail.

They found Jessie trying to lift the sapling with its heavy root ball. He looked at Sudie, who was still sniffling a little bit.

"Can y'all help me tote this to the hole?"

Sudie nodded, and the three of them lifted the sapling and set it into the hole. "I'll take it from here," he said, shoveling dirt around it.

Sudie and Grover walked out of the cemetery entrance with Biscuit leading the way, and as they did, the wind picked back up. They were passing by the Bamboo Forest when Sudie stopped. "Do you think God's mad at me for calling Him stupid?"

"If there is a God," Grover said, "He'd be a pretty sorry one to get bent out of shape because some girl in a little town in the middle of nowhere called Him stupid."

"I'm not some girl," Sudie said. "I'm Sudie Johnston, and this isn't the middle of nowhere. It's Asheville, North Carolina."

"If God spent His time jumping on people every time somebody called Him something," Grover said, "He'd never get anything done."

Grover was relieved his sister didn't say anything else. These God talks tired him out. With their mother dead and their father gone so much, Grover needed Sudie to believe in God. It took some pressure off him. Also, a microscopic cell of himself wondered if he was wrong, if maybe there was a God. Even if he couldn't manage to believe, he liked to think that his sister believed enough for the both of them.

CHAPTER TWO

NO ONE LEFT TO BLAME

On a Saturday morning one week later Grover smelled the sandalwood. He'd been working on a new weaving in his workshop in the Bamboo Forest. He'd reached into the shoebox and pulled out a bloodred sugar maple leaf. He carefully worked it in with the other leaves, then stepped back, blew into his hands to warm his fingers and looked at his work.

He breathed in. There it was. The unmistakable sweet smoky smell. His mother had burned sandalwood incense every morning at her altar upstairs. He looked around but saw nothing except bamboo. He pictured how it used to be in their house every morning. Their father, a thin, balding man with bright eyes made even brighter somehow by his thick, bushy eyebrows. He moved easily around the kitchen, cracking eggs, stirring grits and turning over the bacon that buckled and shriveled in the frying pan. Upstairs their mother sat straight-backed on a little round cushion, chanting and ringing her brass bowl in front of a fat, smiling, little wooden Buddha. When their father called them all to breakfast, she would come downstairs in her robe and sit at the kitchen table, smelling like sandalwood.

Grover looked through the shoebox of leaves. Red oak, tulip poplar, basswood, ash, beech, sycamore, Japanese maple, red maple, sugar maple, paper birch and weeping cherry. He picked out a narrow yellow birch leaf and worked it in. He'd gotten up early this morning, on a Saturday even, put on a coat and hat and headed out to the Bamboo Forest just after daybreak. The weaving, his biggest yet, was about half finished. It hung from a section of bamboo that he'd tied at eye level between two bamboo stalks. The more leaves he'd worked into it, the more the weaving caught the morning breeze, lifting and falling as if it breathed.

Loud caws. Shadows glided through the air. Black, shiny wings. Something had startled the crows. They settled back into the bamboo, flapping and cawing. A couple of years ago he'd found the dangling skeleton of a crow that had somehow gotten caught in the bamboo and hung itself.

The Bamboo Forest took up half a vacant lot next to Grover's house. The half without bamboo was a field that kids sometimes played softball or football in. The rest was bamboo—a maze of footpaths worn by generations of kids' feet. Grover had been coming here since he was old enough to walk. Years ago his mother had given him a small bow saw and a Swiss Army Knife, and he'd made spears, blowguns, bows and arrows. He learned how to lash the bamboo to make chairs, tables, fences and gates.

As he got older, Grover didn't come as much to the Bamboo Forest. Like his friends, he rode his bike or skateboarded or went inside and watched TV. But for the past six months all he'd wanted to do, all he could *stand* to do really, was go outside and put things together—sticks, grass, leaves—anything he could get his hands on.

Something whizzed over his head. He heard a crack, looked up and saw his weaving crumpled on the ground. A soccer ball rolled to a stop beside him as someone came crashing through the bamboo.

A small boy with big ears and freckles stepped into the clearing. "Whoa, I didn't know this was back here," he said.

"This yours?" Grover held up the soccer ball. His heart pounded,

"I was practicing with my left foot," the boy said. "What is this back here? A hideout or something?"

Grover threw the ball hard at the boy, then picked up the weaving, which had been torn from the section of bamboo it had been tied to but otherwise looked okay. He turned over the weaving, gently running his hand over it.

"What is this place?" the boy asked.

"You almost smashed a month's work!" Grover snapped. Well, technically a couple of weeks' worth but he wanted the boy to feel bad about what *could* have happened. He turned the weaving over a couple more times and, when he saw it was okay, began to calm down.

"What're you making?" This boy looked familiar, and his

accent sounded familiar too. "Is this your hideout?" He walked around the neat piles of bamboo arranged by size and length, the piles of grasses, leaves, pinecones and small branches from other trees. A bamboo lean-to occupied the middle of the clearing. Underneath the lean-to sat a small bamboo table and chair where Grover worked when it rained.

"It's my workshop," Grover said, picking out a bamboo section from the pile.

"This isn't no workshop," the boy said. "This is outside."

Grover opened a big toolbox. He had several handsaws—one with a curved blade, another with a big square blade, a couple with long narrow blades. Some with large teeth, some with small. He had rubber bands, twine, string, electrician's tape, duct tape. Nails, screws. He pulled out a big ball of twine, then took his Swiss Army Knife, which he always kept oiled and sharpened, out of his pocket. He cut off four lengths of the twine, and retied the weaving to the bamboo section it had been hanging from, then, with a couple more pieces of twine, retied the whole thing back to the bamboo stalks.

The boy went up to the weaving, gently touching it.

"Don't!" Grover said. "You've done enough already."

Holding his hands behind his back like he was in a museum, the boy studied the weaving, then looked around the clearing, then looked back at the weaving. "Now I get it," he said. "You're some kind a artist!" The boy pointed at the weaving. "And this is your art!"

"I wouldn't call it art exactly," Grover said.

The boy cocked his head one way and then the other as he studied the weaving. "I'm not sure what else you *could* call it."

Grover remembered where he'd seen the boy. One morning last week Grover had been in the front yard looking for the *Asheville Citizen-Times* when a tired-looking van pulling a very large U-Haul trailer rattled up to the house across the street, which Jessie owned but rented out. A mother and her two kids had climbed out of the van. The mother looked young to be somebody's mother, at least younger than Grover's mother. The kids were this round-faced, big-eared boy here and a tall, dark girl with long black hair. After a while, a huge pickup had pulled in front of the rental house. It had a Confederate decal on the rear window, a *Bread Not Bombs* sticker on the bumper and an umbrella in the gun rack. A man Grover'd guessed to be the father got out. He helped them unload the U-Haul, but then a couple of hours later he climbed back in his truck, shouted "So long, Sis" to the woman and drove off. Grover hadn't seen him since. Not that he'd paid much attention. Families came and went in the rental. It wasn't worth the effort to make friends with renters. One day you'd be playing with them, the next day they'd be gone.

"Name's Clay." The boy held out his hand. "I'm real sorry about knocking down your art."

Grover looked at the boy's hand. He'd never had another kid want to shake hands. "Grover" is all he said as he shook the boy's hand.

"Grover? Now that's an interesting name. A mighty interesting name. Don't believe I know a single soul with that name.

I have a cousin name of Sturgess, but I've never met a Grover."

"I'm trying to finish this." Grover bent down to his shoebox.

"Oh, sure, Grover," he said. "You go right ahead. Don't mind me."

"I don't like people watching me work."

"Don't blame you, Grover," he said. "I'll be quiet as a mouse."

Grover turned on the boy but something in his eyes, something easy and open, made it hard to stay mad. Grover sighed, then turned back to his work. He wove a birch leaf into the bamboo, then bent down to pick out another leaf.

Clay bent down with him, peering into the shoebox. "Where'd you get all the leaves, Grover? Back home we learned that it's when the chlorophyll drains out that you get your colors. A funny thing if you think about it. You don't know a leaf's true colors till it's dead."

Grover shot the boy a look.

Clay put his finger to his lips, then whispered, "Quiet as a mouse, Grover."

Grover went back to his weaving, surprised the boy knew a word like *chlorophyll*. He searched for another leaf in the shoebox. He'd always used his mother's shoeboxes to bury his pets that had died over the years—three salamanders, a frog, a turtle, too many goldfish to count and a guinea pig. When he'd gone into his mother's closet a few weeks ago to get this shoebox, his heart had begun to pound. The silent stacks of shoeboxes made him feel like he'd stepped into a mausoleum.

‡   ‡   ‡

Grover wasn't sure how much time had passed when he reached into the shoebox for another leaf and found it empty. He noticed the sun overhead. Noon already? He'd been working for five hours! He looked around for Clay, but Clay was gone. With his stomach growling, he headed home for lunch.

Grover lived with his father and Sudie in a green, two-story, hundred-year-old house. Grover's room faced out on the Bamboo Forest. From his downstairs window all he could see was the calm, cool green of bamboo stalks. Sudie's downstairs room looked on to a bright goldfish pond with tall grasses growing on the far side.

Sudie, who'd always been a late riser, sat on the couch in her pink flannel pajamas, watching a cooking show and eating a grapefruit half. Biscuit was curled up on the couch beside her. On TV a man wearing an apron, who spoke with a French accent, chopped up a red pepper so fast it was a blur.

"Daddy gone to work already?" Grover asked. He went out to the kitchen and made a peanut butter and honey, then sat on the couch with Sudie and watched the man, who was named Jacques Pépin, chop up a few more vegetables and toss them into a skillet. Watching the chef pull a brown loaf of bread out of the oven, Grover noticed the dusty DVD player underneath the TV. It was one of the few technological things their mother had let them have, because, she said, they could watch movies as a family. And last year their mother had surprised everyone by giving Grover an iPod for his birthday, making him promise to use it only at bedtime. It was to replace the worn CD player he'd kept on his nightstand. Ever since he was little he'd needed music to go to sleep.

Sudie squeezed grapefruit juice into her spoon. Their mother had had to make her eat fruits and vegetables. Now Sudie ate a grapefruit every morning, packed her school lunch box with carrots, peppers and apples or grapes and made sure they all had at least two vegetables for dinner. Sudie had been like that with a lot of things. Their mother had always been after Sudie to make her bed and pick up her room. Now Sudie kept her room as neat as a pin.

After Grover ate his sandwich, he took his sister's and his plates out to the kitchen, rinsed them off and put them in the dishwasher. When he came back, he told Sudie he was going back to his workshop.

"I want to see how it's coming," Sudie said, turning off the TV. "Can you wait a second while I change out of my pjs?"

While he waited, Grover roamed the front yard, looking for the morning paper in the tall grass. Their mother had been the one to keep up the yard. Now the grass and the hedges had gotten out of hand. Grover cut it himself every now and then, but one day Sudie had been watching a program on the show *Nature* about letting your grass and hedges grow to make your yard a home for birds and small animals. "We're a refuge," she said, and sent off for a little plastic sign that said *Certified Backyard Wilderness.* She hung it from the abelia bush, which had grown to the size of a VW Bug. Grover didn't bother mowing after that.

A couple of crows cawed from the maple, flew away and settled in an overgrown nandina.

Sudie came out dressed and wearing a coat, and Biscuit followed behind her. As they walked over to the Bamboo Forest, she said, "How come you don't show Daddy your weavings?"

"He never asks to see them," Grover said.

"When he's busy with work," she said, "he forgets about everything else."

The truth was that their father had never seemed to think much of the things Grover made. More than once he'd overheard his parents argue about him. His mother saying that Grover was talented and had *vision*. His father replying that might be true but that the boy could be a good student if he spent half the time studying that he spent in the Bamboo Forest. *He is a good student*, his mother would say. But he knew what his father'd meant. He wanted Grover to be like Sudie, born making As.

The longer his mother had been dead, the more his father had seemed to worry about Grover's grades. When Grover received a couple of Cs on English papers a few weeks ago, his father started making Grover and Sudie walk over to the Wolfe house so he could check his homework. Now Grover was only able to work in the Bamboo Forest after supper, and only after he showed his father his completed homework. With daylight savings switching back to regular time in a couple of weeks, it'd be dark after supper, and then how would he work in the Bamboo Forest?

"What is that?" Sudie walked over to a stake on the edge

of the Bamboo Forest. It had a red ribbon tied to it. "There's another . . . and another."

A pit opened up in his stomach as Grover saw that stakes had been driven in along the edges of the Bamboo Forest. He hadn't noticed these this morning. He'd been too busy working on the weaving. Or someone had put them in the ground while he was eating lunch.

"What do they mean?" Sudie asked.

"I don't know," he said. He sounded miles away from himself. He remembered the afternoon his father had been driving him and his sister home from soccer practice. They'd seen their mother walking along Charlotte Street, with Biscuit trotting ahead of her on the sidewalk. Their father pulled over, rolled down his window and asked if she needed a ride. She shook her head and said she was going to Videolife to pick up a movie and that she and Biscuit both needed the walk. "See you in a little bit," she said as they pulled away. Something made Grover turn around and look back out the rear windshield at his mother. She waved. He didn't wave back. He'd started to. Probably every time she'd ever waved at him before, he'd waved back. But this time he'd felt childish, embarrassed that someone might see him wave to his mother. Besides, why wave good-bye to someone he was going to see in forty-five minutes?

"Grover," Sudie said, tugging on his coat sleeve. "What do the stakes mean?"

"I said, I don't know!" He bent down and took hold of the stake. He tried to jiggle it but it didn't move. It must've been pretty deep in the ground. He tried to pull it up but it wouldn't give. He tried again, this time with both hands, and remembered reading in *The Once and Future King* how the boy Arthur strained to pull the sword from the stone. With a couple more tugs, Grover slid the stake out of the ground and held it up.

Sudie tried to pull up the next one. Feeling bad about yelling at his sister, Grover went over and tugged on it. "Give it a try now," he said, letting her pull it the rest of the way out of the ground. They went all around the edge of the Bamboo Forest, him loosening the stakes and Sudie pulling them out. In the end they each had an armful.

"What'll we do with them?" Sudie asked.

Grover thought about piling them up in his workshop. He could make something out of them. That was a stupid idea. Whoever put them there in the first place might find them. So he and Sudie started home with them, keeping an eye out for anyone who might see them.

"What y'all got there?"

They hadn't seen Clay juggling the soccer ball in front of his house. He'd stopped when he saw them and ran across the street.

"Oh, no," Grover groaned. "Not that kid."

"Clay?" Sudie said.

"You know him?"

"I've kicked around a soccer ball with him a couple of times. He's all right."

Clay trotted up to them. "What y'all toting?" Grover realized the boy's accent was like the people up in the mountains where his family went to get their Christmas tree every year.

"Somebody put stakes in the Bamboo Forest," Sudie said, holding up her armful.

"Sudie," Grover hissed.

"Surveyors," Clay said. "Saw them over there yesterday."

"You did?" Grover asked.

"I want to be a surveyor when I grow up," Clay said, bending down to pet Biscuit. "You get to be outdoors. Not cooped up in some old office all day. My daddy was a surveyor." He glanced at the stakes. "Those boys are going to be none too happy about you pulling those up. If I was you, I'd do a mighty good job of hiding them. Maybe even de-stroy the evidence."

Grover and Sudie went inside with the stakes, and Clay started to follow them. But Grover said, "See you later" and shut the door on him.

"That kid doesn't take a hint," Grover said, dropping his stakes on the floor.

"He's just being friendly," Sudie said, piling hers on top of Grover's.

"There's a fine line between being friendly and being a pest," Grover said.

"There's a fat line between being nice and being rude." Sudie stood at the window, watching Clay walk back across the street.

"He might tell somebody we pulled up the stakes," Grover said.

"He's not like that," Sudie said.

"You better hope you're right," Grover said. He had to admit that, even if Sudie was his little sister and two years younger, she had a sixth sense about people. If she thought Clay would keep his mouth shut, he probably would.

"What're we going to do with all these?" Sudie asked, toeing the pile of stakes.

"We can't leave them here or Daddy'll find out."

Grover studied the woodstove that sat in the middle of the den. Their father heated with it as much as possible to cut the oil bill. Every summer Jessie brought a load of wood that his father loved to split and stack at the side of the house.

"Be back in a second." Grover ran out into the yard, snapping some dead twigs off the abelia bush and the privet hedge. His father had taught him that the best kindling came from the bottom of bushes and trees where it was kept dry by the limbs above. Coming from under the abelia, Grover saw Matthew, Jessie's assistant, in his Army coat and wearing a backpack, walking in the direction of the cemetery. Grover waved but Matthew didn't wave back. He couldn't tell if Matthew was ignoring him or just hadn't seen him.

Back inside, Grover set the twigs by the woodstove and, as he balled up some newspaper, asked Sudie to bring the stakes over to him.

"What're you doing?" She carried over an armful of stakes and dropped them beside him.

"*Deeeee-stroying the evidence.*" He arranged the twigs in a miniature tepee over the ball of newspaper, then lighted a match to the newspaper. When the fire was going good, he stacked the stakes on top. The new wood popped and snapped, sending sparks out into the room, which Sudie was quick to stomp on.

Sudie sat back down beside him. Both watched the stakes flame up inside the woodstove. "Did you hear what Clay said about his daddy?" she asked.

Grover paused. "That he was a surveyor?"

"That he *was*," she said.

"Probably has some other job now," Grover said. "He *was* a surveyor, now he's a plumber or a lawyer or a doctor or something."

"There's no father over there now," she said.

"Maybe he's finishing his job somewhere," Grover said. "They moved ahead of him to get settled."

"Maybe," she said.

Grover watched his sister watch the fire. He and Sudie had become parent detectors, sensing whether a kid had a full set of parents, if their parents were married or divorced, alive or, every now and then, not.

After he'd fed the last stake to the fire, he closed the door to the stove and turned the damper down, so it'd burn steady.

There was a scratch at the front door and a bark. Grover opened the door for Biscuit, who trotted in and jumped onto the couch. He was about to close the front door when he noticed Clay's big sister across the street sitting on the cinder-block steps, reading. Had she been there the whole time? She sat like he'd often seen her, with her legs crossed Indian style, her elbows on her knees and her head bowed over a book in her lap.

He closed the door. Sudie had turned on the TV and sat down on the couch with Biscuit. *This Old House* was on. "Maybe they won't put any more of those stakes in the Bamboo Forest," Sudie said.

Grover knew that pulling up a few stakes wouldn't stop whoever from doing whatever they planned. He almost said that, and in the old days, when their mother was there, he would've. When she was alive, he could say out loud what he was thinking. He could test out his worries. Now he fought to keep his worries not only from his sister, but from himself.

He sat down with Sudie, and Biscuit whined at Grover.

"He wants you to pet him," Sudie said.

"I don't feel like it," Grover said.

"It's not his fault, Grover," she said. "You can't blame Biscuit."

"I don't." He petted Biscuit, but Sudie was kind of right. Every time he saw Biscuit, he pictured him running into traffic and their mother running after him. The police had determined that the driver hadn't been speeding yet hadn't had time to stop.

Grover did his best to watch the TV. Men with New England accents were fixing up a two-hundred-year-old farmhouse. He liked this show. He liked seeing the old houses brought back to life. But after a while, what happened was what sometimes happened when he watched TV. He saw what the TV saw. This afternoon what the TV saw was him and Sudie huddled on the couch with Biscuit between them—the three of them adrift in the living room.

Chapter Three
He's Not Himself

That night Grover walked with Sudie down Edgemont as streetlights buzzed and flickered on. Their father had called and said that he'd meet them at Jessie's. It had turned much colder that afternoon. Grover and Sudie wore sweaters that smelled like the cedar chest. For the first time this fall, Grover had had to get his and his sister's sweaters out of the chest in the upstairs hallway. He'd always loved the dark chest that had first belonged to their grandmother's grandmother and had been protecting Johnston sweaters from moths for generations. Its bright smell was old and safe. As he'd dug through the folded sweaters, he stopped. Last Easter, like she had every Easter, their mother had carefully folded the family's sweaters and put them away. He remembered walking past her as she sat there, setting sweaters into the chest. At the time he hadn't thought a thing about it. But now he knelt beside the chest, stroking the sweaters, holding them to his face, breathing in their bright cedar smell.

As Grover and Sudie walked down the street, leaves blew along the sidewalk, making a dry scrambling sound. In the distance dogs gave test barks to see if other dogs were out there. Grover'd always liked fall with its cold and its early dark. He liked seeing into the lighted rooms of neighbors' houses. He liked watching them cook or sit down to supper or watch TV together. He wondered if his neighbors knew what they had. How quick they could lose it. How in one millisecond it could all be gone.

Gone. The word couldn't have sounded more like itself. *Not there anymore* boiled down to a single syllable, a solitary word. *Gone.* A word Grover had felt in his bones ever since that late afternoon in April when she hadn't come back from her walk. Biscuit had shown up, his broken leash trailing behind. Their father had been on the phone to Videolife, when they'd heard sirens.

Grover and Sudie walked up Jessie's stone walk, lined by leaf-shaped lights. Jessie lived in a small old Spanish stucco house with an arched front porch, a red tiled roof and big wavy glass windows that shimmered tonight with candlelight from inside. His yard stayed neat: the grass mowed, the shrubs trimmed, the beds mulched. Still, he wasn't like some of the neighbors who Grover's father called Yard Nazis—neighbors, most of them old with not much else to do except watch over their yards, swooping down on kids if they set foot on their lawns.

They found Jessie in the kitchen, turning over pieces of chicken sizzling in a frying pan. Without his big hat, he looked smaller. He'd tied his long gray hair back in a ponytail, and wore an apron that had printed in big bold letters across it, *The South*

— 27

Shall Rise Again, and under the words was a drawing of a plateful of biscuits. Jessie already had several golden brown pieces of chicken draining on a paper towel on the counter.

"Daddy said he'd meet us here," Sudie said.

Tippy and Merlin, Jessie's two cats, rubbed against their legs. Tippy was strictly an indoor cat. Merlin spent the day outside but came in at night. Merlin liked to slip into neighbors' houses when they weren't looking. He'd tried slipping into Grover's house but stopped after Biscuit had chased him out a few times.

"If y'all will set the table and fill the tea glasses," Jessie said, checking the rice in a pot on the stove.

Grover and Sudie went to work, knowing which drawer held the silverware, which cabinets held the plates and glasses. Jessie and their parents had been friends so long that he felt like one of the family. They'd always eaten at Jessie's on Saturday nights. Over the past six months, they'd eaten even more at Jessie's, at least Grover and Sudie had.

Grover'd gotten down the plates and filled the tea glasses and Sudie'd set out the silverware and napkins, when their father walked in. He had on his tweed coat and a loosened tie. His face was dark with evening stubble, and he frowned to himself. He bent down and absentmindedly petted the cats.

"Help yourself," Jessie said, nodding to the refrigerator.

Their father took a brown bottle of beer out of the refrigerator and opened it with the *First Baptist of Asheville Church* church key magnet on the side of the refrigerator.

"Daddy, Grover's making his best weaving yet," Sudie said.

"Another amazing one," said Jessie, who stopped by Grover's workshop now and then. "To tell you the truth, I haven't seen anything quite like Grover's weavings."

Their father smiled vacantly as he pulled out a chair and sat at the kitchen table. He sipped his beer, then set the bottle down and looked at it. He'd always had circles under his eyes, but they'd become almost black, like all his worries had pooled there.

"How are things at work?" Jessie asked, lifting the lid on the pot of rice, then replacing it.

Their father looked up. "Hmm?"

"How are things at the Old Kentucky Home?" Jessie asked. That was the name of the Wolfe house, the boardinghouse that Thomas Wolfe's mother had run and where Wolfe had lived some as a boy. Wolfe had divided his time between his father's house and his mother's boardinghouse a few blocks away.

"I met with the county manager last week," their father said, taking a sip of beer. "She says that with the economy the way it is, they have to make cuts where they can, and that they can't cut schools or essential services."

"Essential services?" Sudie asked.

"Like the fire department or the garbage pickup," Grover said.

"The Thomas Wolfe house is an essential service!" Sudie said.

"I'd like to think so," their father said, smiling that vacant smile again. "But the county manager said if we can't get attendance up by the end of the year, they'll have to cut our budget in half."

"In half?" Jessie asked.

"I'll have to lay off staff, and if I lay off staff, we'll have to cut back hours, and if we cut back hours, we'll have even fewer visitors and pretty soon they won't just be cutting our budget, they'll be closing us down." He took another swig of his beer. "And I, along with a lot of other folks, will be out of a job."

"It won't come to that," Jessie said.

"Delbert Lunsford has been talking to the other commissioners about replacing me."

"Nobody listens to him," Jessie said.

"*Somebody* must," their father said. "He manages to get elected every couple of years."

The upstairs of the Wolfe house had burned several years ago. Somebody, they never found out who, had thrown a burning rag through an upstairs window in the middle of the night. Grover'd been too young to remember the fire, but he did remember the big blue tarp that stayed draped over the burned roof for years. Delbert Lunsford, a longtime commissioner and a realtor, had had it in for their father ever since he'd organized opposition to Lunsford's idea to bulldoze the burned house and sell the land to a hotel chain.

Instead of being bulldozed, the house had been restored with money their father had raised over several years. Before the fire the house had been a plain, ugly, run-down old white house. Grover'd seen pictures. The restoration, which came some years after the fire, brought new life to the house. His father had worked hard to bring the house back to how it first looked. Outside, it had been painted bright yellow, and inside, all the furniture, all the walls, all the floors had been restored to their new old selves.

Their mother liked to say it was a *reincarnation*. Still with the house closed so long, attendance had never recovered.

Jessie served everyone's plates in the kitchen. The four of them sat down to eat. Jessie reached for Grover's and Sudie's hands. And their father took their hands too. Everyone bowed their heads except Grover.

"Lord," Jessie said, bowing his head, "we thank you for this sustenance. Amen."

Grover liked Jessie's blessings—short and sweet. Not like Aunt Paula, their father's sister. Her blessings went on so long that food would have to be taken back into the kitchen to be reheated. But it had been good to have Aunt Paula around for their mother's funeral, breaking up the weepy silence of all the red-eyed mourners with her loud sobbing, her swooning and swaying over the coffin and her crying out for Jesus to welcome her precious sister-in-law into His sweet embrace.

They'd been eating a while, and Jessie had their father cracking up with a story about a wealthy widow who was twenty years older and whose yard he'd landscaped for years. The other day she'd said her house was too big to be alone in and asked Jessie if he'd like to "shack up" with her.

Their father laughed. "'*Shack up*'?"

"Her very words," Jessie said, raising his hand like he was taking an oath.

"And what'd you say?" their father asked.

"I said I appreciated the offer but that I was looking for more of a commitment."

Their father laughed again. Grover'd always liked eating at Jessie's. Since their mother died, he'd liked it even more. Jessie could always make their father laugh.

"Someone put stakes in the Bamboo Forest," Sudie said.

Stunned at his sister's timing, Grover glared at her across the table.

What? she silently mouthed.

"I haven't seen any stakes," Jessie said.

"Well, they're not there *now*," Sudie said.

Grover let his head drop to his chest.

"I wonder if he's finally selling?" their father said, setting down a drumstick and wiping his fingers with his napkin.

"Wouldn't be surprised," Jessie said. "I've heard his daughter might be pressing him for the money. She has two kids going to college."

"With the price of land in Asheville these days," their father said, taking a swig from his beer, "it's got to be worth at least a hundred thousand."

"I'd say twice that," Jessie said.

"Wait a minute," Grover said. "Somebody *owns* the Bamboo Forest?" In all the years he'd worked in the Bamboo Forest, never had it occurred to him that anyone might own it. How could anybody own the Bamboo Forest? It was like someone owning the sky or the clouds or the sun. Even today when he'd seen those stakes, it hadn't registered that anyone might own the Bamboo Forest.

"Maybe he's just having the property reappraised," Jessie said.

"Who owns it?" Grover asked.

"Lunsford," Jessie said.

"The commissioner?" Grover asked, looking at their father.

"He owns a lot of land around Asheville," their father said.

"He can't sell the Bamboo Forest," Grover said, sounding panicked.

"He owns it," their father said. "He can do whatever he wants with it."

Grover watched their father sip his beer. "Is that all you have to say?" His voice trembled. "Is that all you have to say about the most important place in our neighborhood?!"

"Whoa there, Son," their father said, holding up his hands. "I didn't mean to shortchange your 'Bamboo Forest.'" He gave Jessie an amused look.

"You always make the Bamboo Forest sound silly," Grover said.

His father scraped at the label on his beer bottle.

"Anybody like another one?" Jessie said, passing the basket of biscuits to Sudie.

"The thing is," his father said, looking up at Grover, "you're getting too old to spend so much time down there, doing those little . . . art projects."

There it was, what his father had been waiting to say to him in all the months since their mother had died.

"They're not little art projects," Grover said. "They're my work!"

"Work?" their father said.

"How about some pie and coffee, Walt?" Jessie said.

"If you spent half the time on your studies that you spend fiddling around in that patch of bamboo," his father said, "you'd be a straight-A student. Like your sister."

"Daddy." Sudie shook her head at their father.

"It's true," their father said. "Grover's a smart boy. . . ."

"Not the way you want me to be," Grover said, his heart pounding.

"What's that?"

"You've already taken away my afternoons in the Bamboo Forest!" Grover said. "The one thing I look forward to during the day! What else do you want from me?"

"I want you to grow up," his father said. "It's time you learn you can't go running off to the bamboo whenever life gets hard."

"But it's okay for you to run off to the Wolfe house?!"

"Grover, I have a lot of people counting on me."

"What about Sudie and me?" Grover said. "We count on you too!"

His father pushed himself up from the table. "I work my fingers to the bone, supporting you and your sister," he said quietly. "You think I like working late? You think I like working on weekends?" His voice rose.

"Walt," Jessie said.

"With your mother gone, my job is all we have! If it goes away, who's going to make a living for us? Can you tell me that, Grover? Who's going to pay the bills?"

"Walt," Jessie said, standing up and putting his hand on their father's shoulder and whispering. "He's just a boy."

Their father kept his eyes on Grover, but as he did, the anger seemed to drain out of them.

"How about some pie and coffee?" Jessie said again.

Their father sighed and sat back down.

"Grover, why don't you help me make the coffee?" Jessie said.

Grover stood shakily and walked with Jessie into the kitchen, while Sudie cleared the table.

"And, Walt," Jessie said over his shoulder, "I've got a box of kindling outside the back door and there's a pile of seasoned wood. It'll be our first fire of the fall."

Their father stared at the beer bottle in his hands. After a few moments he got up and went outside. They could hear him out back picking through the wood. The one thing their father loved about as much as he loved Thomas Wolfe was making fires.

"He's not himself these days," Jessie said in a low voice.

Grover measured out the coffee into the coffeemaker, his hand trembling so much he spilled coffee all over the counter. He started to clean it up.

"Don't worry about it," Jessie said as he finished measuring the coffee.

"Lately he's gotten so uptight about me going out to the Bamboo Forest," Grover said, keeping his voice low. "And he's on me all the time now about my grades. You'd think I was flunking."

"It's not you he's upset about," Jessie said.

"It sure feels like it's me."

"If your mama was alive she'd know how to make him feel better. He misses her."

"Who doesn't?" Grover snapped. But he knew Jessie was right. Their mother had kept their father's spirits up after the Wolfe house burned, during the long hard years when it looked like it might never reopen. He'd worked even longer hours than he worked now and traveled to Raleigh sometimes two or three times a week to raise money.

After the coffee was made and dinner dishes left to soak in the sink, they carried their pie and their father's coffee into the den. Their father, looking more like his old self, shifted the wood with a poker in the roaring fire he had going. He set the poker by the fireplace, making a metal rattle.

Sudie handed him his piece of pie. "Here you go, Daddy."

Their father sat on the couch, and Grover set his father's mug of coffee, which he always took black, on the coffee table in front of him.

"Thanks," their father said quietly and looked up. Grover saw the old softness in his father's face and the new lines in his forehead that had appeared in the last six months. He remembered how once every week or two, Jessie would come over to stay with Grover and Sudie, while their parents went out to supper alone. He remembered how his father would always be in a good mood on those nights, laughing and joking with Sudie and him. He remembered how his mother would walk into the living room, wearing one of her nice dresses and a pair of her glittery earrings, and his father's eyes would light up as if seeing her for the first time.

They'd finished their pie. Jessie and Grover were playing chess on the floor by the fire, and their father was sitting on the couch, sipping his coffee with Sudie beside him, when there was a knock at the front door. Sudie ran to the door and led a woman back to the den. Dressed in green hospital scrubs, she had a wide face sprinkled with freckles, deep green eyes and a smile that reminded Grover of Glinda the Good Witch in *The Wizard of Oz*, one of the few DVDs they owned.

"I hope I'm not interruptin' your supper," she said.

"Leila," Jessie said. "Have you met Walt Johnston?"

"Don't get up," she said.

Their father stood anyway. "I meant to get over and welcome y'all to the neighborhood before now," he said. As soon as you started thinking their father didn't notice anything, like new neighbors for instance, he up and did.

"And this is Sudie and Grover," Jessie said.

"You're the boy Clay met over in the canebrake," she said. "He says you're quite the artist. I didn't mean to interrupt y'all's game," she said, glancing at the chessboard. "I told Emma Lee when I got home from work this evening I'd help her put together a bookshelf we bought. Now I can't find my Phillips. Must've lost it in the move."

Jessie went to the back of the house to get a screwdriver from his toolbox, leaving the woman and Grover's father standing there.

"Your daughter's a reader?" their father asked.

"Emma Lee was born reading," she said.

So that was the name of the girl who sat on the steps all the time. *Emma Lee.*

"Reading is a rare ability in kids these days," their father said. Grover had never been all that great a reader. When he was nine years old, he fell off his bike, hit his head and got a concussion. Grover remembered sitting in the doctor's waiting room, trying to read *Highlights* magazine. He could read the individual words but they didn't add up. Lately Grover had struggled with reading like he was walking around with a concussion; the words didn't add up. In fact almost everything that he did and everything he felt these days didn't add up.

"Jessie tells me you manage the Thomas Wolfe house," the woman said.

"He's the *director*," Sudie said.

"I read *Look Homeward, Angel* when I was in college," the woman said. "But tried picking it up again a couple of years ago and couldn't get through it."

"I get that a lot," their father said. Sometimes he sounded like he'd written the book himself.

"Then I don't feel so dense," she said.

"It's Wolfe who's dense," their father said. "At least his sentences can be." He smiled.

"Emma Lee's read about everything the man ever wrote."

"If y'all come by sometime I'd be happy to give you a personal tour," their father said. Grover noticed their father's Southern accent got stronger talking to this woman, like it did whenever he talked to a repairman or a gas station attendant or anybody who had a thick accent.

"I went through the Wolfe house years ago," Leila said. "Before it burned."

"You need to go through again," Sudie said.

"You wouldn't believe the place now," their father said.

"'A phoenix risen from the ashes,'" Sudie said, quoting what their father had said in the *Asheville Citizen-Times* about the renovation.

"Emma Lee would love a tour," Leila said. "So would I."

"Great," their father said, sounding livelier than Grover could remember him sounding in a long time. It gave him an uneasy feeling.

"You work at St. Joseph's?" their father said, nodding at the woman's scrubs.

"I'm an obstetrics nurse," she said.

"She helps deliver babies," Sudie whispered to Grover.

"I know what it means," Grover whispered back impatiently.

"Both our kids were born at St. Joseph's," their father said.

Jessie came back in with a screwdriver, and the rest of the chocolate pie wrapped in tinfoil.

"I can't take your pie," the woman said. The long flat way she said "pie" was like a sentence all by itself.

"There's plenty more where that came from," Jessie said. "Good luck with the shelf. You need any help?"

"I'm pretty handy," the woman said.

"Is the house working out okay, Leila?" Jessie asked. "I know that electric baseboard isn't the best heat."

"The house is fine, Jessie. We're plenty warm. After a lifetime of splitting and toting wood for Nanna's woodstove, I'm happy to come home from work and just turn a knob."

One of Jessie's cats had come up and was rubbing against her leg. "Merlin's been visiting us pretty regularly." She bent down and petted him. "He likes to sit in the front window and watch the birds." She looked up at Jessie. "I feed him a little something every now and then."

"If he ever gets to be a pest," Jessie said, "toss him out."

"Emma Lee and Clay like him visiting too," she said. "My mother has always had dogs. She's never liked cats. She doesn't trust them."

After the woman left, their father and Sudie settled back on the couch, and Grover and Jessie went back to their game in front of the fire.

"Nice woman," their father said, getting up and putting another log on the fire. Grover could feel how his father's mood had improved.

"They've been through a lot," Jessie said, not taking his eyes off the board. "Lost her husband in Iraq."

Their father shook his head. "It's everywhere."

Grover knew Sudie was remembering what Clay had said. *My daddy was a surveyor.* He looked at his own father, who stared at the fire. Death, Grover had figured out, wasn't really the funeral or the headstone or everybody saying how sorry they were. Death was a long, painful correction in thinking.

That night Grover couldn't sleep. He'd been lying in bed with his door open, listening to George Harrison's *All Things Must Pass* on his iPod. It had been his mother's favorite album. Grover listened to it almost every night. He liked the gentle, dreamy music. Sometimes, just before he fell asleep, he'd find himself standing on the edge of some dark pool, looking down with the music echoing all around him. Sometimes, if he was lucky, he'd catch a glimpse of his mother's face, like a faint moon, rising out of the deep, dark water.

The music usually helped him fall asleep. But on this night even George Harrison couldn't help. The house was quiet when he slipped out and walked over to the Bamboo Forest. He took a flashlight but the moon was so bright he didn't need it. He walked to his workshop and sat on an old tree stump in the middle of the clearing, listening to the night breeze rattle the bamboo leaves. A screech owl tittered nearby and in the distance a train whistle blew. Grover patted the old stump. It was hard to believe that anyone would or even could sell this place. How long did he have? How long before bulldozers mowed down the Bamboo Forest? He'd seen it happen in plenty of other places around town. One day there'd be grass and trees and maybe even a creek. The next day there'd be nothing but ragged roots and ground so torn up and red that it looked like it was bleeding.

Grover thought about his father saying he was too old to be doing *those little art projects*. Maybe he was. He had to admit that when he thought about it, it was pretty silly for a twelve-year-old boy to sit around, trying to weave grass and leaves and sticks together. He saw something—a small ghost drifting toward him. His heart began to pound. But before the apparition reached Grover, Biscuit came trotting up ahead of it. The ghost turned out to be Sudie in her robe.

"I heard you get up," she said, sitting beside him on the stump.

Biscuit gave a little yip and disappeared into the bamboo. He'd probably smelled a rabbit.

"Daddy didn't mean all that tonight," Sudie said.

"He meant it, all right," Grover said. "And maybe I am wasting my time."

"Don't be stupid," Sudie said.

"Is *stupid* your favorite word these days?"

"I can't help it if a lot of things are stupid lately," she said.

They sat on the stump a minute, listening to the screech owl. Biscuit gave another little bark as they heard him scamper around in the bamboo.

"Besides," Sudie said, "you couldn't stop making things if you tried."

Grover expected this was true. He made things in spite of himself. Oftentimes he'd be sitting around and find himself in the middle of weaving grasses or arranging rocks or stacking sticks. Things came together under his hands.

"Can we go back to the house?" Sudie said, standing up. She hugged herself, shivering. "I'm getting cold."

"You go on back," he said. "I'm not ready to."

"Then I'm not going back either." Sudie sat back on the stump, crossing her arms against the chilly night air. She pulled the little cylinder necklace out from under her pajama top and held it. The two of them sat there, listening to the bamboo rattle in the breeze. The screech owl had gone silent.

"Can we go back, please?" Sudie said.

"Okay, okay," he said, getting up.

"Come on, Biscuit," Sudie called, and after a minute, the little dog emerged from the bamboo and ran ahead of them. She took Grover's hand.

Before, Grover would've pulled away. Before, he wouldn't have been caught dead holding his little sister's hand.

Chapter Four

The New Girl

Grover was supposed to be reviewing for the big spelling test tomorrow. But he'd thought of a new idea for a weaving and started sketching in the margins of his spelling composition book. Loud caws and the flash of a crow's wing made him look outside the classroom window. Matthew, Jessie's assistant, passed by the front of the school. When Grover looked back, the rental house girl, Clay's sister, stood just inside the classroom doorway. She had on an old-timey button-up coat that made her look older and taller. Mrs. Caswell and the girl talked quietly, then the girl went back to the cloakroom to hang up her coat.

"Class, we have a new student today," Mrs. Caswell said when the girl returned. "Please welcome Emma Lee Roundtree. Where are you from, Emma Lee?"

"Mit-chell Coun-ty," the girl said, her accent as thick as her brother's. She wore faded jeans, a blue flannel shirt and running shoes. "We lived with my grandmother up on Roan Moun-tain."

Whispering, sprinkled with a few giggles, went up from the class.

Mitchell County was where Grover's family drove every year to find a Christmas tree. Their father always complained it was a long trip and a waste of gas. But every year their mother won out and they made the trip. This year, without their mother around, their father would surely just buy a tree at a lot in Asheville.

"Welcome to Isaac Claxton Elementary, Emma Lee," Mrs. Caswell said.

"Thank you, ma'am," she said.

More whispers and giggles, but Mrs. Caswell shot the class a look.

"I understand your father serves in Iraq," Mrs. Caswell said.

"Until he was killed," Emma Lee said.

Mrs. Caswell's face went pale. "I'm sorry. I misunderstood what I read in your file. I'm so sorry."

"It was four years ago," Emma Lee said matter-of-factly. "His helicopter was shot down."

Mrs. Caswell rubbed her brow. "Why don't you sit in the desk behind Grover Johnston?" She walked Emma Lee to the empty desk behind Grover's.

Emma Lee glanced at Grover as she sat down behind him, but he wasn't sure she recognized him.

At lunch Grover's class lined up to go to the cafeteria. Mrs. Caswell's room was on the third floor, so they had to walk down three flights of stairs. Fifth and sixth grades were on the third floor; fourth and third grades on the second floor; and second grade, first grade and kindergarten were on the first floor. The older you got, the higher up you went in the building. The stairs had dips worn in them from eighty-nine years of children's feet. Built in 1922, Isaac Claxton was the oldest school building still in use in Western North Carolina, a fact Grover and every other student had had drilled into them from the moment they'd walked through its fort-sized doors. Other Isaac Claxton facts: It had been constructed out of bricks covered with a layer of polished concrete and the building's style of architecture was federal, which as far as Grover could figure meant square-ish and with columns. To Grover it had always looked like a cross between a bank and a prison.

When they reached the first floor, they walked down the long kindergarten/first grade hall, which, as they neared the cafeteria, smelled of corn dogs and cooked cabbage. The bulletin boards outside the classrooms were decorated with fall leaves ironed between wax paper. Grover paused, noticing some red oak leaves that would go good in the new weaving. Thankfully, the stakes hadn't reappeared in the Bamboo Forest.

Grover's class quieted down as they passed the principal's office. They could see her at her desk, working. Unsmiling and gray-haired, Mrs. Dillingham resembled George Washington so much that an *anonymous* artist had drawn a picture and taped it to the front door of the school. That the drawing was too good to have been done by anybody but Grover was not something Grover had thought about when he'd taped it up. It was two years ago, and his class had been studying the American Revolution.

Like most of his art, the picture had just come to him: Mrs. Dillingham stood at the front of a boat with her arms crossed over her large chest while teachers rowed her across a river. It was titled *Mrs. Dillingham Crossing the Delaware*. Mrs. Dillingham never said anything about it. Instead she had it framed and hung it on her office wall.

A few doors down, past the assistant principal's office, they passed a door with *Counselor* stenciled on it, and a pale rectangle where his mother's name used to be. His mother's office door had always been open unless she was meeting with a kid or parents. Everyone at Isaac Claxton had loved his mother. Whenever his classmates had found out the school counselor was Grover's mother, they'd say he was the luckiest kid in the world. And he'd tell them, the grass is always greener. The mother's always nicer. He'd tell them they didn't have to put up with having their mother around all the time at school. But now, with her gone, his mother seemed even more with him. Everything he saw, everything he did, everywhere he went, somehow or other ended up reminding him of her. His school, his neighborhood, his house, his whole life was booby-trapped with memories of her.

As he was passing, her office door opened. His heart skipped a beat. Instead of his mother, a short, young, blonde woman came out carrying a brown paper lunch bag. She pulled the door closed behind her.

"Grover," said Miss Snyder, the new counselor, who walked along beside him in the line. "How are you?"

"Okay," he said.

"Come by and visit with me sometime," she said.

Grover felt Miss Snyder look at him but he didn't look back.

"See you later," she said, then walked on ahead.

When Miss Snyder had first arrived, she'd met with Grover and Sudie together. She'd told them how sorry she was and to let her know if they ever needed anything or just wanted to talk. Sudie had gone to see her many times. Grover never had. He wasn't a big talker in the first place. Plus, he knew from having a mother who was a counselor and who was always trying to dissect her son's feelings about every little thing that Miss Snyder would sooner or later try to get him to talk about his feelings. To Grover, talking about feelings was about as much fun as throwing up.

After lunch Grover's class went outside to recess. Ashley Galloway and some other girls played four square on one end of the basketball court. Grover and Sam Newcomer, who lived up the street on Edgemont, played HORSE on the opposite end of the court. Grover and Sam had been friends for as long as Grover could remember. When they were little, they had played in the Bamboo Forest all day. As they'd gotten older, they'd ridden bikes through the neighborhood, skateboarded and on weekends often spent nights at each other's houses. Grover'd preferred spending the night at Sam's, because Sam always had the latest computer game and Sam's parents didn't mind if they played them late into the night. Grover never mentioned this to his mother, although he was pretty sure she knew why he was yawning so much the next day.

But since the accident, Grover hadn't spent much time with Sam, keeping to himself in the Bamboo Forest. Sam had come by early on, asking him to go ride bikes or come try out his new PlayStation but Grover always had weaving to do. About all that was left of their friendship was playing HORSE every day after lunch. Grover never won but it was a tradition, and the boys never felt free to do anything else until they'd played their one game.

After his shot swished through the basket, Sam said, "The new girl is pretty." Emma Lee sat across the playground, underneath a huge sycamore, reading.

"She moved into the rental house," Grover said. He caught the ball, shot and the ball bounced off the rim. "H," he said.

"Have you talked to her?" Sam's second shot swished through the basket.

"Why?" Grover asked. His shot missed the basket altogether.

"You have to get over this." Sam shot, another swish.

"Get over what?"

"Your fear of intimacy." Sam's father was a psychiatrist.

"Speak English," Grover said.

"Your fear of the opposite sex," Sam said.

"I'm not *afraid* of girls," Grover said.

"You never talk to them."

"I talk to Mira."

Grover looked in the direction of a black girl who was playing hopscotch with a group of girls off to the side. Mira Hodges was the smartest girl at Claxton. Like Grover, she lived in Montford. Sometimes he called her when he forgot to write down their homework assignment. *Mira, this is Grover. What was our social studies homework?* She'd tell him. He'd say, *Thanks*, and hang up. Mira left a card on his desk that she'd made. On the front, she'd drawn a hand holding out some flowers, and on the inside it said, "I'm so sorry about your mama." He kept it on his dresser.

Sam made a long shot that swished through the net.

"Nice shot, Sam!" Ashley waved from the other end of the court.

Sam waved back halfheartedly.

"You have to get over your fear of intimacy," Grover said in a low voice.

Ashley had flirted with Sam for years and expected him to take her to the Claxton Christmas Waltz, a sixth graders' dance the school had been holding every year since 1922. All sixth graders had to attend. Most kids went to the dance in safe clumps of boys and girls.

After Sam skunked Grover at HORSE, Daniel Pevoe, a tall black boy who'd transferred in this year, and was real competition for Sam, began to play him. Grover sat off to the side and pulled a worn Rubik's cube out of his coat pocket. Jessie had slipped it into his hands at the funeral home. It got Grover through not only the visitation, but the funeral and the whole afternoon and night of people coming to his house, bringing food and telling him and Sudie how sorry they were. It got him through months of sleepless nights, and through all the being in places he did not want to be, which was everywhere except the Bamboo Forest.

After recess, his class went back inside, and as Grover sat down at his desk, the new girl tapped him on the back.

"Are you named after the Grover in *Look Homeward, Angel*?"

How'd she know? Most kids thought he was named after a Muppet.

"Mama told me your daddy runs the Wolfe house," she said.

Instead of looking through a baby name book, Grover's parents had flipped through Wolfe's novel for both Sudie's and Grover's names. Grover was named after a character who died early. Why couldn't they have named him one of the normal brother names in the book, like Ben or Steve?

Later that afternoon, when Mrs. Caswell was writing extra credit challenge words on the blackboard, the new girl tapped him on the back again.

"You're a good artist," she whispered.

Grover stared at her blankly.

"My brother took me over to your mama's grave."

"Who said you could go over there?" Grover whispered.

"It's a free country," she said.

He turned back around, but she tapped his shoulder.

"I like your tapestries," she said.

In a little while, he felt the girl tap him again.

"Now what?" he asked.

"You can't keep her to yourself," she said.

"What are you talking about?"

"The dead belong to everybody," she said. "Take it from me."

Grover looked at her a minute. "It's none of your business!"

"Grover, do you have something you'd like to share with the rest of the class?" asked Mrs. Caswell.

"No, ma'am," he said.

Grover sat there, looking straight ahead, but his mind was on this new girl sitting right behind him. He waited for her to tap his back again and when she did he was going to let her have it.

It was only about half an hour later, when Mrs. Caswell was in the middle of a lesson on the Cherokee Indians, that Grover had calmed down enough to hear what the girl had called his weavings. *Tapestries*.

‡   ‡   ‡

Every day at recess the new girl read underneath the sycamore tree, and every day Grover stole glimpses of her while Sam beat him at HORSE or while he worked his Rubik's cube. Who knew what else she'd figured out about him? He needed to keep an eye on her, which was hard to do with her sitting behind him. In class, she was smart. Right up there with Mira. More and more Mrs. Caswell called on Emma Lee instead of Ashley or one of her friends. Grover overheard those girls whisper things about the way she dressed, the way she talked.

The new girl had been at Claxton about a week when one day at recess while Grover played Sam in HORSE, Mrs. Caswell sat down and started talking to Emma Lee. After a while, Mrs. Caswell hugged her and got up. Mrs. Caswell stopped by where Ashley and her friends played four square, said something to them and then walked on up to the top of the hill where Miss Shook, the other sixth-grade teacher, sat on the teacher's bench.

Miss Shook had been Grover's fourth-grade teacher. Tall, fat and jowl-faced, she yelled a lot, wasn't too bright and didn't like boys, especially quiet boys like Grover. Often when he had been sitting quietly doing his work, she'd call on him, saying, "What are you up to, Grover?" One time she'd accused him of cheating on a math test. It was only after his mother proposed that Miss Shook give him another, harder test and Grover still made a 100 that Miss Shook left him alone. Lucky for Sudie, Miss Shook had been moved from fourth to sixth grade last year.

Ashley and her friends had stopped playing four square and were talking something over. They didn't look so eager now. He saw them draw straws. Ashley must've lost, because she was the one who, slowly and looking back at her friends, walked over to Emma Lee. Emma Lee looked up from her book. Ashley flipped her blonde hair back over her shoulder, tilted her head and, looking everywhere but at Emma Lee, said something Grover couldn't hear.

Emma Lee closed her book and followed Ashley to where they'd been playing four square. She began playing with them. She was taller than all of them and quicker too. Even in that long coat of hers. Sam had finished skunking Grover when Ashley and her friends, looking irritated, came down to their end of the basketball court. Emma Lee followed behind, grinning.

Grover noticed Matthew standing out on the sidewalk in his old Army coat, looking through the fence in their direction, his fingers curled around the chain-link fence.

"Who won?" Sam asked the girls.

Ashley smiled, and putting on a fake mountain accent, said, "Emuh Leeeee diyud."

Emma Lee's smile faded, her brown eyes darkened and she went still.

"Are you boys finished?" Ashley asked. "We want to play HORSE. You want to play with us?"

"That's okay." Sam backed up a little.

Ashley turned to the other girls. "Should we play HORSE? Or should we play another game?"

"Like what?" asked Stacey.

"Yeah," said Marcie, "like what?"

"Hmmm," Ashley said, tapping her chin and frowning. She snapped her fingers. "I know!" She turned to Emma Lee. "Let's play H-I-L-L-B-I-L-L-Y."

Grover wasn't positive what happened. All he knew was that one minute Ashley was standing and the next she wasn't.

"What happened here?" Mrs. Caswell asked. Grover didn't see how his teacher had covered so much ground so quickly.

"She . . . she slapped me," Ashley said in a surprised, trembling voice. She gingerly touched her cheek where a hand mark slowly bloomed. The other girls helped her up and dusted leaves off the back of her sweater.

"Emma Lee?" asked Mrs. Caswell. "Why did you slap Ashley?"

"She knows good and well why," Emma Lee said calmly.

"We were trying to include her, like you asked," Ashley said.

By now most of the kids on the playground had gathered around.

"Did anyone else see what happened?" Mrs. Caswell looked around the circle of kids.

Grover looked at his feet.

Mrs. Caswell took Emma Lee's arm. "We'll have to pay a visit to Mrs. Dillingham."

As Grover watched Mrs. Caswell lead Emma Lee away, he and all the other kids knew what going to Mrs. Dillingham meant. That's when he remembered seeing Matthew, but when Grover looked to where he'd been standing along the fence, he saw Matthew was gone.

The bell sounded that recess was over. As Grover and Sam walked toward the building, Mira came over and asked, "What happened?"

"They called her a hillbilly," Sam said.

Mira shook her head and sighed. "Those girls . . ."

"It wouldn't matter if Mrs. Dillingham knew," Sam said.

Grover was sure his friend was right. Mrs. Dillingham always said she didn't care why somebody hit somebody. It was an automatic suspension. Still, he couldn't help admitting that he wouldn't have minded if Emma Lee never came back to school.

‡   ‡   ‡

When Mrs. Caswell finally returned with Emma Lee, Emma Lee disappeared into the cloakroom, probably getting her backpack. When she came back out, she'd taken off her coat. She walked to her desk, pulled out her science book and started reading. Grover glanced across the room at Sam, who gave a shrug. Everyone in the class was looking at Emma Lee. Never had anyone who'd hit anyone escaped suspension. Grover wondered if Mrs. Caswell had somehow convinced their principal to give the girl another chance. He went back to reading his science book, but he kept thinking about his mother and how she would've taken him aside and asked him to look out for the new girl. He went back to his science book one more time but he couldn't absorb the words on the page.

Unable to stand it any longer, Grover set down his book and with an exasperated sigh said, "Hillbilly!"

Mrs. Caswell looked up from a paper she was grading. "Pardon me, Grover?"

Grover felt his classmates look up from their books. "Ashley called Emma Lee a hillbilly. That's why she hit her."

"I see," said Mrs. Caswell, looking at Ashley, who was looking at Grover like *Do I know that kid?* It was probably the first time since they'd made that hygrometer together back in third grade that Ashley had noticed him.

Mrs. Caswell slid her chair back, got up and walked slowly to Ashley's desk.

"I didn't *call* her anything," Ashley said.

"No?" asked Mrs. Caswell.

"I said I wanted to play a game called . . . that word he just said."

Mrs. Caswell cocked her head. "What word was that?"

"The one he just said," she said again, her face getting redder.

"I didn't hear Grover very well," she said. "Can you tell me what the word is?"

Ashley lowered her head. "Hillbilly," she whispered.

"I'm sorry, Ashley," Mrs. Caswell said, "I didn't hear you."

"Hillbilly," Ashley said a little louder, her voice trembling.

"What is the definition of *hillbilly*?" Mrs. Caswell asked.

Ashley didn't look up.

"I asked you a question, Ashley," Mrs. Caswell said.

Ashley looked up. "Please, Mrs. Caswell," she said, sounding like she was about to cry.

Mrs. Caswell crossed her arms, still waiting for an answer.

Ashley ducked like she was trying to curl up into a ball and disappear.

"Can anyone help Ashley come up with a definition for *hillbilly*?"

No one spoke.

Daniel Pevoe raised his hand. Daniel sat in the front row where Mrs. Caswell could help him catch up with his work. With Mrs. Caswell's help, he'd been passing all his subjects.

"Yes, Daniel?"

"*Hillbilly* is kind of like the N-word . . . "

The class gasped.

". . . except it's talking about mountain people."

Mrs. Caswell just looked at Daniel a moment as all kinds of whispering went on throughout the room. "Thank you, Daniel," Mrs. Caswell said slowly as if needing time to think. "You raise a very good point." She turned to Ashley. "Don't you think Daniel raises a good point?"

"Ma'am?" Ashley said.

"We were all surprised, even shocked, by Daniel's comment, yet I think he's making a pretty accurate comparison." Mrs. Caswell turned back to Ashley. "Would you ever call Mira the N-word?"

"Of course not!" Ashley said. "That's a horrible, horrible word! I've never said that word before in my life!"

"I'm glad to hear it," Mrs. Caswell said. "It is a horrible word. But according to Daniel's comparison, *hillbilly* is a pretty horrible word too."

"It was a game," Ashley said weakly.

"Oh, I see," said Mrs. Caswell. "You weren't calling Emma Lee a hillbilly. You just wanted to play a game called H-I-L-L-B-I-L-L-Y."

Ashley's head slumped to her chest, like she was about to melt right out of her chair and collect in a miserable puddle on the floor.

"You owe Emma Lee an apology," Mrs. Caswell said.

"I'm sorry," Ashley whispered.

"It's been my experience," said Mrs. Caswell, "apologies are delivered best when one is standing and looking the offended party in the eye."

Ashley slowly stood up, walked over to where Emma Lee sat and said, "I'm sorry." What surprised Grover was that it sounded like she meant it.

Almost half an hour later, the class had gone back to work. Ashley was at her desk, her eyes rimmed in red. With his mother no longer bothering him, Grover had finished the assigned reading on clouds, answered the questions and even contributed to the class discussion on the difference between cumulus and nimbus. Somehow Sam had moved the discussion from clouds to storms to hurricanes, which got Mrs. Caswell off on a story about a cat she'd read about that had survived Hurricane Katrina by floating in a salad bowl for a week.

Grover felt a tap on his shoulder.

"You didn't have to go and do that," Emma Lee whispered.

Grover thought about it. "Yes, I did."

They looked at each other a minute.

"Oh," she said, looking into his eyes. "*She* made you do it."

"What are you talking about?!" he said, louder than he meant.

"Grover," said Mrs. Caswell, "do you have something you'd like to share with the class?"

"No, ma'am," Grover said, turning back around in his seat.

Who in the heck was this girl who read him like one of her books?

CHAPTER FIVE

D IS FOR DEAD MAN

He felt his report card burning a hole in his backpack. It was Tuesday, the day after the Emma Lee incident. Grover and Sudie had walked out of Isaac Claxton and headed up Montford Avenue toward downtown and the Wolfe house. Grover'd forgotten that first quarter report cards were being given out today. Unlike the other kids, he hadn't slid his out of its little manila envelope, but had stuffed it deep into his backpack. The past couple of weeks there'd been more Cs and even a D. He'd never had a Ð on anything in his life. This might very well be the first D in the history of the Johnston family. Mrs. Caswell had asked that the tests and papers be signed by his father. Instead of showing them to his father, Grover had forged his father's signature. He was amazed he hadn't been caught. Of course it wouldn't make any difference. His father would see his report card and it'd be all over.

They passed Reader's Corner, a small used-book store with a

black-and-white cat named Tom after Thomas Wolfe, who always sat in the front window. Grover often stopped here with Sudie and would sit and pet Tom while Sudie picked out books. Their father kept a tab at the Reader's Corner, which he'd pay at the end of every month. Their mother had loved Reader's Corner. Two blocks farther up they passed Videolife, another little store, but with movie posters plastered all over the windows. Grover's heart always sped up whenever they passed Videolife.

"Look, Grover, they have *Fantastic Mr. Fox*." Sudie stopped, looking longingly at a poster. "Maybe we could rent just one movie?" She held up her finger. "Just one."

"Come on, Sudie," Grover said impatiently, taking her hand and pulling her along. Sudie kept looking back over her shoulder at Videolife as they walked on up Montford.

"I don't see why we can't rent just one," Sudie said.

What Sudie didn't know, and what Grover and his father agreed never to tell her, was that their mother had been walking up to Videolife to get *Fantastic Mr. Fox*. She'd asked Videolife to call her as soon as it arrived. She'd wanted to surprise Sudie.

They crossed the bridge that led into downtown. The bridge was the overpass of I-240, a busy four-lane expressway with cars and tractor trailer trucks rumbling beneath them. Built thirty years ago, I-240 cut through the middle of Asheville, dividing Montford and other Asheville neighborhoods from downtown. Their father hated it because in its construction they had bulldozed Thomas Wolfe's birthplace and made a big wide wound in Beaucatcher Mountain.

They crossed into downtown and entered the Grove Arcade—a long building built in the 1920s with immense winged lions guarding the doors. They walked down the long hallway, which glistened with polished marble and granite. Sunlight slanted through the high windows, so that the bright light and deep shadow reminded Grover of a famous painting he'd seen in some art book. The painting was of a church, but that's all he could remember.

The Grove Arcade had been renovated into a kind of mall, with shops down both sides. People lived in condos on the second floor. The original architect's drawings, displayed in the middle of the building, showed that it was planned to have twelve stories above it, a small skyscraper, where people would live above the shops. The Depression had hit and the project ran out of money, and they never built above the first few floors.

Businessmen in coats and ties, and businesswomen in high heels and suits, using the building as a cut-through, walked fast to one important meeting or another. Tourists strolled around, lugging shopping bags and pausing in front of store windows. A few street people lounged on benches beside grocery carts full of their belongings. Young street people, what their father called quasi street people, wore backpacks and camped downtown in alleys and vacant lots. A lot of them wore their hair in dreadlocks. Many carried drums, and, on Saturday nights, a huge drumming circle gathered in Pritchard Park, the drumming echoing off the buildings and carrying all the way to Grover's house.

Grover's family would walk downtown on Saturday nights and watch the drumming, which went on for hours. People danced in the center of the circle. Sometimes Grover's mother would try to pull their father into the circle to dance, but he almost always refused. Their mother would go into the center of the circle and dance by herself, swaying and turning around, closing her eyes and smiling like the drumming had taken her some other place. Watching his mother dance like that, Grover sometimes felt he didn't know her.

With the report card in his backpack, Grover was in no hurry to reach their father's office. They stopped at Bean Streets Café, a coffee shop, on the way to the Wolfe house. Every morning their father gave them enough money to stop after school and buy hot chocolate and a doughnut. After they got their hot chocolates, Grover and Sudie sat at a table in the lower section of Bean Streets. It was like somebody's den with old sofas and big cushioned chairs to sit in. A woman mannequin's arm reached down from the ceiling, its nails painted bright red.

Grover liked Bean Streets because Mr. Critt, the owner, who lived upstairs and often walked around in a robe and bedroom slippers, was a painter and displayed his own paintings on the walls. They were never of any particular thing. You might make out a tree or a telephone pole or a tennis shoe or a bicycle, but whatever it was would always be caught up in crazy swirls of colors. His paintings looked like little framed nightmares.

Grover and Sudie sat at their usual table, a giant checkerboard, with the pieces in the little drawers underneath. Sudie started to get them, but Grover shook his head.

"You don't want to play?" Sudie asked.

"Not in the mood."

"What's wrong?"

"He's going to kill me."

"How come?"

"My report card," he said.

"What'd you get?"

"Haven't looked." He glanced down to his backpack on the floor.

"Why not?" she asked.

"It's gotta be bad."

"Why don't you get it out? Maybe it's not so bad."

He looked at his backpack but didn't move.

"I'll get it out." She reached for his backpack.

"Sudie!" He grabbed the backpack from her.

"You've got to look at it sometime."

He sighed, unzipped his backpack and dug out his report card. He slid it out of the manila envelope and started to open it. But then he handed it to his sister.

Sudie unfolded the report card and began to read. "It's not so bad," she said. "A B in social studies. An A in math." She looked up at him and smiled. "An A in physical education." She paused. "A C- in science."

"Ah," groaned Grover. "I told you." Science had always been one of his best subjects.

She turned the report card to another page. He watched her read it. She looked up at him, biting her lip. She shut the report card and slid it toward him.

"What?" he asked.

She scratched her forehead, then, looking around, lowered her voice. "A D in English."

Grover sat back in his chair. "D is for dead man."

"It'll be okay," Sudie said, leaning across the table toward her brother.

"Are you kidding? He was expecting my grades to improve by coming to study at his office, not get worse! Heck, he might even think I messed up on purpose." He stared at the report card for a minute. "I'm a dead man."

"Stop saying that." Sudie sipped her hot chocolate.

Grover kept staring at the report card. Then it came to him. "Unless . . ."

"What?" she asked.

"Unless you don't show him *your* report card."

"How will that help?" Sudie asked.

"If you don't show him yours, then he won't know report cards have come out, and he's too worried about the Wolfe house right now to remember." In fact he'd never seen his father so preoccupied.

"But . . ." She paused. "We have to get them signed."

"I can take care of that," he said. "I've been signing my papers and tests the past few weeks. I've got Daddy's signature down."

"Grover, that's not right!"

"I knew he'd kill me if he saw those Cs and Ds. Besides, I didn't want to worry him."

Sudie narrowed her eyes at him.

"Mostly I didn't want him to kill me." He put his hands together like he was begging. "Come on, Sudie. I need your help."

"I don't know," she said. "It's like lying."

"Sudie, please." He took his sister's hand. "Daddy won't let me near the Bamboo Forest if he finds out about this. And life without the Bamboo Forest . . . well . . . "

She crossed her arms.

"I mean *you* wouldn't be hiding anything bad," he said. "You've got straight As." Sudie always had straight As.

"He's going to find out sooner or later," Sudie said, uncrossing her arms and sitting up.

"By then I'll have pulled my grades up," Grover said.

"I don't know." Sudie looked down at Grover's report card.

Grover took his sister's hand again. "You're my only hope."

"Daddy'll be wondering where we are," Sudie said.

As they were getting up, Grover noticed a guy sitting at a table by the window, drinking coffee and underlining with a big yellow highlighter in what looked like a textbook.

"Did he look familiar to you?" Grover asked Sudie as they walked outside.

Sudie looked back at the guy in the window. "Isn't that Matthew? Jessie's assistant?"

Grover saw she was right. He hadn't recognized him. Instead of the worn Army jacket, he wore a UNC Asheville sweatshirt.

His hair was neatly combed and his pale face shown like he'd just taken a shower. Still, there was something about him that seemed sort of off. The crooked way he held his mouth, like a slight but permanent scowl. Jessie often hired what seemed to Grover pretty eccentric students. Their father had said Jessie had a soft spot for misfits. Thinking about all this as he and his sister headed for the Wolfe house, Grover realized that he himself had been hired by Jessie for a number of jobs. What did that say about him?

‡   ‡   ‡

The parking lot of the Wolfe house was empty except for a big bus that said *First Baptist Church of Charlotte* across the side. Inside, a large group of old ladies chattered around the displays. Grover noticed their father's office door closed. Little Bit, their father's gray-haired secretary, was at the copy machine.

"He's in there with a couple of commissioners." She looked toward their father's office and sighed.

"Is one of them Mr. Lunsford?" Grover asked.

"Afraid so," said Little Bit under her breath. Barely five feet tall, Little Bit had been their father's secretary for as long as he'd been director. "From the looks on their faces, I doubt they had good news for your father."

She handed Sudie and Grover each a sheet of what she'd been copying. It said, *A Thomas Wolfe Christmas,* over a drawing of the Thomas Wolfe house with a wreath on the door. *Come celebrate an authentic 1900s Christmas as Thomas Wolfe and his family might have celebrated. The house will be decorated in authentic early twentieth century decorations. Snacks and refreshments will be offered. School and church groups welcome.*

Little Bit kept her eye on the closed office door. "Your dad thinks it's a pretty crazy idea. To tell you the truth, I'm surprised he's even letting me do it."

Two tour guides came out of the break room, brushing doughnut crumbs from their blazers. Joanna was a short-haired blonde woman just graduated from UNC Asheville who'd started leading tours last year and who, to Grover's fascination, had a tattoo of a green vine along her collarbone. Dwight, the other guide, was a middle-aged man older than their father who had been leading tours almost as long as Little Bit had been secretary. Dwight had written a couple of short biographies of Thomas Wolfe sold in the gift shop. The expert way that Joanna and Dwight circled up the crowd of chattering old women, divided them into two groups and led them off into the house reminded Grover of a nature show he'd seen about sheepdogs working their flocks.

Grover and Sudie went to the break room, which, since it was usually empty and since Little Bit kept it stocked with Krispy Kreme doughnuts, was where they did their homework. They'd taken their books out of their backpacks when they heard their father. They peeked around the corner and saw Mr. Lunsford. He was a thin, nervous man, whose eyes never rested on any one person for long, like he was always checking to see if someone more important might've walked into the room. Behind Mr.

Lunsford was a short, bald, red-faced man, who Grover recognized as another commissioner.

"Oh, hey, kids," their father said.

"Are these yours?" the bald commissioner asked.

"Grover and Sudie," their father said. "This is Commissioner Renfro and Commissioner Lunsford."

"Nice to meet y'all," Mr. Renfro said.

"Absolutely," Delbert Lunsford said, picking up a flyer off Little Bit's desk.

"'*A Thomas Wolfe Christmas*?'" Mr. Lunsford said, reading it and looking up at their father.

"We're hoping it might increase our numbers," their father said.

Mr. Lunsford rubbed his forehead.

"It was my idea," Little Bit said, stepping up to Mr. Lunsford. "For one thing, I think teachers will welcome something to do with their classes around this time of year."

"Interesting idea," Mr. Lunsford said, "but who's paying for these decorations and these refreshments?" Mr. Lunsford's eyes paused on Little Bit but then shifted back to their father. "The taxpayer, I imagine."

"We're hoping they'll pay for themselves," their father said.

Mr. Lunsford didn't say anything.

"Worth a try," Mr. Renfro said. "Might be just the thing to turn this place around."

Mr. Lunsford set the flyer back on the stack. "I hope it works, Johnston. For your sake. Come on, Renfro."

Mr. Renfro shook their father's hand and followed after Mr. Lunsford. Their father, looking grim-faced, walked the two commissioners through the lobby and disappeared through the foyer with them.

"That man's always had it in for this place," Little Bit said, going back to copying. Little Bit looked to make sure the men were gone. "They say Wolfe modeled a character after Lunsford's great-grandfather in one of his books and apparently the Lunsfords never forgave him. Your father is all that stands between Delbert Lunsford and the wrecking ball."

Grover and Sudie went back into the break room and sat down to do their homework. In a minute their father walked by the door and stopped at Little Bit's desk. Grover got up to try to overhear what they were saying.

"I'm sorry, Walt," Little Bit said. "Seems my idea has gotten you into hot water."

"If it wasn't the Wolfe Christmas, he'd find something else," their father said. "Are the kids here?"

"They started on their homework," Little Bit said overly loud as if to say if they weren't working on it, they better start.

Grover grabbed his social studies book and opened it, but as he did, his report card fell right by the door. Panicked, he couldn't move. Sudie jumped up, grabbed his report card, sat back down and slid it under her math book as their father walked in.

"Hey, Daddy," Sudie said sweetly.

"I've got to go over to city hall for another meeting," their father said. "I'll be back in an hour or so." He started to leave but came back, pointing his finger at Grover. "Double-check your homework. I'll go over it with you tonight."

Grover nodded, his heart pounding from the close call.

They watched him walk back across to his office, grab his coat, say something to Little Bit and then trudge out the front door, his head bowed like he was walking into a stiff wind.

Sudie waited till he'd gone out the front door, then pulled Grover's report card from under her math book, handing it back to him.

"Thanks," he said.

"Daddy doesn't look very good," Sudie said.

Grover and Sudie started studying. Grover was going over his spelling words when Sudie handed him her report card. "Sign it."

"Really?" Grover said.

"I don't think Daddy seeing your report card would be such a good thing right now. For you or him."

He took out a pen and carefully signed their father's name, then handed it back to her.

She looked at the signature, raising an eyebrow. "That's pretty good."

"I've been practicing," Grover said.

Sudie put her report card back in her pack, then looked at him. "You better get your grades up."

‡　‡　‡

As Grover had guessed, their father had been too preoccupied with work to remember their report cards, which they'd returned to their teachers Wednesday morning. Grover'd held his breath, afraid that somehow Mrs. Caswell might discover his forgery and contact his father. But nothing happened. Every afternoon for the rest of the week when Grover and Sudie came to the Wolfe house, things went as they had been going for a while—their father would be on the phone with some official, sounding angry or desperate or both. *Now, Christopher, I promise we'll get those numbers up. We just need a little more time.* Either that or he'd come storming back from some meeting, slamming his satchel on his desk. *They don't get it. All these guys think about is the bottom line.*

Their father was irritable and liable to snap at Grover and Sudie. In the evenings they'd buy take-out and sit in front of the TV, watching the *PBS NewsHour*. Grover couldn't help thinking how calmly the newscasters told them about wars, earthquakes, famines, the worst things in the world. Yet they never seemed upset.

After the *NewsHour* Grover and Sudie would clean up, while their father sat in the den making calls. These conversations didn't always go so well, and their father would hang up grumbling. Sudie and Grover cleaned up the kitchen as fast as possible to get out of there. Sudie, with Biscuit following her, would go to her room to study and Grover would head to the Bamboo Forest.

It was Friday night, three days since Grover and Sudie had returned their report cards to their teachers. They'd eaten supper and Sudie and Grover were cleaning up. Their father had been in a foul mood during dinner. He'd heard a rumor that the board of commissioners was considering moving the Wolfe house and selling the land to a hotel developer.

"Maybe *A Thomas Wolfe Christmas* will get attendance up," Sudie said.

"Lunsford's right! It's a waste of the taxpayers' money!" Their father laughed a desperate laugh. "*A Thomas Wolfe Christmas*! It's an oxymoron."

"What's an oxymoron?" Sudie asked.

"Then why are you letting Little Bit go through with it?" Grover asked their father.

His father sighed and his face softened. "Honestly, I don't know." Little Bit had a special place in his father's heart. She'd stood by him when the house had burned, working long hours for no extra pay, helping him raise money.

After dinner, their father got on the phone. As soon as Sudie and Grover had cleaned up, Sudie hurried off to her room and Grover left for the Bamboo Forest, carrying his toolbox and a couple of flashlights. It had been getting dark earlier. He'd figured out how to set up the flashlights so he could spotlight his weavings and work at night. He was nearly finished with a new weaving, or *tapestry*, as Emma called it. He'd made a big grid out of bamboo, his biggest yet, then started weaving in evergreen limbs he'd cut from hemlocks, pines, fir and a Norway spruce in the neighborhood. It made a kind of furry, prickly, green tapestry. Because it was a Friday night and not a school night, his father would probably let him stay out later.

It was an unusually warm night, like it sometimes got before a storm. Grover had discovered he enjoyed working in the dark. He was aware of the night air on his skin, the bright Christmasy smells of the evergreens, and all around him the bamboo creaked and rustled in the wind. With the tapestry spotlighted, it was like that was all there was, the work in front of him. Nothing else mattered. As he wove the limbs within the circle of light, he'd feel part of himself step back from the work, like he'd become two people—the doer and the watcher.

Grover had been working for about half an hour and was weaving in one of the limbs Jessie had said he could cut from his hemlock bushes. Thunder echoed in the distance and lightning flickered faintly but Grover was too caught up in his work to worry about it. He heard someone coming through the bamboo. Biscuit appeared at his feet. He grabbed one of the flashlights and pointed it toward the noise. Sudie appeared in the light, shading her eyes with her hands.

"He found out!" she said.

"What are you talking about?"

"Mrs. Caswell just called," she said. "I heard Daddy say, 'What low grades?'"

"Oh Lord," Grover said.

"He's coming," she said. "You better get out of here."

"Where would I go?" He began picking up his tools and putting them in his toolbox with Sudie helping him.

"Go over to Jessie's . . ."

"Grover!" It was their father's voice. They heard a loud crashing through the bamboo.

"Run to Jessie's," Sudie said, pushing him. "I'll finish cleaning up."

"*Grover!*" their father shouted again.

"Too late," Grover said as he shined the flashlight in the direction the crashing was coming from. Their father appeared in the light, scowling. He walked up to Grover and slapped the flashlight out of his hand. The flashlight clattered to the ground and went dead. The only light now was from the one flashlight spotlighting the tapestry.

"How dare you!" their father growled.

"I can explain . . . ," Grover said.

"How dare you forge my signature!"

"Daddy, he was afraid you'd get mad," Sudie said.

"He was right about that," their father said.

"You shouldn't get mad at him. . . ."

"Get out of here, Sudie," their father said, staring at Grover. "I know you were in on this too!"

"Daddy . . ." Sudie took hold of their father's arm, but he shook her off and she fell. Biscuit gave a low growl.

"Go on, Sudie," Grover said, his voice trembling. He could only half see his father in the light. He couldn't see his expression. It was like the shape of his father had been taken over by this angry creature. "Go on back, Sudie," Grover said. "It'll be okay."

His father laughed an angry laugh, not taking his eyes off Grover.

Sudie looked at them a minute, then, grabbing up Biscuit, tore through the bamboo.

"Did you really think you'd get away with it?" his father said.

"I thought I could pull my grades up," Grover said, quietly.

"Never did I think a son of mine would stoop to such a thing," his father said.

"All I did was put your signature on a few things."

"I'm glad your mother's not alive to see this!"

Grover felt the breath go out of him.

"She would be devastated," his father said. "Just devastated!"

"She'd be devastated, all right," Grover said, unable to control himself. "She'd be devastated to see what kind of father you've turned into! She'd be devastated that she couldn't count on you, even when she's dead!"

What Grover heard next was silence. An empty silence that was full of nothing but a long, aching hurt that rushed at him from everywhere. A siren cried somewhere in the distance. He braced himself for a fist to his chest or a slap to his face. Not that their father had ever hit either of them, but there was no telling about the man standing in front of him. He glared at Grover. There was a crack of thunder, and a flash of lightning lit up his father's face, an angry mask. His father turned toward the tapestry that sat green and still in the spotlight. He walked over and snatched it down.

"No, Daddy, please don't . . . ," Grover begged, taking hold of his father's arm. His father shook him off, and Grover found himself, like Sudie, on the ground. There was another crack of thunder, louder, and a brighter flash of lightning.

"Daddy, please, that's my best one yet," Grover said, getting back up.

"It's over," their father said. As he held the weaving in front of Grover, he tried to rip it in two but the bamboo frame was too strong. Instead, he tossed it into the darkness. "No more playing in the blasted Bamboo Forest!"

Seeing Grover's toolbox, he picked it up and hurled it into the bamboo, tools and twine scattering everywhere. He turned to the lean-to and the table and the chair that Grover had built from bamboo, and began kicking and smashing them.

Grover was too stunned to move as he watched his father, like some wild animal gone berserk, tear his workshop to shreds. Every now and then lightning would flash and he'd see his father clearly, like he was watching a series of snapshots of his father destroying his workshop. When his father had finally finished, he stood there, catching his breath. Grover could feel him getting calmer.

He turned to Grover and with something close to his old fatherly tone said, "Son, ever since your mother died, you've done nothing but come out here and be all by yourself. You ought to be out doing things with other kids. Otherwise, you'll never get over . . ."

The anger Grover felt right then toward his father was something he'd never felt before in his life. It was more than anger. It was hatred so pure and hot that it seared the back of his throat. Grover felt the hair on the back of his neck stand up and a bolt of lightning shot right down in the middle of the Bamboo Forest. The thunder was so loud it seemed to come from inside him.

"The wrong one died," Grover said quietly. He started to run out of the Bamboo Forest. He tripped over something and went sprawling, hitting his knee on a stump or a rock. It hurt but he picked himself up and ran and didn't stop, didn't even slow down. It lightninged and thundered again. Then it began to rain. He kept running, not knowing where he was going till he ran through the gates of the Riverside Cemetery, down the little roads, past hundreds of headstones, arriving at his mother's headstone. Something warm ran down his shin. He pulled up his pant leg and, in the faint glow of a streetlight, made out a thin line of blood that had trickled down his shin.

He slumped against his mother's headstone, the rain coming down. "How could you leave us?" he shouted. He looked around at all the weavings that Jessie kept arranged so neatly around her headstone. In the faint light and slickened by the rain, they looked like shiny skeletons. Nothing close to what he'd dreamed of making for her. The bones of dreams.

"I'm the crazy one," he said. "I'm the crazy one making things for a dead mother!" Wiping the rain from his face, he gazed at her headstone, waiting for an answer. He got up and started kicking the weavings and kept kicking them, feeling a dark satisfaction as he kicked weeks and weeks of his work around the grave. "Dead, dead, dead, dead, dead!"

Strong arms wrapped around him from behind. "Leave me alone," he cried, thinking it was his father. "I hate you!" He tried to pull away, but the arms held him tight, then slowly turned him around.

"It's okay, darlin'." A woman's voice. A woman hugged him. He smelled a medicine smell like at the doctor's office. "It's all right, sweetheart," she said, patting his back. At her touch, Grover felt something loosen down deep inside him, something that had been stuck there since that evening his mother hadn't come home. He began to tremble, and at first didn't recognize the sounds of his sobs.

CHAPTER SIX

GONE TO VIDEOLIFE

Grover could tell by the light through his window that it was mid-morning. Put out with himself for sleeping late and missing perfectly good work time in the Bamboo Forest, he hopped out of bed. The ache in his knee and the bandage wrapped around it brought last night rushing back. The yelling, the smashing, the splintering. The lightning snapshots of his father destroying everything in his path. Workshop, weavings, months of work—not there, not there, so not there anymore.

He fell back on his bed and remembered the rest—how Emma Lee's mother had been on her usual evening walk through Riverside last night when it had begun to storm and she had happened to see him; how they'd run into Jessie and Sudie trotting up the street in the rain toward them; how they'd found their father on the front porch in the dark, crying into his hands and saying over and over, *I'm sorry, Caroline. I'm sorry. I'm so sorry*; how Emma Lee's mother had made Grover change out of his wet clothes, then cleaned the gash in his knee and bandaged it; how Jessie had led their father, looking pale and exhausted, upstairs and put him to bed; how Jessie and Emma Lee's mother had whispered in the kitchen to themselves; how Jessie said he'd spend the night on the couch; how Emma Lee's mother had put Sudie to bed, and Jessie sat on the end of Grover's bed till Grover felt his eyelids getting heavy.

Grover climbed out of bed and looked out his window at the mid-morning light filtering through the bamboo. The worst part hadn't been his father wrecking his workshop. The worst part had been seeing his father cry. Grover hadn't seen him cry once since their mother had died. Not when he had come back from the hospital. Not at the funeral. Not even after the funeral when everybody came back to their house with plates and bowls and platters of food. It shook Grover to see his father cry. It made him wonder for the first time if maybe their father missed their mother as much as he and Sudie did.

He smelled something he hadn't smelled in a long time. Bacon. Then he heard laughter. Pulling on his jeans, he limped as quietly as he could on his stiff knee down the hall toward the kitchen. He peeked around the corner. Jessie stood at the stove, flipping pancakes; Emma Lee's mother stood beside him, turning sizzling bacon over in the frying pan; Emma Lee was setting the breakfast table; and Sudie, still in her purple pajamas, sat on the couch and watched *Sesame Street* with Biscuit curled up next to her.

"There he is," Jessie said.

"Let's have a look," Leila said, covering the frying pan. She had Grover sit at the kitchen table and roll up his pant leg. "You won't need stitches," she said, carefully unwrapping the bandage. She took a bottle of hydrogen peroxide from a bag, poured some over the cut, which bubbled, stinging a little. She dried the cut and put a big Band-Aid over it. She handed Grover the bottle of hydrogen peroxide. "Pour some of this over it every morning and every night before you go to bed and keep it clean."

Grover felt almost dizzy with all these people in his kitchen. Was this a strange dream? Or had last night been the dream, the nightmare?

"Daddy's down at the Bamboo Forest," Sudie called from the couch.

"Clay's with him." Jessie slid a couple of pancakes onto a plate and put it in the oven to keep warm.

"Emma Lee," Leila said, "why don't you and Grover go tell them breakfast is ready?"

"Yes, ma'am," Emma Lee said, setting a fork on a folded paper napkin. "Come on." She grabbed Grover's arm and led him toward the door before he had a chance to say that going to see his father was the last thing he wanted to do.

"Get a jacket," she said, taking down her coat from one of the pegs along the foyer wall, where coats and sweaters hung. "It's turned cold."

"I don't need a coat," Grover said, pulling away. Opening the front door, he felt a blast of frigid air. He turned around and Emma Lee held his coat out to him.

As they walked over to the Bamboo Forest, Grover noticed

the sky was a stunning blue, as if last night's storm had swept away all lingering clouds. The only signs of the storm itself were a few fallen branches and water beading like diamonds in the grass and on the tips of bare tree limbs. The air was light, wintry, and Grover found himself walking into a new season.

"What's going on?" Grover asked as they headed down the street toward the Bamboo Forest.

Emma Lee didn't say anything.

"Why are y'all making breakfast in my house?"

"*Somebody* needs to," she said.

"Y'all don't really know us," Grover said.

"Where we come from, neighbors help each other," Emma Lee said. "Besides, your daddy called us this morning."

"He did?"

"To apologize for last night," Emma Lee said. "And to thank Mama."

As they neared the Bamboo Forest, Grover felt a familiar tightness push up into his chest. He had a flash of last night—his father slinging his tapestry into the bamboo, then his tools, then all the smashing. He stopped. "I'm not going."

"Whatever," Emma said, shrugging, "but I gotta tell them breakfast is ready." As she walked through the field and disappeared into the bamboo, several crows flapped out of the grass.

The wind rustled the bamboo leaves.

Grover sighed and started across the field, entering the path through the bamboo. He tried to brace himself. Last night had seemed not quite real, like walking around in a nightmare. The lightning had given him glimpses, but he hadn't been able to really see. He tried to prepare himself for the mess he was about to find. He heard them coming back through the bamboo, slipped off the path and crouched down. Emma Lee, Clay and Grover's father passed right by him.

"I believe we've got his workshop looking pretty good," Clay said.

"I appreciate your help," Grover's father said, passing within inches of Grover and not seeing him. His father looked pale, hollow-eyed and exhausted, but there was something about the warm tone of his voice that Grover hadn't heard in a long time.

"Guess he went on back," Emma Lee said, glancing right where Grover was hidden, meeting his eyes, yet walking on.

"If he's like me," Clay said, "the boy's probably got a appetite on him."

Grover waited, shivering and watching his breath come out in little clouds. A crow cawed. He stepped out of the bamboo and walked along the path till he came to the open circle. He couldn't bring himself to look. Slowly he lifted his eyes.

Had he lost his mind? The place seemed as it had always been. The lean-to, his worktable, even his chair were all there, together and standing. His neat piles of supplies were as he'd left them. His toolbox, which his father'd hurled into the bamboo, sat underneath the lean-to. Grover went to it, finding only a little dent in the side. He opened it. His saws and his twine were all back in the drawers. They weren't in the drawers he kept them in, but most everything seemed there.

Then he looked up. On the other side of the clearing, hanging where he always hung his tapestries, was the tapestry he'd been working on. He walked up to it. A few of the evergreen limbs were broken or missing but most of it seemed to be there.

"Those bamboo grids you make are tough."

Grover turned around and saw his father standing there.

"I came back for your toolbox," his father said, walking up. "Sudie reminded me you always bring it back to the house."

Grover looked around at his workshop. "When did you do all this?"

"I got up early," his father said, "and came out here to repair things as best I could." He looked at Grover like he was waiting for a judgment.

Grover turned away and looked at the tapestry. Did his father think he was going to get off that easy?

"Clay helped me." His father picked up a stray length of bamboo and set it in a pile. "I'm very sorry about how I've been these past few months."

Grover believed him, but he still couldn't get past the wall of his anger. A flock of crows flew overhead, settling into the bamboo on the far side of the workshop. Grover thought of his mother and how she would've said to try with his father.

"I'm sorry about what I said last night, that the wrong one died," Grover heard himself say. Then, surprising himself, he said, "I didn't mean it."

"Sure you did," his father said, starting to put his hand on Grover's shoulder but seeming to sense Grover wasn't ready for that. "Who wouldn't wish the mother over the father? It's perfectly natural. In fact, it shouldn't be any other way."

His father reached out and stroked Grover's tapestry. "There's not a night that goes by I don't wish it had been me who'd gone to Videolife instead of your mother." He sighed. "But what came to me this morning was this," he said, rubbing his temples. "We'll have to settle for me."

Grover looked at his father.

"How's your knee?" his father asked.

"Okay," Grover said.

His father was looking at the tapestry. "I meant to ask, was it you who came out here last night, after I . . . lost it?"

Grover shook his head.

"This morning when I first got here," his father said, "your weaving was already hanging back up. And your toolbox was sitting there with some of the tools already back in it."

"Maybe Clay?" Grover said.

"I asked Clay and Emma Lee and Leila, and I asked Jessie, and none of them came out here last night afterward."

"Sudie," Grover said.

"She didn't go anywhere last night and didn't wake up till a while ago."

Looking at the tapestry that blew slightly in the wind, Grover felt goose bumps rise on his arms. Was his mother still here in some way? Was this somehow her doing?

"Grover?" his father asked.

"Nothing," Grover said.

"Let's go eat breakfast." His father picked up Grover's toolbox.

Grover started to take the toolbox from him but his father said, "I've got it."

Then his father put his arm around Grover's shoulder and started to lead him back home. At the edge of the Bamboo Forest, Grover nearly tripped over a red-ribboned stake in the ground. So that's what he had fallen over last night.

"They're back," his father said. Somehow Grover had missed the flagged stakes that had sprouted overnight like new bamboo shoots.

So much time had passed since he and Sudie had pulled them up that he'd believed they wouldn't reappear. Grover frantically grabbed hold of the stake he'd nearly tripped over and worked it back and forth, but it was in deep.

"Stop!" his father said. "If Lunsford finds out my son has pulled these up, he'll have my job for sure."

Grover let go of the stake. He hadn't thought of that.

His father sighed and set down the toolbox. "Oh, what the heck!" He looked around. "Come on. Grab hold." His father bent over and took hold of the stake. "Maybe between the both of us . . ."

"Are you sure?" Grover asked. He bent down, taking hold of the stake with his father. They both pulled, but it still didn't budge.

"They put these in extra deep," their father said, grunting as he kept pulling. Grover pulled with all his strength and just as he'd decided once and for all that the world was a bleak and hopeless place, the stake moved and slid ever so slowly out of the ground.

Chapter Seven

A Big Old Grass

Later that afternoon, with their father gone to the Wolfe house and Sudie sitting by the woodstove reading a Ramona book, Grover decided he'd take care of something that had been bothering him since he'd woken up. He went out back, got their wheelbarrow and a rake from the shed and headed to Riverside. The day had turned colder, and it made the wheels of the wheelbarrow squeak. He was rolling the wheelbarrow up the street when he noticed Clay kicking the soccer ball against the side of his house. In the cold air, it made a ringing sound.

Grover tried to hurry past, but when he sped up, the wheels squealed louder.

"You working in the Bamboo Forest?" Clay asked, running over.

"I'm going over to the cemetery," Grover said, not stopping.

"Need some help?" Clay asked. "Mama says yard work is my long suit."

"That's okay," Grover said. He was embarrassed that he'd kicked the tapestries at the grave all around last night and didn't want Clay to see what a mess he'd made.

"Back home I took care of the family plot," Clay said. "I used to mow and weed-eat the whole thing. I was careful not to nick any of the old gravestones." He sighed. "I sort of miss taking care of it. Of course I miss that Mama paid me good too."

"See you," Grover said and started back up Edgemont, the wheelbarrow still screeching. He glanced back and saw Clay walking slowly back toward his house, his shoulders slumped. Clay halfheartedly kicked a walnut that bounced up the street.

"Now that I think about it," Grover called to him, "I probably could use some help."

Clay walked along with him, talking the whole way up the street, past the Bamboo Forest and through the big iron gates of Riverside. When they reached his mother's grave, Grover was surprised to find that someone had already straightened up. Jessie must've come by. The tapestries all seemed to be in one piece.

"I don't understand," Grover said, picking up a couple of the smallest weavings. "I kicked these all over the place last night. I thought they'd be smashed to pieces."

Clay picked one up and tugged on it. "These weavings of yours don't tear up." Clay handed it to Grover.

Grover pulled on it, gently at first, then harder.

"Remember that first time I met you?" Clay said. "Kicked the soccer ball right into one you were working on. That ball didn't hurt your weaving hardly at all. You know why?"

"Why?"

"Bamboo's strong," he said. "We did a section in my science class on it back at Bakersville Elementary. They use bamboo in Asian countries to frame houses. They even make big buildings with it. It stands up to earthquakes better, because it's flexible and strong too. You've been framing your weavings with the toughest thing there is. Plus you tie some mean knots to hold 'em together." Clay talked more about bamboo, as they straightened up a little more around the plot. "Technically bamboo's a grass. A big old grass, still it's a grass."

As Clay helped him pick up and rake around his mother's plot, Grover remembered the funeral. It had been a clear warm Saturday in early April. The warmest day they'd had so far. Jonquils and bright pink and red azaleas had been in bloom throughout the cemetery. Riverside was so crowded with mourners that people had to park all along Edgemont Road and walk several blocks to the grave. Many were teachers, others were families and students who had gotten to know Grover's mother during the fifteen years she'd been at Claxton. Some students were now grown men and women and had families of their own. In all the years they'd lived next to the cemetery, never had Grover seen such a crowd. At the center of what must've been hundreds of people, Grover and Sudie sat with their father under a tent with other close friends and family.

The urn with their mother's ashes sat on a small pedestal above a neat square hole Jessie had dug. Sudie sat next to Grover, her face about to crumble as it had crumbled so many times that week. She clutched the tiny silver cylinder attached to a necklace that hung around her neck. Grover had stuffed his in his pocket. Nancy, the Buddhist priest, a friendly woman with warm green eyes and very short gray hair, had given them the cylinders before the funeral, telling them they contained a sprinkling of their mother's ashes.

During the ceremony Grover worked the Rubik's cube Jessie had given him, and Sudie leaned against their father and petted Biscuit, who, in the middle of the ceremony, had somehow threaded his way through the crowd and appeared beside Sudie's chair. Nancy spoke for a while, talking about what a kind, generous and patient person Caroline Johnston had been. Grover guessed that was true. But Nancy didn't say anything about how unreasonably strict their mother could be, never letting them watch TV on a week night, not letting them leave the table till they'd eaten all their vegetables or not letting them go anywhere till their rooms were picked up. She didn't mention anything about how every now and then their mother would lose it and scream at them, like whenever Sudie and he argued about whose turn it was to do the dishes or when they left dirty clothes or dirty dishes in the middle of their rooms. Mostly she'd been a good mother. Mostly she'd been a good wife. Mostly she'd been a good counselor. But listening to Nancy praise his mother, Grover felt he was hearing about someone he only vaguely recognized.

"Bamboo sends out these things they call rhizomes underneath the ground," Clay said as they finished raking up the grave. "Which is how come it spreads so easy."

"Rhizomes?" Grover asked. Every now and then the Bamboo Forest sent out shoots underneath the fence that miraculously sprouted up several yards into the cemetery. Jessie often had to cut them back. Sometimes Grover would notice a new green shoot sprouting right out of a grave itself.

As they were heading out of the cemetery, the boys passed Jessie, who had a wheelbarrow too. His was piled with broken tree branches that had fallen in last night's storm.

"Thanks for straightening up Mama's grave," Grover said.

Jessie stopped. "I haven't been over there today, and Matthew'd said he was planning to take today off, so I don't know who it could've been."

Grover thought about the weaving and the toolbox his father had found this morning. He looked back in the direction of his mother's grave and felt a tingle travel up his spine.

CHAPTER EIGHT
ALL THAT'S LEFT

Thomas Wolfe eyed Grover from across the kitchen, the writer's pale moon of a face floating in the middle of his father's apron. His father poured batter into a waffle iron and closed it, the batter hissing. The apron had been a fund-raising attempt. On the apron, Wolfe frowned, his hair uncombed, his eyes dark and tired like he'd been up all night writing. Not a very appetizing picture. Grover hadn't been surprised their father had been stuck with a closet full of them.

It was Monday morning, over a week since the terrible night their father had lost it, and he'd started making breakfast for them again. He had been leaving Grover and Sudie to eat Cheerios, Wheat Chex or instant oatmeal. Now he was back in the kitchen. Grover had never appreciated their father's breakfasts as much as he did now. Big stacks of pancakes and link sausages; French toast sprinkled with powdered sugar; homemade whole wheat biscuits with scrambled eggs, bacon and grits.

"Order up." Their father placed before them plates of Belgian waffles, swimming in syrup and butter. He filled their glasses with milk, poured himself a cup of coffee, then sat down with his own plate of waffles.

There'd been a general sigh of relief in the house. On most afternoons now their father let Grover and Sudie walk home after school instead of having them come to his office. This gave Grover more time in the Bamboo Forest. Their father stayed pretty late at the office. And after supper, he still made business calls, trying to get support for the Wolfe house, but he didn't sound as desperate or angry.

Another new thing. Every night, after about an hour of making calls, their father would get Sudie and Grover to sit with him and watch a little TV, something their mother never would've allowed on a school night. They'd watch *Nature* or *Nova* or *History Detectives*.

Last night they'd been watching *Antiques Roadshow*. The program was set in Savannah, Georgia. A man had brought in a face jug—a big pottery jug with a face on it—bug eyes, wide grinning mouth and big ears that were handles. Grover had never seen anything like it, and started thinking how he might make one out of creek clay. Grover and Sudie and their father started guessing how much it was worth.

The expert, a pretty woman with long black hair that sort of reminded Grover of Emma Lee, pointed out features on the jug with a little wooden pointer. The more she described it, the more Grover could tell it was something special.

"A thousand dollars," their father said.

"Two thousand!" Sudie blurted.

"Ten thousand!" Grover shouted, just before the expert said, "And I would insure this for fifteen thousand!"

"All right!" Grover said, raising his fist. Then he suddenly stopped.

"Grover," their father said, "are you okay?"

He nodded but didn't say anything, and he sat watching the rest of the show in silence.

That night he couldn't sleep. He'd forgotten his mother, and while watching *Antiques Roadshow* of all things! What kind of ungrateful son would forget about his mother who'd only died months ago? How many other times during the day did he not think about her? Although he hadn't wanted to admit it to himself, for some time he'd noticed he hadn't been thinking about her as much. Which made him wonder if she still thought about him, wherever she was. Was that what death was—everybody forgetting everybody?

He lay there with his iPod, listening to *All Things Must Pass*. He'd listened to the album all the way through. Not knowing what else to do he turned on his reading lamp and reached for the copy of *Look Homeward, Angel* he kept on the bottom of his nightstand. He blew the dust off the cover and opened to the first page. He'd only read a few pages when there was a knock at his door and his father came in.

"You're reading?" His father tilted the cover so he could read the title. "You gotta be kidding me!"

"Puts me right to sleep," Grover said.

"*Look Homeward, Angel* as sedative," his father said. "That's a marketing idea I hadn't thought of. Why can't you sleep?"

"Don't know," Grover said, setting the book facedown on his lap.

"Bad for the binding." His father gently took the book, folded a Kleenex to mark Grover's place, then closed it and set it back on Grover's lap. "Is something bothering you?"

Grover shrugged. He wasn't used to his father asking about anything other than his grades. Their mother had been the one to ask questions. A little too many questions. She'd ask him how his day had been or what he'd done in class or what he was working on in the Bamboo Forest. Pretty normal-seeming questions. He knew she asked not so much for the answers as to measure how he was feeling. Her questions were like the probes they sent to Mars to analyze what the planet was made of.

"Miss Snyder called," his father said.

Grover sat up. "What'd *she* want?" he asked, his heart beating faster.

"To encourage you to come see her," he said. "She thought it might help you feel better."

There was that word, *feel.*

Grover crossed his arms and looked straight ahead.

"Nobody's going to make you," his father said.

Grover looked at him out of the corner of his eye.

"We thought it might be a good idea to talk to someone," his father said.

We thought! His father and Miss Snyder had talked enough to become a *we*?

"I don't want to see her."

His father walked to the window. Just enough light from Grover's lamp spilled out into the side yard to highlight the green ribs of the Bamboo Forest. His father rubbed his forehead. "If your mother was here . . ."

Outside, the wind rustled the bamboo.

"I don't think about her as much," Grover said.

His father turned back to him.

"Sometimes I don't even feel all that sad," Grover said.

His father sat on the bed beside him. "It's okay to feel better."

"It's not okay to forget her," Grover said, sounding angry, but he wasn't sure who he was angry with.

"When your mother was alive, did you think of her all the time?"

"No."

"That didn't mean she wasn't there, did it?"

"But now remembering her is all that's left," Grover said.

"Is it?" his father asked, but it didn't sound like he expected Grover to answer. More like he was asking himself the question.

"What about you?" Grover asked. "Are you forgetting her?"

His father wrapped his hands around his knee and leaned back. By this time of night, he always looked like he needed another shave. He had bags under his eyes and there was a softness in his face that made him look older. "If you're asking do I feel better some days, I do. Other days I miss her so bad I can hardly bring myself to get out of bed in the morning."

Grover remembered seeing his father cry on the porch that night after he'd torn up his workshop. It was one thing to have a father who was cranky and stormed around the house, a father he could be good and mad at. It was another thing to have a father whose voice shook, who even cried. It embarrassed Grover, and he didn't know what to say or do. His father sat on Grover's bed for a while. Grover couldn't remember the last time his father had sat with him.

‡   ‡   ‡

Grover zipped up his coat and ducked into its collar, trying to cut the wind. It was early November and the weather was freezing, the coldest morning Asheville had had so far this year. The wind burned his cheeks. Sudie, who read the weather in the paper every morning, said it would be twenty-one degrees this morning. "The wind makes it feel like below zero," Sudie said, pulling her scarf up around her face.

They stared with envy whenever a car passed. "Lucky dogs," Sudie muttered as she waved to friends who waved from the toastiness of their Volvo station wagon.

Their father had started them back walking to school. Grover, Sudie and their parents used to walk the several blocks to Isaac Claxton, and then their father would cross over into downtown and walk a few more blocks to the Wolfe house. After the accident, their father had driven them. He hadn't seemed to have the energy to get everyone ready, including himself, soon enough to walk. But Grover guessed the main reason their father drove was because of how their mother had died. If Sudie or Grover just walked down Edgemont, their father always looked them in the eye and said, "Watch out for cars."

As they passed the Bamboo Forest, Grover checked for new stakes. He did this every morning. His father had helped him pull up all the stakes, which wasn't easy. More and more, working in the Bamboo Forest made Grover feel part of something bigger. More and more he felt like, as weird as it sounded, he was working with the place itself. The bamboo sections practically laid themselves into grids, tree branches wove themselves between the bamboo sections and leaves arranged themselves into patterns. Nature was the artist and he its assistant.

Several blocks from school, the Roundtrees' van passed them. The brake lights came on, and they pulled over to the curb. Clay rolled down his window. "Y'all want a ride?!"

It was the first time Grover'd noticed the American flag decal and the *Support Our Troops* sticker on their bumper.

"Hop in," Leila said.

"You have room?" their father asked, which made Grover and Sudie look at each other. Hadn't he just finished telling them walking was good for them?

Clay climbed out of the car and opened the sliding back door, revealing Emma Lee, who looked up from a book. Clay climbed into the very back seat and Sudie climbed in next to him. Their father took Clay's seat up front next to Leila. Grover climbed in, shut the van door and slid in next to Emma Lee, who glanced up at him, then went back to reading her book.

"Look what I made." Clay held up a Cheerios box with rubber bands strung across an open hole in the side. "Emma Lee helped me with it last night." He strummed it.

"Let me try," Sudie said.

He held it out to her.

Emma Lee seemed deep into her book. At first Grover and Emma Lee hadn't talked much after that morning when she'd taken him down to the Bamboo Forest to find his father, the morning after his father had torn up his workshop. Grover had felt uncomfortable around her. She'd observed his family at its worst.

One day on the playground Emma Lee had sat down beside him when he was working his Rubik's cube and, out of the blue, said, "The war changed our daddy. He'd always been real sweet. Never spanked us, never hardly raised his voice. The last time he came home on leave we didn't know him. He hollered at us and threw things and sprained Mama's wrist and gave her a black eye. She'd just finished the paperwork to file for divorce the day we heard." Since then Grover hadn't felt as weird around her.

"You better come see it before time runs out." Grover's father was talking to Leila.

"Asheville wouldn't be Asheville without the Thomas Wolfe house," Leila said. "It's a major landmark."

"That's what I keep telling commissioners," his father said.

"And what do they say?"

"They say if it's such a major landmark, why are attendance numbers so low?"

"Maybe we could come over some afternoon," Leila said, looking in the rearview mirror at Emma Lee and Clay.

"Sure," Emma Lee said.

"Emma Lee and Clay could walk over with Grover and Sudie after school one day," their father said.

"It's Jessie's assistant." Sudie was looking out the window at Matthew walking along Montford with his backpack, sipping from a Bean Streets cup.

"I'm glad Jessie hired him," their father said.

"You know him?" Leila asked.

"He's a history student from the college," their father said flatly. "I gave him a little help with a research project a couple of years ago. Last spring he had sort of a breakdown and dropped out. But he's back now and re-enrolled." He looked out the window at Matthew.

"You don't sound too crazy about him," Leila said.

"Oh, he's okay," their father said. "Jessie's right to give him work."

They rode along in silence for a minute, then Leila started in telling a story about a girl who'd delivered her baby at the hospital yesterday. The girl had never told the father she was pregnant with their baby. "The poor boy never figured it out till last night in the middle of eating pizza at Frank's she looked up at him and told him her water had broken. The next thing he knew they were at the hospital and she was giving birth to a nine-pound boy."

"Was she heavy in the first place?" Clay asked, strumming his Cheerios box.

"Skinny as a rail," Leila said.

"How could he not know?" their father said.

"He said he figured she'd been stopping by the Krispy Kreme a little too often."

His father laughed a big laugh that seemed to come from deep down in him. It caught Grover off guard. He remembered a night a couple of years ago when his father was driving them back from El Chapala, their favorite Mexican restaurant across town. Grover had been sitting in the back with his sister, and up front his father and mother were talking about something. Suddenly, their father burst out laughing, then their mother started laughing. They both laughed so hard, their father finally had to pull over. It was at times like those that Grover was reminded how much of a couple his parents really were, making him feel excluded and safe at the same time.

Chapter Nine

Wait Up

After being dropped off in front of the school, Sudie and Grover started up the Claxton steps with Emma Lee and Clay. Miss Snyder happened to walk in at the same time, and Grover held open the big door for her. She smiled at him, and, remembering she wanted to see him, he looked away.

The whole rest of the day Miss Snyder was everywhere. When he was in the library, she was at the desk talking to the librarian. In the cafeteria, she was in the line ahead of him. Later in the day, when he was delivering something to the office, she was walking up the hall toward him. That afternoon when Sudie and Grover stopped by Bean Streets for hot chocolate and a game of checkers, Grover looked up and saw her standing over them.

Sudie jumped up and hugged her. She was always hugging Miss Snyder and her teachers whenever she saw them out in public.

"I don't think I've ever beaten Sudie at checkers," Miss Snyder said.

"You haven't," Sudie said, sitting back down across from her brother.

Miss Snyder watched them long enough for Sudie to do a double jump and take two of Grover's men.

"She's following me," Grover said to Sudie after Miss Snyder had left.

"All the way to Bean Streets?" Sudie asked.

"She wants me to come see her."

"I like going to see her," Sudie said. "All we do is play checkers or hearts or booby trap."

Grover stopped himself from saying that the only reason Miss Snyder played games with her or any of the other Claxton kids was because it was her job. It was her job to get at kids' feelings. Their mother had played games with kids too. She'd once explained to him that playing with little kids was a better way to understand them than asking direct questions. Grover didn't say anything more about Miss Snyder to Sudie. It was good for his sister to have someone to talk to. *She* needed it.

The next day, Mrs. Caswell was at the board, diagramming a sentence. She'd said that back in the Dark Ages when she was in sixth grade everyone had to learn how to diagram a sentence. She didn't expect the class to learn how, but she thought they should at least see what a diagrammed sentence looked like. Grover didn't care about the *subject* and the *predicate* and all the other names of the parts, but he loved the look of it, the design it made, like a tree turned on its side. He was imagining a whole forest of diagrammed sentences, when there was a knock at the door and Miss Snyder came in. Grover's heart raced as the two women went out into the hall.

With their teacher out in the hall, the kids in the class turned to each other and started talking in low voices, whispering and giggling.

Emma Lee leaned forward. "Teachers are never talking about what you think they're talking about."

They heard Mrs. Caswell and Miss Snyder laugh out in the hall.

"See?" Emma Lee said, whispering behind him.

After a minute Mrs. Caswell came back, clapping her hands to quiet everyone. "Back to work." She picked up the chalk and finished the sentence she'd been diagramming.

Grover didn't trust it. Mrs. Caswell wouldn't say in front of the whole class that Miss Snyder wanted to see him. She'd tell him at the end of class after everyone was gone. When the bell sounded and the class lined up to go to lunch, Mrs. Caswell didn't even glance Grover's way. He lingered, pretending to look for something in his desk, but she just looked at him over her glasses.

"Found it," he said, picking up a pencil, and ran to catch up with the line.

As Grover's class passed Miss Snyder's office, the door was closed and no light came from the bottom of the door, which was how Grover used to tell if his mother was in. His mother used to intercept him on his way to lunch. Sometimes she pulled him out of line, took him into her office and shut the door. She'd tell him to be nice to a particular boy or girl. She'd never say why. He'd know it was because the kid's parents were divorcing or someone in their family was sick, had maybe even died. As he passed Miss Snyder's closed office door, Grover realized he'd become one of those kids his mother had told him to be nice to.

After lunch, Grover went out on the playground. Miss Snyder stood with Mrs. Caswell and Miss Shook, talking.

"You're shooting worse than usual." Sam fished the basketball out of the juniper bush. Grover watched Sam swish another shot.

Shouts went up on the other side of the playground as Emma Lee, who'd launched the kickball all the way to the chain-link fence, streaked around the bases.

Most days Emma Lee played kickball with Mira and some other girls. Although Ashley and her friends hadn't called Emma Lee a hillbilly or anything else after that day in class, they never invited her to play with them.

"Earth to Grover," Sam said, holding the basketball out to Grover.

"Oh, sorry." Grover took the ball.

"I'm glad to see you've finally taken an interest in the opposite sex."

"I don't think of her like that," Grover said, shooting and missing.

"You think of her like she's a boy?" Sam asked.

"Well, no."

"So you must think of her as a girl," Sam said.

"I think of her as a person," Grover said.

"Not a girl?" Sam asked, retrieving the ball.

"Nope."

"Just a person?"

"Yep."

Sam stood there a minute, holding the ball against his hip and looking across the playground where Emma Lee trotted into the outfield. "Well," he said, "she sure is a pretty person."

"Miss Snyder called my father," Grover said, glancing in the counselor's direction. "She wants me to come see her."

"About what?" Sam said.

"And you call yourself the son of a psychiatrist?"

"Oh, about *that*," Sam said. "Well, you have seemed kind of down."

"Kind of down?!" Grover said. "My mother gets run over by a car and I'm 'kind of down'?" His voice shook.

A couple of kids in the outfield of the kickball game looked toward them.

"Calm down," Sam said, looking around.

"Daddy said I didn't have to go see her," Grover said.

"Then don't," Sam said.

"What if I *should* go see her?" Grover shot the ball and missed.

"'Should go'?" Sam said, catching the rebound.

"What if that would be the best thing to do?"

"Then go see her."

"I don't want to go see her," Grover said.

"Then don't!" Sam shot the ball from a good twenty feet out. It swished.

"Would you go see her?" Grover asked.

"For you?" Sam asked. "I don't see how that would work."

"No," Grover said. "Let's say you needed to talk to someone about something like, say . . . a dead mother. Would you go see her?"

"Sure," he said, not hesitating as he looked toward where Miss Snyder leaned up against the building, talking with the teachers.

"You would?"

"You bet," Sam said, "Miss Snyder is hot."

Grover looked at his friend.

"What?" Sam said. "She has nice legs."

"You're hopeless," Grover said.

Sam tossed the ball to Grover, who walked out to the spot from where Sam had just swished the ball. He totally missed the basket but Daniel Pevoe, who was waiting to play Sam, caught it.

"HORSE," Grover said under his breath as he walked off the court.

‡   ‡   ‡

That afternoon Mrs. Caswell sent Grover down to the office to get a box of chalk. He liked these errands. He got to see another side to Claxton as he walked past all the classrooms with kids at their desks hard at work. It was kind of like being backstage in a play. On the way back from the office, he noticed that a bright line of light shined along the bottom of Miss Snyder's office door. She was in.

He was still standing there trying to decide whether to knock when the door opened.

"I thought I heard someone." Miss Snyder motioned him into her office.

"I wasn't stopping by. I'm on my way back from the office."

"Why don't you come on in?" Miss Snyder asked.

"Mrs. Caswell will wonder where I am," he said, his voice shaking a little.

"I'll call her and tell her you've stopped by." She picked up her office phone and dialed. Grover heard Mrs. Caswell pick up on the other end.

"Jill," Miss Snyder said into the phone, "this is Brenda. Grover Johnston has stopped by my office. Do you mind if we visit for a little while?" Miss Snyder nodded, then said, "Thanks." And hung up. "Mrs. Caswell says we can visit as long as we like."

There was something in the way Miss Snyder had sounded on the phone with Mrs. Caswell that told Grover the two women had talked about him. He'd fallen into their trap.

"Would you like some hot chocolate?" Miss Snyder asked, taking out a couple of mugs and two packs of instant hot chocolate.

Grover loved hot chocolate, but knew what she was up to. He shook his head.

"You sure? I'm going to make some for myself."

He paused. "Okay," he said, telling himself even if she did bring him hot chocolate, she wasn't getting anything out of him.

"I've got to run down to the cafeteria to get some hot water," she said. "I'll be right back." Miss Snyder left him sitting alone in her office. This was the first time he'd been in his mother's office since she'd died. He looked around. Miss Snyder had asked their father if he would mind her keeping some of the same pictures and toys their mother had had till the end of the year. She'd told him she didn't want to just swoop in and immediately put up all new pictures. Like their mother hadn't existed.

There was a framed print of a scene from *Goodnight Moon*. A big poster of Max dancing with the monsters from *Where the Wild Things Are*. A calendar of Van Gogh paintings Grover had given her last Christmas. His mother loved art and every year Grover gave her a calendar of some famous painter's paintings. Last year it had been Picasso. The year before, Renoir. The year before that, Chagall. Grover flipped through the calendar, reading the little notes his mother had made. The last date she'd written something was April 5. She'd written in her neat print: *Lunch with Grover*. The next day she was hit.

Grover walked over to the shelves of toys his mother had used with kids. There were things mixed in he'd never seen before. One was a Rubik's cube like he'd never seen. Not a cube exactly, more pillow-shaped. He picked it up. Ten rows by ten rows. It would take a genius to solve this. He began moving the rows around but when Miss Snyder returned he quickly set it back on the shelf.

"You found my V-CUBE," she said, handing him a warm mug of hot chocolate.

"Thanks," he said, taking a sip. "Is that what it's called?"

"I ordered it from a company in Greece," she said, pulling her chair around from behind her desk to sit across from him. "But as soon as I saw it I knew I was in over my head."

"It looks hard," Grover said, his eye going back to the V-CUBE on the shelf.

"I bet you could work it." She took the V-CUBE off her shelf and handed it to him.

They drank their hot chocolate in silence. In between sips of his hot chocolate, Grover would pick up the V-CUBE, trying to work it. Grover wondered if Miss Snyder had gone and gotten hot chocolate to give him some time alone in the office. He remembered what Sam had said and glanced down at her crossed legs. But then he looked away. He tried to clear his head, telling himself he wasn't going to fall into this trap. He set his hot chocolate on her desk. "I know why you're doing all this."

"Doing all what?"

"The hot chocolate and the cube and all."

"Why?"

"To get at my feelings."

"Is that what I'm doing?"

"My mother told me that's how counselors do it. You get kids playing and comfortable and everything, so you can observe them and get at their feelings."

"And that's a bad thing?" she asked.

Grover shrugged. "Maybe not for some kids."

"Like your sister maybe?"

"Yeah, it's good for Sudie," he said. "She's big on feelings."

"But you?"

"I hate 'em." He crossed his arms and stared at the floor.

"Really? All feelings?"

"If it's a feeling," he said, "I pretty much hate it."

"So you hate being happy?"

"Well, no."

"Isn't happiness a feeling?"

"Okay," he said, looking at her, "I don't hate *one* feeling."

"Excited? You hate being excited. For instance, when you're excited about working on your tapestries?"

"How do you know about my tapestries?"

"You're getting to be a pretty famous artist around town." She sipped her hot chocolate. "What about smart? Do you hate feeling smart when you work an especially difficult math problem?"

She *had* been talking to Mrs. Caswell.

"So, we've come up with at least three feelings you don't hate. I imagine there are a couple more."

Grover looked back toward the calendar hanging on the wall. "Mama always wanted to know how I was feeling."

"So what did you say to her whenever she asked you how you were feeling?"

"Nothing." He paused. "Or I'd say I didn't want to talk about it or I'd go to my room or outside to make something in the Bamboo Forest." He looked again at the calendar. "Can I have that at the end of the year?"

"You can have it now if you like."

"Keep it till the end of the year. I'd just like to have it then."

"Of course," she said. "Will you come see me again?"

"I didn't come see you in the first place. I was passing by your office and you opened the door."

Grover sat back in his seat, working the V-CUBE. He didn't say anything, and neither did Miss Snyder. Outside the closed door, he heard some kids' voices—a class on its way down the hall, out to recess. The couple of times he glanced up from the V-CUBE, Miss Snyder was watching him.

"You miss your mother?" she finally asked.

Grover shrugged. "Who wouldn't?"

"Hansel and Gretel," she said.

He looked up. "She was a stepmother."

"You know, I think you're right about that," she said.

He worked the V-CUBE a little more. "One thing I never got about that story," he said.

"What's that?"

"What kind of father takes his kids out in the woods and leaves them?"

He worked the V-CUBE for a couple more minutes. When he got up to leave, she asked, "Will you come back to see me?"

"I said I didn't come to see you in the first place," he said.

"Well, the next time you're running an errand for Mrs. Caswell, I hope you'll stop by." She lifted up the V-CUBE. "We'll be waiting."

Grover was pretty far down the hall before he admitted to himself that Sam was right. She did have pretty legs.

CHAPTER TEN
FOR ALL I CARE

The afternoon the realtor stabbed a For Sale sign on the edge of the Bamboo Forest, Grover'd been hard at work on his biggest tapestry yet. Eight feet high and five feet wide, it was so big he rested the bottom on the ground and lashed it to several growing bamboo stalks to hold it upright. At school he sketched and drew in the margins of his schoolwork. He headed to the Bamboo Forest the moment he got home from school. He worked after supper, weaving by flashlight till his father called him in.

This afternoon Clay had come over and hung around while Grover worked. Clay made it his job to keep the workshop neat, picking up leaves or sticks or branches that Grover had stripped away from the bigger limbs. Clay helped cut up the bamboo sections for the big grid, and Grover taught him how to lash them together. Under Grover's careful supervision, he even wove in some limbs himself. Mostly, Clay did what he was doing at the moment, sitting cross-legged on the big stump and talking.

"I've got a mind to contact Guinness World Records," Clay said. "This one might be some kind of record."

Grover wove in a pine branch he'd come across on the way home from school.

"By the time you finish this, it'll take half the neighborhood to tote it to the plot."

Biscuit came from nowhere, and Clay leaned down to pet him. In a moment Sudie appeared on the edge of the workshop. "Come quick," she said.

Grover dropped the limb he was working on, and he and Clay followed Sudie to the edge of the Bamboo Forest. Sudie motioned them to stop, grabbed up Biscuit and held him, then pointed to a shiny Mercedes pulled up next to the field. They watched as a woman in an expensive-looking coat and glossy high heels lifted a metal sign out of her trunk, walked to the edge of the field, then—like this was something she did all the time—plunged it into the ground.

Grover flinched.

Biscuit started barking, but Sudie clamped her hand over his snout.

The woman wiped her hands and looked around. Grover, Sudie and Clay ducked. The woman closed her trunk, climbed into her car and drove away. They waited till they were sure she was gone, then walked up to the sign. Grover'd known what it said the minute he'd seen the woman. Here it was—a tombstone for the Bamboo Forest:

Lunsford Realty

Lot for Sale

2+ acres

Contact Maureen Abdalla

Call 555-1389, ext 312

Grover's chest began to ache and his mouth suddenly felt full of ashes.

"Aren't you going to pull it up?" Sudie asked.

He stuffed his hands into his coat pockets.

"You're going to leave it there?" she asked.

"It won't make any difference," Grover said.

Sudie gave Grover a disgusted look, then began to tug on the sign. She pulled and pulled, but it wouldn't come up. She kicked it and it made a tinny rattle. Her arms flopped by her sides, and she started in the direction of home with Biscuit behind her.

"Where are you going?" Clay called.

She kept walking but hadn't gone far when a shiny BMW slowed and then backed up. The window rolled down. The driver, a big bald man in a coat and tie, seemed to be writing down the number on the sign. Sudie ran back and planted herself in front of the sign.

The man rolled his window down farther. "Hey, kid, you're blocking the sign."

"It's not for sale," Sudie said.

"That's not what the sign says," the man said.

"Get out of the way, Sudie," Grover said.

At the sight of the sign, something in Grover had shut down.

Gone. First his mother, now the Bamboo Forest. And he himself felt gone. Gone from every place he'd ever known. Deep-down-in-his-soul-nobody-home gone.

"Listen, honey," the man in the car said, "will you move so I can see the phone number? Then you can stand there the rest of the day for all I care."

Sudie crossed her arms. The man got out, slammed the car door behind him and walked toward Sudie. Biscuit barked.

"All I need is the phone number," the man said, walking around to the other side of the sign, but Sudie kept moving around with him. Biscuit barked and growled.

"Get out of his way," Grover said.

"Come on, kid." The man took hold of Sudie's arm.

"No." Sudie hugged the sign.

The man's face reddened as he pried Sudie from the sign.

Clay ran at the man but he just swatted Clay out of the way.

"Hey, mister! Your car!" Matthew, who was wearing his old Army coat and must've been on his way to work, was out in the road, pointing toward the BMW, which was slowly rolling down Edgemont, the driver's side door wide open.

"Oh Lord." The bald man ran after it and, finally catching up with it, jumped in the driver's seat, bringing it to a stop.

In a burst of anger, Grover jerked the For Sale sign out of the ground, ran to where the car had come to a halt and swatted the trunk.

"Hey! What the—" The bald man jumped out of the car and came toward Grover.

"You want to see the sign!" Grover shouted. He swung the sign at the bald man, who jumped back in the car. "Well, here you go! Here's the sign!" Grover swatted the car again. The bald man started the car, the tires squealing as he sped out of sight.

Grover stood in the middle of the road, catching his breath. Sudie and Clay came up beside him.

Emma Lee came running up the street, a book in her hand. "What in the world?"

Clay nodded at the sign that Grover was only half aware he still held.

"Oh, no," Emma Lee said.

"I don't reckon that old boy will be buying it," Clay said, nodding in the direction the car had disappeared.

"They'll be plenty more where he came from," Grover said grimly.

"Where'd that Matthew fellow go?" Clay said.

"There he is," Sudie said, pointing up the street where they saw him walking through the cemetery gates.

Grover started back in the direction of the Bamboo Forest, and as he did, he hurled the sign into the thickest part of the bamboo. He charged up the path. Back in his workshop, he stood in front of the tapestry. He kept seeing the For Sale sign. *For Sale. For Sale. For Sale.* He looked at his tapestry. *Tapestry, my eye,* he thought. It was just a bunch of bamboo and sticks crammed together. It wasn't anything really. He thought of all the hours he'd wasted out here, messing with leaves and sticks and limbs, trying to make them into more than they could ever be.

He sat down on the ground, feeling light-headed. Like the time he'd gotten hit in the head. Like he was floating above everything, looking down on his life. As he sat there with his elbows propped on his thighs and his chin resting in his palms, the yellow carpet of bamboo leaves beneath him began to spin— slowly at first, then faster, until it blurred into a Saturday in early spring just before everything changed.

Most of the drive up to the Blue Ridge Parkway, past Cold Mountain and past Mount Pisgah, Grover sat in the back, stewing about being dragged along on another hike. He barely noticed the deep green rhododendron and laurel moving in the breeze, the spring water dripping down the moss-covered rocks or the purple waves of mountains that went on forever. When he was smaller he loved going on these hikes, but somewhere along the way his parents had turned into slowpokes, always stopping to look at wildflowers or birds, trying to identify them in one of their many guidebooks. And Sudie, who'd always been a slow hiker anyway, was slower than ever, bending down to look at every butterfly, bee or spider. Grover barreled ahead, but his parents never let him get too far ahead. They never let him leave behind the lumbering embarrassment that was his family.

They pulled into the parking lot of Graveyard Fields, a kind of flat-bottomed bowl with waterfalls at both ends. The trail followed a big creek, where they could wade, skip smoothed river rocks and look for salamanders. Some people said Graveyard Fields got its name after a farmer's herd of cows had died in a sudden deep freeze. Another story was that it was named after a big fire that left tree stumps singed and gray, resembling tombstones. Grover liked theorizing how it got its name. But this afternoon he couldn't shake being irritated. He stayed ahead for a good part of the way. His mother kept calling, "Grover, wait up!" and he'd wait till he saw them appear around a bend in the trail.

These hikes had become a trial for him. His father had often offered for Grover to stay home and work in the Bamboo Forest, but his mother insisted he go. She said it was important that they do things as a family. Grover didn't see what was so important about doing things as a family. He'd spent the last twelve years doing things as a family.

His family spent half an hour on a shoal in the creek, turning over river rocks and catching salamanders. The cool air, the wet sweet smell of the creek mud on his hands and the water gurgling over the rocks worked on him. He remembered looking up from hunting for salamanders and seeing his mother squatting on the little beach and, with his father's help, turning over a big flat rock. His sister stooped beside them, hands cupped just above the water, ready to scoop up any salamander that might be hiding underneath.

But once they were back on the trail, he kept trying to go ahead, even with his mother calling out to wait up. A few days later his mother would be hit by a car. If only he had known that this hike through Graveyard Fields was the last his family would ever take, he would've waited up.

Shadows flickered past, and he heard crows settling down in the bamboo. He looked around at the fading light in the Bamboo Forest. How long had he been sitting here? He stood, thinking he should probably get home, but he couldn't resist picking up the pine limb he'd been working with and weaving it into the big bamboo grid. He picked up another limb and wove that in. Then another and another. The more he worked, the better he felt. He'd been working for a while when he stepped back to see how his tapestry was shaping up.

"You do good work."

Startled, Grover put his hand to his chest.

Emma Lee was sitting on the sycamore stump.

"How long have you been sitting there?" he asked, his heart racing.

"A while," she said.

"I never heard you," he said.

"We're one quarter Cherokee. We know how to sneak up on people." She smiled. "Man, you really jumped."

He sat down beside her on the stump, looking at the tapestry.

"You're a real good artist," she said.

Grover shrugged, never knowing what to say when people complimented his work.

"You say 'Thank you,'" she said. The more he was around Emma Lee, the more he was afraid to think much of anything, for fear that she would read his mind.

He looked at the tapestry. "Maybe I'll finish it before the bull-dozers come."

"That's no way to think," she said.

"Well, you gotta admit, it's pretty hopeless."

"I don't have to admit a thing," Emma Lee said.

Grover looked at her.

"If you go around thinking things are hopeless," she said, "then you have no reason to try, do you?"

Try. Hadn't his mother used that word all the time? As long as you try, she used to say, that's all anybody can ask. Grover looked around. He lowered his voice. "Did my mother send your family to be our neighbors?" Grover felt embarrassed as soon as he'd said it.

"Not that I know of," Emma Lee said, "but God works in mysterious ways."

"I don't believe in God," Grover said, crossing his arms.

"Because of what happened to your mama?"

"That didn't help," Grover said.

"Losing Daddy made me believe even more," Emma Lee said. "It's my only hope of seeing him again."

"You want to see him again?" he asked. "Even after he hurt your mother like he did?" Ever since Emma Lee had told him what happened with her father, he'd figured she was glad to be rid of him.

"In Heaven he'd be back to his old self." She said this like there wasn't a doubt in her mind. "I think you believe in God. If there wasn't a God, then there'd be no Heaven. There'd be no place for your mother to be."

"How do you know what I believe?" He jumped off the stump and walked over to the tapestry, adjusting a limb that was a little out of place. "Besides, believing is for kids. Believing is something people outgrow." He looked back at her. "Or at least they ought to."

"You can never outgrow God," she said.

He didn't say anything.

"I see God in your art."

"Where?" Grover looked at the tapestry.

"It's not like that," she said. "It's not something you can point to. It's just a feeling I get whenever I look at your weavings." She got up, came over and gently laid her hand flat on the woven limbs. "Like I'm looking through a window onto a world I never knew was there."

"Really?" Grover said, scratching his head and looking at the tapestry. "All I do is put things together." He shrugged. "It's more like things put themselves together. Like I'm helping nature get a little more organized. Like I'm part of something . . . I don't know . . . something way bigger." He felt silly for saying it.

"That's what I'm talking about," Emma Lee said. "Something way bigger. That's God."

"It is?"

"What else could it be?" she asked.

He picked up a new limb from the stack that Clay had neatly arranged and began working it in between the others. "I don't believe in God."

"Maybe your head doesn't," Emma Lee said, watching him work, "but your hands sure do."

CHAPTER ELEVEN

TRY NOT TO THINK ABOUT IT

It was a Friday afternoon, one week before Thanksgiving, when Grover, Sudie, Clay and Emma Lee walked down the front steps of Claxton after school and headed up Montford Avenue in the direction of downtown. Last night Leila Roundtree had called their father, asking if they could tour the Wolfe house this afternoon. Grover and Sudie were to take Clay and Emma Lee downtown and meet Leila and their father at the house.

Montford was a long, wide street and the cold wind blew uninterrupted all the way from downtown. After a few blocks, they ducked into Reader's Corner to warm up. The first thing Grover always noticed when he walked into Reader's Corner was the musty smell of used books. An old, comfortable smell. And even though he wasn't a big reader, being around books other people had read made Grover feel at home.

Byron, the owner, was a short, round woman with long white hair and spectacles perched on the tip of her nose—a female

Benjamin Franklin. She sat at a desk surrounded by boxes of books, going through them and writing prices in pencil on the inside cover.

Grover took Clay over to the window to show him Tom, who pushed his head against Grover's hand and purred loud enough to hear across the store.

"Emma Lee's died and gone to heaven," Clay said. His sister stood in the middle of the store, taking in the shelves sagging with books.

"This is Clay," Sudie said to Byron, "and that's his sister, Emma Lee."

"Hey," Clay said. He turned back to Emma Lee. "Sis, we can't stay long."

Emma Lee, having already picked up a book, didn't say anything.

Clay leaned toward Byron and said in a low confidential tone, "She's a bookaholic."

Byron looked over her spectacles at Clay. "We get a lot of those."

Emma Lee disappeared around the corner of a bookshelf, still reading the book. "Uh-oh," Clay said, going after her. "Now Emma Lee . . ."

Watching Clay go after his sister, Grover remembered that one day he'd been behind her at Claxton and watched her walk down the hall, her long black hair swaying. It had taken his breath away. Up until that moment he hadn't really seen her, at least not like *that*. Now he'd be in the middle of doing homework or washing the dishes with Sudie or working in the Bamboo Forest, and suddenly there'd she'd be, walking down the hall at Claxton, her long hair swaying.

"How's the weaving going?" Byron asked. She was one of the few people he could talk to about his tapestries.

"I'd rather be in the Bamboo Forest," he said. Ever since the woman had stuck the For Sale sign in the Bamboo Forest, Grover had felt his time there running out.

"We're taking Emma Lee and Clay to tour the Wolfe house."

"It's kind of you to take time out for your friends. You always were a generous boy." She looked at him over her spectacles. "You come by it honestly." Grover wasn't sure if she meant his mother or his father. But Grover could never look into Byron's clear eyes anymore without seeing what she'd seen that warm evening last April just as she was closing her store:

She had locked the front door and had been closing out the cash register when there was a knock at the window. Grover's mother had been outside, walking past with Biscuit on the leash. She often stopped by to talk to Byron and buy a book or two but this time she'd waved and walked on. Byron heard sirens a little later though she hadn't thought anything of it.

Grover never minded stopping by the Reader's Corner with Sudie. He wasn't interested in the books so much. He mostly liked petting Tom, talking to Byron and looking through the very window where their mother was last seen alive.

After they left, they'd walked two blocks and the wind blew harder.

"I'm freezing," Sudie said, shivering and looking longingly at Videolife as they passed by the store.

"Why don't we stop in there?" Clay said.

Grover stared at the store. "We've only got a few more blocks."

"Your sister looks cold," Emma Lee whispered into his ear.

Sudie's cheeks had turned holly berry red. "For just a minute," he said.

With his heart pounding, Grover followed them inside. He hadn't stepped in here since the day their mother hadn't come home. Videolife was small, about a tenth the size of Blockbuster across town but had a lot more movies, especially old movies. The shelves, almost as close together as the ones in Reader's Corner, were packed with DVDs and old VHS tapes. Big hand-written signs dangled from fishing line above the sections: *Keep You Up at Night Scary, Too Deep for Us, Great Old Ones, Strictly for Grown-ups, Okay for Everybody, Basically for Kids* and *Stupid in the Stupidest Sense.*

On late Friday afternoons Grover and Sudie would walk down here, meet their parents and decide on a movie together, which wasn't always easy. They'd get take-out from a little restaurant called The Weeping Duck, then go home and watch the movie and eat wonton soup, egg rolls, and Grover's favorite, shrimp fried rice.

Sudie and Clay had gone straight to the *Pretty New* section and found *Fantastic Mr. Fox.* They were reading what it said about it on the back of the DVD.

"Let me know if you need any help," said the guy behind the counter. He had a goatee and wore a turtleneck. He was watching a TV mounted high up on the wall in one corner where a Woody Allen movie was playing. Their father loved Woody Allen. He would laugh and laugh at his movies. Most of the time, Grover didn't see what was so funny.

Sudie looked up at Grover hopefully, clutching *Fantastic Mr. Fox* to her chest. Grover shook his head. Sudie sighed and set it back on the shelf.

"It's just one little movie," she said.

Grover wasn't about to tell Sudie why just the sight of his sister holding that DVD made him feel almost sick. He'd never tell her that his mother had asked him, when Videolife had first called, if he would pick up the *Fantastic Mr. Fox* DVD that the store was holding for them after school. He'd never tell her that he'd forgotten about it till the day he'd seen their mother through the car's rear window, headed toward Videolife with Biscuit.

"Sure there isn't anything I can help you with?" The guy behind the counter glanced away from the movie.

"We just came in to warm up," Grover said.

"Stay as long as you like," the guy said, looking back at the TV. But the way he said it made Grover wonder if he knew who they were.

Grover wandered over to the *Funny as All Get-Out*, picking up a DVD of *Fawlty Towers*, a British TV comedy that used to make their mother laugh so hard she'd be wiping away tears. Someone sneezed. He looked up to see Matthew, in his UNC

Asheville sweatshirt this time, looking at a movie, reading the back of the case. Grover quietly set the DVD back in its place, and then quickly stepped around the corner and headed back to find his sister and the others.

‡   ‡   ‡

They crossed the overpass that led into downtown, passing city workers who fought the wind to hang garlands, wreaths, giant yellow candles and Christmas lights. The workers were decorating for the Christmas parade tomorrow, which was on the Saturday before Thanksgiving.

Grover, Sudie, Clay and Emma Lee ducked into the Grove Arcade. In the entryway, a red-cheeked man dressed in a Salvation Army uniform rang a bell for donations. Clay dug into his pocket, pulled out a crumpled dollar bill and dropped it into the big hanging pot.

"Merry Christmas to y'all," the man said as the four of them walked on inside.

The first thing to hit them was the warmth, the feeling coming back into their hands and faces, as they looked at the long glistening hallway. Shafts of afternoon sunlight filtered down through the high windows, looking touchable.

"Monet," Emma Lee said to herself, staring down the hall.

"I gave the fellow a dollar," Clay said to his sister.

"Not *money*," she said impatiently. "The painter. It's like that painting by him." She looked down the hall. "Of the cathedral."

"Exactly!" Grover said, looking at her. One year Grover'd given his mother a calendar of Monet's paintings.

Sudie showed Emma Lee and Clay the model in the middle of the building of how the architect had originally designed the building with a twelve-story tower above the shops, a small skyscraper. Grover had heard this a million times, but it was only now that he thought what it must've been like for the architect. How disappointed he must've been to have worked so hard on something and created such a beautiful building on paper but never seen the whole thing built.

The arcade was busy with Christmas shoppers. Grover had always been struck by how early Christmas seemed to start downtown. Their father said it was good for business. He said that some stores made most of their money during the holiday season.

A group of people had gathered in the center of the arcade where three musicians—a banjo player, a fiddler and a guitar player—played old-time Christmas music. The fiddler, a bearded man, had left his case open, and it was full of coins and dollar bills. They played fast and hard. People tapped their toes and clapped in time. It was the kind of music that was difficult not to smile to.

"Man, they're hot." Clay took off his backpack and started to clog.

"Clay's won the clogging competition at the Lamar Lunsford Festival every year since he was four," Emma Lee said.

"Look at that hillbilly go," said a well-dressed older man to a woman in a fur coat. Grover could tell from his accent that he was not from the South.

"My brother is *not* a hillbilly!" Emma Lee had whirled around and faced the man.

"I didn't mean anything by it." The man laughed and looked at his wife, then back at Emma Lee. "I think your brother is one hell of a dancer."

"Don't call him a hillbilly," Emma Lee said, her jaw working.

"I really don't see the problem . . ."

"You heard the girl!" Another man stepped up to the well-dressed man. Grover had noticed him standing behind them, listening to the music with his wife and two little blonde-haired girls. He had long hair, wore a ball cap and a hunting jacket.

"I didn't mean anything by it." The well-dressed man wasn't laughing now and his face had turned pale. "Tell him, Gertrude." He turned to his wife but she pressed her lips together as if this wasn't the first time her husband's mouth had gotten him in trouble.

"I wouldn't call nobody a hillbilly," the man in the ball cap said, leveling his eyes at the well-dressed man, "not if you expect to live a long and healthy life."

"Is that a threat?!"

"It's one of them health advisories."

The well-dressed man started to say something but seemed to think better of it. He took his wife's hand, and they disappeared through the crowd.

"'Preciate it," Emma Lee said to the man in the ball cap.

He gave her a wink and nodded toward the band. "The fella's right. Your brother's good." He stepped back and joined his family. Grover saw the sad look flicker across Emma Lee's face as she watched the man's little girls take their father's hands and lean back against him.

The band shifted into a faster song, and as the fiddle sped up, so did Clay's footwork. More people gathered to listen to the music and watch him dance. Emma Lee shrugged off her backpack and joined her brother. Other people stepped out of the crowd, joining Clay and Emma Lee, and pretty soon it seemed as if half the people in the Grove Arcade were dancing.

"Come on." Emma Lee waved Grover up.

He thought about going up, but his feet wouldn't move. He knew good and well that if his mother had been there, she'd have been dancing right in the middle of them.

‡   ‡   ‡

Grover watched Emma Lee drink her hot chocolate. He didn't know if it was the cold or the dancing, but her cheeks had reddened and her eyes glistened. They had stopped in at Bean Streets long enough for Sudie to beat Clay in checkers.

"Oh, gross," Emma Lee was muttering under her breath.

A dreadlocked couple kissed and stuck their tongues into each other's mouths right in front of their table, where Mr. Critt had hung a sprig of mistletoe on the tip of the mannequin arm coming out of the ceiling.

"Make me gag," Emma Lee said louder.

Grover laughed, nearly spraying hot chocolate everywhere.

"Don't knock what you haven't tried, sister," the dreadlock girl said to Emma Lee. She nodded toward the mistletoe. "Why don't you and your boyfriend give it a whirl?"

"I'm *not* her boyfriend!" Grover said.

"Never too early to start," the dreadlock guy said, then, as if he was demonstrating, kissed the dreadlock girl another long kiss. The couple sauntered off toward their table in the back, his hand in her back pocket.

Grover couldn't bring himself to look at Emma Lee. He kept his eyes on the checkerboard as Sudie quickly finished off Clay. When he finally did look up, the expression on Emma Lee's face wasn't at all what he'd expected. He couldn't be sure but he thought she looked a little hurt.

‡ ‡ ‡

"In case you hadn't noticed, my sister has a thing for Thomas Wolfe," Clay said as Emma Lee ran ahead and disappeared into the Old Kentucky Home. Clay looked at the rocking chairs lined up on the long porch.

"The guests used to sit out here in the summers," Sudie said. "A long time ago, people stayed in boardinghouses like this when they visited Asheville. Now they stay in hotels." She pointed to the Renaissance Hotel, a huge, ten-story hotel across from the Wolfe house. "Daddy says the Wolfe house has been in the hotel's shadow since the day it was built."

Shading his eyes with his hands, Clay frowned up into the

sky, looking over at the hotel and then back at the Wolfe house. "Now I may be wrong. Wouldn't be the first time. But unless I'm sorely mistaken, the path of the sun over these two buildings is such that the Wolfe house would never find itself in that big old hotel's shadow."

Inside, the first thing Grover noticed was the bright smell of pine and fir. Along the edges of the main exhibit room lay wreaths, a small stack of cut fir trees and another neat pile of garlands made from pine branches. Emma Lee was already at the exhibits, stopping to read every word, something Grover hadn't done in all the years he'd come here. Little Bit and several of the tour guides were draping garlands around the main room.

"He's in his office," Little Bit said, handing a garland to a tour guide on a ladder.

"You really are having a Thomas Wolfe Christmas," Sudie said.

Little Bit glanced off toward their father's office. "I thought your daddy would have a fit when he saw the bill. Instead, he said to make sure I got whatever I needed." She lowered her voice. "His mood has improved lately."

Grover walked to his father's half-open office door and found him standing at his desk with Leila beside him. They were looking at an open book on the desk. The way they leaned together, almost touching, gave Grover an odd feeling. He knocked.

Leila and their father stepped back from each other.

"Come on in!" his father said. A tinge of red crept across his father's face. "I was showing Leila a first edition *Look Homeward, Angel.*"

When Leila Roundtree looked up from the book, it hit Grover how pretty she was and how she wasn't just somebody's mother. He thought about how his father had accepted rides from the Roundtrees in the mornings, how he and Leila had started going on walks after supper, how he came back from those walks in a good mood.

His father led the Roundtrees through the house, starting downstairs, taking them through the dining room, the kitchen, the piano parlor, the sunroom parlor and then upstairs to the bedrooms. He showed them the room where Wolfe's brother Ben had died. Even without reading the book, Grover'd heard his father's spiel enough to know that Ben, Wolfe's older brother, was the angel in *Look Homeward, Angel*.

With no other visitors around, his father unhooked the velvet ropes and let the Roundtrees walk throughout the rooms. Emma Lee hardly said a word the whole time. She seemed to soak it all in. One of the last rooms they visited was the bedroom where Wolfe's father died.

"This is the very bed he died in," Grover's father said.

"I'll be," Clay said.

"Was he like Gant in the book?" Leila asked.

"A funny guy," his father said, "full of life, quoted long passages of Shakespeare, built roaring fires and on occasion given to excess."

"Given to what?" Clay asked.

"Drank too much," Sudie said.

As Grover's father led Leila and Clay on down the hall to

another room, Grover noticed Emma Lee linger. She laid her hand flat on the bed where Wolfe's father had died. Grover came and stood beside her.

"They know of at least eleven people who died in this house," Grover said.

He heard his father's voice down the hall. Grover placed his hand on the bed. "Course everybody who ever lived in this place must be dead now."

Emma Lee looked at him.

"Wolfe's father. His mother. His brothers and sisters, all dead. Every boarder whoever stayed here has to be dead. And Wolfe's been dead since 1938."

"What are you saying?" Emma Lee asked.

Grover shrugged. "Just that everybody's dead."

"Or getting there," Emma Lee said.

Careful to replace the felt rope, Grover led Emma Lee in the direction his father had taken Leila and Clay and Sudie, but found himself leading her down the hall toward the sleeping porch where Wolfe spent many nights and where he'd had to share the room with whatever boarder might be staying there at the time. It was Grover's favorite room because it had so many windows and was lighter than the rest of the house.

"He never knew from night to night where he'd have to sleep," Grover said. "Or who he'd have to share a room with." He pointed to the two beds that took up most of the room. "His mother was so cheap she'd squeeze as many beds into a room as she could. She even rented to people with tuberculosis. When he died of tuberculosis of the brain, they said he might've caught it from having to sleep in boarders' beds."

They could hear his father's voice down the hall as he reeled off facts about Wolfe's seven brothers and sisters. Outside, the wind whistled and a loose shutter tapped against the house. Grover reached for Emma Lee's hand.

She looked at him and then down at his hand holding hers.

Her hand was warm and rough at the same time. He let go.

They didn't say anything. The wind whistled outside and the shutter continued to tap against the house. The two of them stood watching the wind in the bare trees and the light fading outside. Down the hall, their families' voices were coming toward them.

Chapter Twelve

MERLIN WANTS IN

"Class, line up for lunch," said Mrs. Caswell. Chairs scraped as the kids lined up with their parents. It was Wednesday, when the school served Thanksgiving lunch and family were invited. Sam's father was in line. Mira's mom. Ashley's mom. Both of Daniel Pevoe's parents and his grandmother too. Almost everyone had a parent with them, some had both. The other night Sudie had invited their father to the Claxton Thanksgiving lunch, but he had a business lunch he couldn't miss. Sudie was disappointed but hadn't said anything. All morning, Grover had held out hope that their father, who was known for surprises, might show at the last minute.

Still in her nurse's uniform, Emma Lee's mother arrived as Mrs. Caswell led the line down the hall. Emma Lee, who'd been quiet all morning, gave her mother a weak smile, and Leila put her arm around her shoulder.

"Is your daddy coming?" Leila asked Grover as the line started down the stairway.

"He's busy," Grover said.

"He has a lot on his shoulders these days," Leila said.

Why did adults always make excuses for each other?

When his class filed past the offices, Grover noticed Miss Snyder at her desk, doing paperwork. He darted into her office. He'd been to see her a few times since the first meeting and had stopped feeling quite so strange passing her office. It didn't feel like his mother's anymore. Miss Snyder looked up from a form she was filling out.

"Would you sit with Sudie at lunch?" Grover asked. "Our father can't come."

"What about you?" Miss Snyder asked.

"I guess I *could* eat with her, but it wouldn't be special."

"What I mean is," she said, "would you like me to sit with you too?"

"That's okay," he said.

"Why is it okay?"

"I don't need anybody sitting with me."

"Why is that?"

"I'm older."

"I see." Miss Snyder rubbed her chin. "So older kids don't need people to sit with them?"

"Well, there's that," he said, "plus talking to people tires me out."

"Like now?" she asked. "Am I tiring you out?"

He glanced back at the passing line of his class.

"Of course I'll sit with her," she said.

In the cafeteria he sat beside Sam, whose father sat across from him, talking and laughing. Dr. Newcomer was a very funny, very nice man and a good father, it seemed to Grover. He'd coached Sam's soccer team for years, had been a troop leader in Sam's Boy Scout Troop and was always doing things with Sam, like taking him camping in the Smokies or skiing up at Wolf Ridge or to see a basketball game in Chapel Hill.

Emma Lee sat on the other side of him, hardly speaking to her mother. This didn't seem to bother Leila, who talked a lot to Mira's mother, the mayor of Asheville and a big supporter of the Wolfe house.

Halfway through the meal, Grover leaned over to Emma Lee and said, "Pretty good turkey, huh?"

Emma Lee smiled but seemed to drift back to wherever she'd been.

After school, Grover went to work in the Bamboo Forest. As usual, Clay came over and helped. The tapestries Grover was working on had gotten so big he needed an assistant to stand on the other side to help him weave in the long limbs.

For Sale signs, like stubborn weeds, had kept sprouting up almost as fast as Grover tossed them into the bamboo. He'd stopped when a police car started cruising their street, slowing in front of the Bamboo Forest. His father said the lot might not sell, that times were tight and few people would be able or willing to pay $250,000 for two little acres. Grover continued to go out to the Bamboo Forest every day, working harder than ever since any day could be his last.

"What was wrong with Emma Lee today?" Grover asked as he pushed a long hemlock limb into an opening.

"This time of year is hard for her," Clay said, taking the limb and sliding it back toward Grover. "It's hard for all of us but it's special hard for Emma Lee."

"How come?"

"Daddy was killed on Thanksgiving four years ago." Clay's eyes looked at him through a slot in the tapestry. "His dying was hardest on Emma Lee. I didn't know him as good since I was so little when he first went over there."

It was about dark when Grover and Clay straightened up the studio, putting everything neatly away. Grover picked up his toolbox, and together Clay and Grover walked out of the Bamboo Forest. The streetlights buzzed on and snowflakes whirled down through the light.

"The first snow of the year," Grover said, putting his hand out. His heart lifted a little at the sight of it.

"Back home they would've had a bunch of snows by now," Clay said.

They walked up the middle of Edgemont, looking up at the snow. When they came even with their houses, Grover heard a cat cry. Merlin sat on the sill outside the Roundtrees' front window. He seemed to be looking at a flame flickering.

"Merlin wants in," Clay said.

"What's with the candle?"

"Every evening from now till Christmas, Emma Lee will light that candle for Daddy and set it in the window. She's done it every year since he died. Says it's to guide his spirit home. The only thing is that it's also Merlin's perch, and when Emma Lee set the candle there, he jumped up and knocked it down. Nearly caught the house on fire. Mama said we have to keep him out whenever Emma Lee lights that candle."

A dark figure walked slowly up the street. Whoever it was, was tired. Grover recognized the battered hat. Jessie had on overalls and muddy work boots and snow collected on the brim of his hat. He looked at Grover's toolbox. "Y'all been hard at it?"

"Grover's working on a monster weaving," Clay said.

"What's that racket?" Jessie walked into the Roundtrees' yard and lifted Merlin off their windowsill and carried him back, holding the cat in his arms like a baby. "Cat, you're one bothersome feline."

"Mama makes us put him out so he'll come home to you," Clay said, petting Merlin. "She says it's important Merlin knows he's your cat."

"Merlin belongs to no man," Jessie said as the cat squirmed out of his arms, dropped to the ground and disappeared into the dark.

Headlights swept across the bottom of the street, and Grover could tell by the engine's rattle that it was his father's car. The headlights lit up the air, showing how heavy the snow fell. Grover and Clay and Jessie moved to the sidewalk as Grover's father pulled even with them. He rolled down his window.

"It's coming down, isn't it?" his father said, sounding like he'd had a good day at the Wolfe house.

"Charles said they're calling for eight inches," Jessie said.

Charles was the big guy who operated the backhoe at Riverside. "Maybe we ought to do our grocery shopping tonight? In case everything is shut down tomorrow."

"We can grab a bite to eat at Five Points and then head over to the co-op," their father said.

"Give me a few minutes to get out of these work clothes," Jessie said. He started up the street.

"Clay," their father said, "I'm glad y'all can join us for Thanksgiving."

This was the first Grover'd heard about the Roundtrees eating Thanksgiving with them. As he watched his father pull into the drive, Grover thought there seemed to be a good bit of communication with Leila that he wasn't in on.

"I better get home," Clay said. "Mama'll wonder where I am. See you, Grover."

"See you," Grover said, picking up his toolbox. He started up the front walk but then turned to watch Clay walk across their yard and disappear inside. The snow was coming down even harder. The candle flickering in the Roundtrees' front window gave Grover a warm and dizzy feeling, like he was falling but being held up at the same time.

‡   ‡   ‡

The waitress refilled Jessie's coffee cup and then their father's.

"Could I get some catsup, please?" Sudie said, looking at the pile of French fries next to her hamburger.

The waitress, a UNC Asheville student, had tattoos up and down her arms, and a nose stud. She pulled a bottle of catsup out of her uniform pocket and set it in front of Sudie.

"And I'd like some parmesan cheese," Grover said.

The waitress grabbed a shaker of parmesan off an empty table across from them. "Let me know if you need anything else."

Five Points Café sat on the edge of Montford and was only a few blocks from their house. Out the window, snow had already collected on Jessie's truck. Jessie'd driven them over in his pickup, which did well in the snow. Jessie and Grover sat on one side of a booth and Sudie and their father sat across from them.

Grover and Sudie had eaten at Five Points since they were little, always with their father. In the mornings it was filled with workmen sitting at the counter, drinking coffee and talking. Their mother wasn't crazy about Five Points, saying the food was greasy, so they only ate there when their mother was away or at a meeting. Eating here tonight had given Grover the uneasy feeling that their mother was just at a PTO meeting or out with her book group.

"And cranberry sauce," Jessie said, taking the pencil from behind his ear and adding to the grocery list he'd made on his napkin.

"And crescent rolls?" Sudie asked, dipping a French fry in catsup. "What's Thanksgiving without crescent rolls?"

Jessie asked their father how the Wolfe house had gone today, and it struck Grover that Jessie had taken over the job of asking the questions their mother used to ask.

"I don't know about this Thomas Wolfe Christmas thing," their father said. "All we have so far is a couple of school groups scheduled for a tour after Thanksgiving."

"That's a good start," Jessie said, just like their mother would've said.

"It'll take a lot more than a couple of high school classes to recoup what we've spent on decorations and advertising," their father said. "It'll take even more to get Lunsford off my back."

"Speaking of the old boy," Jessie said. "How'd your talk with him go?"

Grover's father frowned at Jessie.

"You went to see Mr. Lunsford?" Grover asked, wiping spaghetti sauce from his mouth with his napkin.

"Sorry about that, Walt," Jessie said. "I forgot it was a secret."

"The cat's out of the bag," his father said, giving Jessie a look. "I went to see him about your Bamboo Forest."

"You did?"

"At lunch today. Was the only time he could work me in."

So that was why his father hadn't been able to come to the Thanksgiving lunch at Claxton.

"I was hoping I might talk him down," his father said.

"You offered to buy it?" Grover's fork clattered onto his plate.

"With your mother's life insurance money coming soon," his father said, "I thought maybe we could afford it. If he'd come down to a reasonable price." He looked at Jessie. "I told him how it had meant a lot to the neighborhood kids over the years and how my son did his art work there but he said he couldn't afford to go any lower. He said he was sorry but he really needed the money for his grandkids' college."

Grover started to eat, but then set the fork back down. The Bamboo Forest was definitely going to get sold. Somehow, up until this moment, and even with the For Sale signs piling up, a part of him had believed it might not happen.

"Then Lunsford gave me a funny look and said, 'You wouldn't happen to know who's been pulling up the surveyor's stakes over there, would you? Or my signs?'" His father rubbed his forehead, looking at Grover and Sudie. "Y'all have to stop pulling up those signs. That's all I need is for him to find out we're behind that."

"I stopped when the police started coming by," Grover said.

"The police?" his father said. "I know the Bamboo Forest means a lot to you two. But Lunsford probably wouldn't mind getting rid of me. So you have to be on your best behavior here on in or the Bamboo Forest might not be the only thing we lose." Grover'd overheard his parents a few years before, when Mr. Lunsford had started talking again about demolishing the Wolfe house, that if their father lost his job and they needed money, they could sell their house. It was paid for.

"Maybe the Bamboo Forest won't sell," Sudie said.

"He's asking about three times what that land is worth," said Jessie.

"Look how it's coming down!" a man said in the booth behind theirs.

The snow fell so fast and thick it looked like the windows had been covered with white sheets. Grover thought how his father had gone to Mr. Lunsford, a man who was as close to an enemy he'd probably ever had, and asked to buy the Bamboo Forest. His father hadn't forgotten him. The sight of all the snow sent a vaguely familiar lightness up through his chest. It had been so long since he'd felt this way that at first Grover didn't recognize what had crept up on him. It wasn't happiness exactly but it was in the neighborhood.

As they were walking out the front door, Matthew happened to be heading in. He stepped back and held the door open for them.

"Thanks," Jessie said.

"Sure thing," Matthew said. He nodded to their father, but didn't look him in the eye.

"Matthew," their father said, smiling a strained smile.

Matthew's eyes lit briefly on Sudie and Grover, then he walked on inside.

"How's he working out?" their father asked Jessie as they squeezed into the truck.

"He's dependable," Jessie said, cranking the engine and turning on the windshield wipers, which wiped away the blanket of snow already on the windshield. "I ask him to do something, he does it."

"Then you did right," their father said. "Hiring him, I mean."

"He says he'll be finishing up his degree this semester," Jessie said.

"That's a good thing," their father said, looking out at the snow. He sounded miles away.

‡   ‡   ‡

As they made room in the refrigerator for the turkey, the lights flickered.

"I'm wondering," Jessie said, "if we might should go ahead and cook this bird in case the power quits on us."

There was a pause when it seemed to Grover everybody must've been thinking the same thing: Their mother had always been the one to cook the turkey.

"They print directions on the turkey," Sudie said.

Jessie lifted the turkey out of the refrigerator and set it on the counter, reading the little square box full of cooking directions on the wrapper.

"What does it say to cook it on?" Grover's father said, turning on the oven.

"Let's see," Jessie said, squinting at the wrapper. "Three fifty."

Grover's father set the dial on the oven.

Jessie rolled up his sleeves as Sudie handed him a pair of their mother's kitchen scissors, then cut off the plastic wrapper and set it aside with the directions facing up. Checking the directions a couple more times, he pulled out the gizzard, the neck and the giblets too, rubbed some olive oil and salt and pepper onto the turkey and started to slide it into the oven.

"Mama always put on a little tinfoil tent to keep it from drying out," Sudie said. Jessie pulled the turkey back out of the oven. "Reckon you can make us one?"

Sudie had already gotten out the tinfoil and was tearing off a section. She folded it neatly into a little tent and set it on the turkey. Then Jessie slid it into the oven.

"Says you want to cook him fifteen minutes per pound," Jessie said, squinting at the directions. "And he's a nineteen pounder, so let's see . . ."

"Two hundred and eighty-five minutes," Grover said. "Or four hours and forty-five minutes."

"Mama takes the tent off an hour before it's done cooking," Sudie said, and then like she'd heard herself use the present tense with their mother, her face darkened a little.

"In three hours and forty-five minutes we'll want to take the tinfoil off," Grover said. "So we'll need to do that at one thirty."

"I'll set my alarm clock," their father said, stifling a yawn.

"I could cook it at my house, Walt," Jessie said, "if you don't want to get up. Cause once you're up, you'd have to wait another hour after you take the tinfoil off."

His father groaned. "I don't know if I can manage that. It's been a long day."

"I'll do it," Grover said. "I'm not tired." The possibility of a big snow was one of the most exciting things that had happened in a while, and Grover was wide awake.

"I'll stay up with him," Sudie said.

"I don't know," his father said.

"Please, Daddy," Sudie said, putting her hands together. "Tomorrow's Thanksgiving. It's not like I have to get up to go to school."

"I guess it won't hurt anything for you to keep Grover company."

"Yes!" Sudie said, pumping her fist.

Jessie went home, saying he'd be back tomorrow to start cooking, and their father stoked up the stove in the living room, then went to bed.

Sudie got into her pajamas, dragged a quilt in from her room and settled onto the couch with a new Ramona book. Biscuit jumped up beside her. Grover pulled a chair to the front window and watched the snow. He studied Jessie's rental house across the street. Before the Roundtrees had moved in, it had seemed a kind of shell that college students, like hermit crabs, moved into and out of. With the Roundtrees over there, it had started to feel different. Tonight, with the white lines of snow collecting on the eaves and along the roof ridge, and the stubborn candle burning in the dark center, there was no denying that Jessie's rental house had become a home.

Grover woke to his watch beeping. He sat up, yawned and stretched. The first thing he noticed was the sweet smell of turkey. He checked his watch. One thirty. Sudie was asleep on the couch with Biscuit. The TV was still on, some BBC news program. The woodstove ticked with heat. Outside, it was snowing, still. He couldn't ever remember a snow like this. The trees and shrubs in the front yard bowed with snow. It must've been close to a foot by now.

He turned off the TV, pulled the quilt up around Sudie and went out to the kitchen. He started to open the oven, remembered the oven mittens, put them on, then slid the turkey halfway out, pulled off the tinfoil tent and slid the turkey back in. He set his watch for one hour, when the turkey would be done.

He stood at the window, looking at all the snow. He had an hour he could actually get some work done. He dug snow boots out of the back of his closet, put two flashlights in his coat pockets, pulled on his gloves and a wool hat and closed the front door quietly behind him. The first thing he noticed was the silence. No sounds of traffic, no barking dogs, no distant sirens. Nothing except the occasional snap of a branch or limb somewhere, giving under the weight of the snow. The snow absorbed house lights, streetlights and lights from downtown, so that it looked like it glowed from within.

Grover started out, but heard Biscuit bark inside. He opened the door, and without looking, the dog took his usual flying leap off the front steps and with a little poof sank out of sight. Now his bark sounded panicked. Grover dug him up out of the snow and held the shivering little dog in his arms. "It's too deep." He set Biscuit back inside the house and closed the door. He slogged his way over to the Bamboo Forest, his boots squeaking in the powdery snow. The bamboo bent over with snow. Some shoots bent all the way over, but when he knocked the snow off they sprang up like catapults, showering him with snow. His studio didn't look like itself. Just a bunch of white mounds. His heart skipped a beat when he saw the weaving he'd been working on bent nearly in half with the weight of the snow. He hurried over, shook the snow off, and as he did, it sprang back into shape.

He pulled out the flashlights, set them in little holders he'd made by lashing some bamboo together. Then he turned them on to the weaving. He dragged a pine limb from underneath a snowy pile, and started weaving it in. He'd never worked in the snow before. He'd never worked at two in the morning before. He'd weave the end of the limb into one side, then walk around and weave it into the other. It was much slower than when Clay helped him, but pretty soon he had the hang of it. He'd weave, walk around to the other side, then weave and walk around again. He liked working this way, in the snow, in the dark, in all the silence. After a while, he became so warm walking back and forth that he ended up unbuttoning his coat and taking off his hat.

As he did whenever the work went well, Grover lost himself. Forgot about place, forgot about time, forgot about himself. He'd finished the limb and was starting on another when his watch beeped.

"Uh-oh!" He grabbed the flashlights, stuffed them into his coat pockets and ran toward the house, but running in the deep snow was like running in slow motion. He'd turned up his walk when he noticed the candle flickering in the Roundtrees' window. Had they meant to leave it burning all night? He remembered a few years ago how a family over on Pearson Street had all burned to death when their Christmas tree had caught fire in the middle of the night.

He crossed the road and walked down their front walk. The yard dipped right in front of the house, so that the bottom of the window was eye level with whoever stood in the yard. Grover pressed against their window, staring into the candle flame. It was a large, sturdy candle, and he didn't see any curtains that might catch fire. He started to turn back when he was startled by a movement above him. A white shadow emerged in the window. The shape of a woman in her nightgown. Leila Roundtree. His heart began to pound. He felt a dry lump in his throat as if suddenly he was in a place he shouldn't be, looking at something he shouldn't.

How long had she been standing there? Or had she just come to the window? She didn't seem to see him. The vague white oval of her face turned toward the street, like she was looking for someone. Who was she looking for? Her husband? His ghost? Or was she looking at Grover's house?

Grover didn't dare move, praying she didn't look down. How would he explain himself? What would the Roundtrees think if they caught him at their window? Yet he couldn't take his eyes off the womanly shape of her, the curves pushing gently against the nightgown.

His watch gave a single beep. The turkey! Grover prayed it wasn't burning, but if it came down to burning the turkey or being caught here at the window staring at Leila Roundtree in her nightgown, the turkey could be charred to a crisp. Just as he was thinking maybe he should make a run for it, the luminous shadow above him leaned into the circle of light. And what he saw made his heart move up into his throat. Holding her long hair back from the flame, Emma Lee leaned in and blew the candle out.

CHAPTER THIRTEEN

SMALL TALK

The next morning Grover woke to a too-bright room. He glanced at his watch. Ten o'clock? He hated being late to the Bamboo Forest. He started to get out of bed, then stopped. Last night. Was it a dream? He heard kids yelling and laughing outside. He went to his window and had to squint at all the sunlight reflecting off what looked like about a foot of snow. Last night had been real, all of it: Walking around outside by himself in the falling snow. Working in the Bamboo Forest in the deep, deep silence. The flickering candle in the Roundtrees' window. The shadow. Emma Lee in the window in her nightgown. This last he remembered with a pang of guilt and a pang of something else—a new feeling that somehow felt familiar, like he'd been away and come back into himself for the first time. Back into his legs, back into his arms, into his feet, into his hands, into his toes, his fingers, into every little cell of himself.

He needed to talk to somebody, and he knew who that some-body was.

Grover dressed and went out to the kitchen, where Jessie, in an apron, was sliding a couple of pecan pies out of the oven and setting them off to the side. Sudie sat at the breakfast table in her pajamas, crumbling corn bread into a bowl.

"Your father left these for you." Jessie took a plate of French toast out of the toaster oven and set it on the table in front of Grover, along with a bottle of maple syrup.

"He walked over to the Wolfe house," Sudie said.

"Wanted to make sure none of those big sycamores had dropped limbs on it," Jessie said. "Good job on the bird." He nodded at the brown, glistening turkey that sat on the counter.

Grover devoured the French toast and downed a glass of milk, then grabbed his coat off the hook by the kitchen door, pulled on his gloves and his hat and stomped into his boots. It was so bright outside he had to shield his eyes with his hand. The storm had passed through in the early morning, leaving the day clear and cold. Kids were out sledding, throwing snowballs, building snowmen.

Grover found Sam at the far end of Riverside, where kids were hurling themselves down a big hill they called Dead Man's Descent.

"I don't believe it," Sam said as he trudged back up the hill, pulling his sled. "Couldn't resist the snow, huh? Where's your sled?"

"I need advice," Grover said.

"What kind of advice?"

"Not right here," Grover said, looking back at all the kids.

The two of them walked down one of the little roads that ran between the headstones, Sam pulling his sled behind him.

Grover looked across the cemetery, then back at Sam. "How do you ask a girl?"

"Ask a girl what?"

"How do you ask a girl to go somewhere with you?"

"In English is best," Sam said.

"I'm serious," Grover said.

"And if you ask me," Sam said, his voice going hard, "that's your whole problem. You're way too serious and have been ever since—" He seemed to stop himself.

"Since what?" Grover asked.

"Nothing," Sam said.

"Since my mother died?" Grover asked. "Is that what you mean? I got serious when Mama was hit by a car?"

Sam turned and started back in the direction of the sledding.

Grover ran up in front of him. "It is sort of serious, Sam. When your mother gets killed, it doesn't make you feel all that great! In case you hadn't noticed."

"I didn't mean it like that," Sam said quietly and stepped around him.

Grover stopped, watching his old friend walk away. "Sam!"

Sam kept walking.

"My mother is dead!" His words echoed off the white hills and came back to him as hard and cold as the snow-topped headstones.

Sam turned around. "So what, Grover?"

The words hung in the air between them.

Sam took a couple of steps back toward Grover. "You stopped riding bikes with me, stopped skateboarding with me, stopped coming to our house." He shrugged. "Stopped being my friend."

"I already told you—"

"Just because your mother's dead doesn't mean you have to be."

The boys looked at each other. Grover was surprised that their friendship had meant that much to Sam. Sam had all kinds of friends.

"I'm sorry I stopped coming up to your house," Grover said.

Sam looked at the ground.

"Will you help me?" Grover said.

Sam gave a big sigh. "All you have to do is wait till you're by yourself with Emma Lee and ask her to the Christmas Waltz."

"Who said anything about Emma Lee?"

"You're hopeless." Sam started up a path up a big hill, pulling his sled with him.

"Okay, okay, so it is Emma Lee."

Sam stopped and waited for Grover, and together they walked up a path lined by great shaggy hemlocks, their limbs bowed with snow. Grover'd gotten more than a few of his limbs for his tapestries from up here. Jessie'd said these trees were the oldest in the cemetery and had been here hundreds of years before there were graves. Grover sometimes thought about all the generations of people these trees had seen buried.

"I held her hand," Grover said.

Sam stopped. "Emma Lee's?"

"Once," Grover said, holding up a finger. "Sort of. When we were going through the Wolfe house."

Sam raised his eyebrows like he was impressed.

"I'm not even sure she really noticed," Grover said.

"Oh, *she* noticed," Sam said.

"How do you know?" Grover asked.

"Girls never *not* notice. Noticing is one of their main things."

"How do I ask her to go with me?" Grover reached inside his coat and pulled out his little sketchbook and his mechanical pencil.

"You're taking notes?" Sam asked.

"What do I say first?" Grover clicked his pencil, getting ready to write.

"'Hello' is usually a good start," Sam said, watching Grover scribble in his notebook. "I can't believe you wrote that down."

"What next?"

"Don't ask her right off. You need to make small talk first."

"Small talk?" Grover asked.

"You need to talk about other things."

"How do I do that?"

"Talk about what you usually talk about. I see you talking to her on the playground and in class too sometimes." Sam looked away. "In fact, you talk to her more than you talk to anybody else these days. Her and her brother."

It had never occurred to Grover that Sam might be jealous

of the Roundtrees. "They're just around," Grover said. "It's not like I go get them. Clay just comes over, and he likes the Bamboo Forest. So does Emma Lee." He kicked at the snow. "But it all feels different now with Emma Lee," Grover said, closing his sketchbook. "After last night."

"Last night?" Sam asked.

"Nothing." No way was Grover going to tell Sam about seeing Emma Lee in her nightgown. "So," Grover said, lifting up his notebook, getting his pencil ready to write.

"You don't want to rush into asking her."

"'Don't rush'," Grover said aloud as he wrote the words and circled them.

"You don't want her thinking it's a big deal to you," he said. "Just be talking to her about whatever it is y'all usually talk about, and then ask her like you just thought of it right then, like it's no big deal."

Grover wrote the words *No Big Deal* in his notebook and underlined them twice. "I never knew asking a girl was so complicated."

"Girls are more complicated than algebraic equations," Sam said.

"Algebra isn't complicated," Grover said.

"Okay, Einstein, so girls are more complicated than . . . than . . . quantum physics."

Grover closed his notebook. "I'll never be able to do this."

"I didn't mean that about quantum physics," Sam said. "I don't even know what quantum physics is."

"I can't do it," Grover said.

"You need a little practice."

"Practice?"

"Role-playing. My dad uses it with his patients. I'll be Emma Lee."

Grover laughed.

"Ask me to go out with you."

"You're serious?" Grover said.

"It'll help, I swear."

"I'm not asking you to go to the waltz with me."

"You won't be asking me, you'll be asking Emma Lee."

"This is totally random," Grover said. He tugged on a low limb of a hemlock, bringing snow down on both their heads. "Did you know that hemlocks might be wiped out in ten years? The woolly adelgid, a tiny insect from Asia, is killing them." Grover looked at the limb. "This would go good in my tapestry."

"You're stalling," Sam said.

Grover let go of the limb. "So what do we do?"

"Let's say you've rung Emma Lee's doorbell." Sam stepped between two headstones and opened an imaginary door. "'Oh, hello, Grover.'"

"Do you have something in your eye?" Grover asked.

"I'm flirting with you," Sam said.

"Gross."

"It's role-playing."

"Emma Lee doesn't blink her eyes like that. You look like an owl."

"Let me try again." He turned away, then after a minute turned back. "Hi, Grover."

"You make a terrible girl."

"Okay, okay," Sam said, turning his back to Grover again. "I think I've got it now." Then he turned around. Before he could get a word out, Grover was shaking his head. "She doesn't fake smile. There's nothing fake about Emma Lee."

"I don't think I'm going to get Emma Lee right for you," Sam said. He lay down on his sled on his stomach and aimed it down a steep hill. "Can you give me a push?" He held up his legs.

Grover took hold of his boots. "What am I supposed to do?"

"You'll figure it out."

Grover ran, pushing Sam over a little hump and then the sled took off on its own. His friend expertly steered the sled between a couple of headstones and then around a big hemlock. He remembered going to the funeral of Lee Sullivan, a tall, redheaded boy who back in third grade had been sledding down a street and slammed into a parked car.

A bunch of crows started cawing loudly overhead. At first Grover didn't see the red-tailed hawk. He just heard its high fierce screech. Then he saw the hawk at the center of all the confusion, getting dive-bombed by a dozen angry crows. What impressed Grover was the way the hawk calmly continued circling, keeping its mile-seeing eyes to the ground, looking for prey.

CHAPTER FOURTEEN

SUIT YOURSELF

When the doorbell rang a little after seven, their father answered it. The door nearly flew open from the wind. Leila came in first, followed by Clay and then Emma Lee, who had a book under one arm. Did she plan to read through Thanksgiving dinner?

"That wind is something fierce," Leila said, pushing her hair back out of her face.

Their father helped her off with her coat. "You look great," he said.

She wore a deep red dress that somehow showed up her face. She had on lipstick and sparkly earrings. Grover felt betrayed to see his father's eyes linger on another woman the way they used to linger on their mother.

"Let me take your coat," Sudie said to Clay.

"Thank you kindly," Clay said, handing her his coat.

Grover stood looking at Emma Lee, who hadn't looked up at him.

"Help Emma Lee with her coat," their father said.

Emma Lee took her coat off herself and held it out to Grover without a word. He'd worried all day that she'd seen him last night standing at her window, staring at her in her nightgown. He carried the coats to his bedroom and laid them on his bed. His bedroom had been where they had always put guests' coats, back when they used to have people over. The wind rattled the bamboo outside his window, a loose shutter flapped against the house and the lights flickered.

Back in the main room, Leila and their father and Jessie sat around the roaring woodstove, sipping from glasses of wine. Jessie had spent the day in the kitchen cooking. Their father had come home mid-afternoon, put leaves in the dining room table, brought up extra chairs from the basement and split a big pile of wood. Sudie and Grover had cleaned the house, shoveled the front walk and picked up limbs that had fallen and piled them in the wood-shed for kindling.

Sudie had taken Clay back to her bedroom to show him her night-light collection. That left Grover sitting off to the side, sipping eggnog while Emma Lee sat by the fire reading her book, her long hair curtaining her face. The fire in the woodstove sputtered when a gust of wind whistled down the chimney.

"This reminds me how it used to get up on the Roan after a big snow," Leila said, looking toward Emma Lee. "We had some mean winds up there, didn't we?"

Emma Lee didn't look up from her book.

"Sometimes it'd blow so hard it seemed like it might shove the cabin right off the side of the mountain," Leila said.

Grover wandered back to Sudie's room. Sudie had been collecting rock night-lights since she was little. Different colored stones and crystals with lights inside them. She had collected dozens over the years, including a couple of lighted fountains with running water. At night, a warm glow came from Sudie's room.

"This room is something else," Clay said, bending down beside one of the night-light water fountains.

Grover sat on a beanbag in the corner. Sudie bent down beside Clay and showed him how, with a flick of a switch, she could make the lights on the water fountain change color.

"Emma Lee's gotta see this," Clay said, getting up. Then he stopped. "On second thought," he said, "maybe another time."

"What's wrong with Emma Lee?" Sudie asked. "She looks sad."

Clay glanced at Grover, and Grover thought, *He knows about me standing out there too! Maybe the whole family knows!*

Sudie's windows rattled with a big gust of wind.

"Our daddy died on Thanksgiving," Clay said.

How could he have forgotten? Grover'd been so ready to feel guilty about last night that he hadn't considered the obvious reason.

When everyone sat down to Thanksgiving dinner, they took hands around the table. Sudie and Clay, who sat on either side of Grover, took his hands. Jessie sat where their mother always had. He'd changed into a nice shirt and his bolo tie. He'd let his hair down and combed it so that it fell gray and shining down to his shoulders. He reminded Grover of a distinguished Civil War general. Jessie bowed his head and so did everyone else. Grover began to feel like he was spying, and besides it was Jessie doing the blessing, so he closed his eyes and bowed his head out of respect.

"Father," Jessie began, "we thank You for the food we are about to receive. . . ."

The wind howled down the chimney and the windows rattled.

"We thank You for the many blessings You have showered upon us. We thank You for being our rod and our staff as we've traveled through a valley we know all too well. . . ."

Grover felt a tingle of warmth up his spine and across the back of his head. Holding hands like this, with his family and Jessie and the Roundtrees, made him feel part of something bigger. It was the same feeling he got in the Bamboo Forest.

"And we thank You for looking after our departed loved ones until such time as we can be reunited in Your presence. In Your name we pray, amen."

"Amen," everyone said, including Grover.

Emma Lee smiled at Grover, like she'd felt what he'd felt. Everyone was smiling, like they'd all felt it. Something about Jessie's blessing had lifted something from all of them.

"Can y'all *please* pass the crescent rolls?" Sudie asked, sounding desperate.

The wind howled in the chimney a long time, the lights flickered and then they heard a slow huge crash, a kind of thunderous tearing sound, like the earth itself was being torn out from under them. The house shook and dishes rattled. Stories Grover had read in the paper about earthquakes and tsunamis in far-off places flashed through his mind. The lights flickered some more, went off, came back on, then went off for good.

‡   ‡   ‡

People had come out, some with their flashlights, to look at the huge tree that had fallen across the street and darkened the neighborhood. Jessie said it was a tulip poplar. Its roots had pulled up out of the ground in a perfect rectangle. The hole reminded Grover of the neat graves Charles dug with his backhoe. After parents had made sure there were no fallen wires, neighborhood kids climbed onto the tree as if onto a fallen giant. Sudie and Clay joined them, disappearing into the maze of limbs. Grover walked up its great trunk, stepping on limbs that only an hour before had been forty feet in the air. Somewhere in that labyrinth of limbs, a hand took Grover's and pulled him up. It was Emma Lee. She pulled him onto a big limb where she was standing.

"Look." She lifted her eyes to the sky. Stars had poured into the space where the tree had stood.

Grover looked at her but she was still looking up. It went through his mind to tell her he'd stood outside her window. He opened his mouth but what came out was "Clay told me about how your father died on Thanksgiving."

She looked at him, then back up the sky.

"And how you light a candle for him."

"He's such a blabbermouth," Emma Lee snapped.

"You were the one who told me we can't keep the dead to ourselves."

She looked back up at the sky and her face softened. After a minute, she pointed to a very bright star. "That's the Dog Star. I know that much."

Back inside, their father had lighted candles around the living room and kitchen. They finished their Thanksgiving meal by candlelight and moved into the den to eat dessert. He opened the doors to the woodstove so that it lit up the room. He refilled Leila's wineglass and his own.

"I forgot to get Merlin in tonight," Jessie said, sipping from a mug of hot tea.

"Will he be all right in the snow?" Clay asked.

"He'll find him a warm place to curl up or slip into somebody's house." Grover watched Emma Lee, who'd already finished her pecan pie and picked up her book again, sitting close by the stove to read.

"Leila," Jessie said, "they won't be getting our power back on tonight, and all y'all have is that electric baseboard heat. I have a kerosene heater I could bring over."

"We'll be fine," Leila said. "We're mountain people."

"Why doesn't everyone spend the night?" their father said. "We've got the woodstove to keep us warm."

Grover looked at his father. He was so different these days. It would've been their mother who suggested everyone stay over. More and more, Grover'd gotten the feeling that his father was trying to do what his mother would've wanted him to.

"I'll be okay." Jessie looked at Leila. "I'm worried about y'all."

"Please stay." Sudie put her hands together. "It'll be like an indoor camping trip."

"Let's spend the night, Mama," Clay said.

"We don't want to put you out," Leila said.

"Clay can sleep in Grover's room and Emma Lee in Sudie's," their father said. "And you can sleep in the guest room."

Emma Lee whispered something into her mother's ear.

"Sweetheart," Leila said, "I think it'll be all right not to light it one night."

"No, it won't," Emma Lee said under her breath. "Especially not tonight."

Leila sighed. "Honey, please . . ."

"Not tonight," Emma Lee said again.

"Emma Lee," her mother said, "our house will be colder than a meat locker."

"But, Mama . . ."

"That's enough, Emma Lee!" Leila said sternly.

Emma Lee went back to where she'd been sitting, picked up her book, but didn't open it. She stared into the fire with a kind of look like she'd made up her mind about something, then opened her book.

‡   ‡   ‡

Grover had told Clay he'd be happy to sleep on the floor in the sleeping bag.

"I like sleeping bags," Clay'd said, wriggling down inside it. "Reminds me of the couple of times me and Daddy camped."

Their father had put a candle in Grover's room, telling him to be sure and blow it out before he went to bed.

"I like your room," Clay said, glancing out Grover's window, where they could make out the ribs of the bamboo by the flickering candlelight. "Feels like we're in the middle of a canebrake." He eyed the bamboo critically. "Some of that needs pruning. I've got a new pair of loppers. . . ." He yawned and scooted down into his bag and turned on his side, facing away from Grover.

"Grover?" he said, turning halfway back.

"Yeah?"

"Just so you know." His eyes met Grover's for a second, then he turned away again. "My sister likes you." He scooted down into his sleeping bag.

Grover felt a tightness in his throat. "She said that?"

"With Emma Lee, it's what she doesn't say that you need to listen to." Clay yawned. "She talks to me about most things but she hasn't said one word about you."

Grover lay there, thinking that one over. After a while, he said, "Clay?"

He didn't answer. Grover got out of bed and leaned over him. He was already asleep. Grover gave him a little shake, but he groaned and turned over. Grover climbed back into bed, blowing the candle out on his dresser.

He heard laughter in the living room. Jessie had gone home,

but their father and Leila had stayed up. As his eyes grew used to the dark, Grover could see outside his window how the bamboo swayed in the wind. He listened to the rustling for a while. Was it the wind? Or was someone outside? Or some thing? In this weather? His heart stopped when a masked face hovered in the window, looking in. He almost cried out. It took a minute to see that the face belonged to a raccoon. Maybe the fall of the great tree had disturbed his nest. With paws pressed against the glass, the raccoon boldly studied Grover's room, then seeming satisfied, lumbered back into the bamboo.

Grover woke late in the night. He'd heard something. He didn't see the raccoon in the window. Clay quietly snored. Grover pressed the little light on his watch that showed the time. One in the morning. He heard the creak of floorboards. Grover pulled on his pants and walked out to the living room. The main room was still pretty warm. Their father had filled the woodstove and turned the damper down.

He heard the front door shut. Looking out the window, he saw Emma Lee in her coat, walking down their walk. Grover grabbed his coat and went out the front door, careful to shut it quietly behind him.

"Hey, Emma Lee!" he called.

Emma Lee turned around and hissed, "You're going to wake them up!"

"Where you going?" he whispered.

"I have something I need to do."

"Can I come?"

"Go back inside before somebody misses us," she said.

The wind had stopped. A full moon was out, showing the great tree sprawled across the road.

"I'll be back soon," she said.

"Why can't I go with you, then?"

"Keep your voice down," she said.

Emma Lee's house was pitch-black dark. Grover still had the flashlights he'd been carrying in his coat from working in the Bamboo Forest. He handed one to Emma Lee.

"It's freezing in here," Grover said. He'd never been in their house. As he shined his flashlight around he saw in the hall a real weaving of what looked like mountains going on forever. "What's that?" Grover asked. He'd never seen anything quite like it.

"Nanna's," she said, heading into the front room.

"Your grandmother weaves?"

"She has a big old loom," Emma Lee said from the front room.

He saw another weaving farther down the hall—of a cabin on a mountainside. He walked into the kitchen and saw a weaving over the sink—cows in a pasture. Everywhere he shined his flashlight was a weaving. There were weavings of sunflowers, of mountain laurel in bloom, of creeks, waterfalls and one of a bridge spanning a river.

Grover came up next to Emma Lee, who stood at the front window, looking out on the moonlit street. He'd never seen his house from over here. The overgrown grass and bushes looked like a snow-covered jungle, and the old dark house rising behind it looked neglected, like the sadness of the past year had seeped through the walls and out into the yard.

Emma Lee struck a match against the side of a box of kitchen matches and lit the big candle. Grover remembered with a start last night standing just outside the window, looking in at her. She pulled up a chair and sat in front of the candle.

"Now what?" Grover asked.

"That's it," she said.

"You came all the way over here to light this candle?"

She stared into the flame.

He shivered. "Well, now that it's lit, can we go back?"

"I'm staying." She folded her arms and watched the candle.

Grover pulled up a chair and sat beside her.

"Suit yourself," she said.

After a while, Grover said, "It's cold in here."

"I'll get us some blankets," she said.

As he watched her light disappear down the hall, he pointed his flashlight at the weaving of the family on the wall. He reached into his coat pocket for his sketchbook. As he sketched by the light of his flashlight, he saw the notes he'd taken from Sam earlier that day in the cemetery.

She came back in, carrying blankets, gave him one, then she wrapped herself in the other. In the flickering candlelight, she looked like an Indian princess sitting in front of a campfire. Candlelight, thought Grover, made the world look old.

He tucked the notebook back into his coat pocket, looked

out at the night, then back at her. He cleared his throat. "How's it going?"

Emma Lee looked at him.

"What have you been doing lately?"

Emma Lee frowned. "You're acting very weird all of the sudden."

"I'm making small talk," he said. "I've been told girls like to have conversations first."

"Before what? Grover, what are you getting at?"

"Forget it." He sighed. "I was trying to ask you to go to the Christmas Waltz. I was *told* girls like conversation before they're asked things."

"Maybe some girls," she said.

"I'm hopeless when it comes to girls." He kept staring at the candle.

"With this girl you're not," she said.

Grover looked at her. "You'll go with me?"

"Yes," she said.

"Oh," he said.

They both jumped when they heard a sudden strange crying. Merlin was outside on the ledge, staring in at them.

"Maybe we ought to let him in," Emma Lee said. "He might be cold."

"But Clay said your mama said . . ."

"I know."

Merlin jumped from the windowsill and disappeared.

Grover sat with Emma Lee for a while longer, staring at

the candle and occasionally looking at her, finding it hard to believe that not only had he asked her but she'd said yes. After a while, Grover felt his eyelids get heavy and he said he was going back to the house. Emma Lee said she'd come in a little while. When Grover opened the front door, something streaked past him into the house. He chased after the cat, back into the front room, where Merlin was already in Emma Lee's lap.

"You want me to put him out?" Grover asked.

She shook her head, petting the cat and yawning.

Grover had started out when Emma Lee spoke, "Thanks," she said.

"For what?"

"Everything."

Grover walked home through the deep snow. He didn't like the feeling of her thanking him for *Everything*. Like she was saying good-bye. He looked back to see her still in the window. Once inside his house, he slowly closed the door behind him so he wouldn't make a sound. Biscuit pranced up to him, sniffing him like he smelled the Roundtrees' house. "Go on!" he whispered. Lowering his head, the dog walked back toward Sudie's room.

Grover was thinking about going back to get Emma Lee when he heard noises coming from the guest bedroom where Leila slept. He noticed a line of flickering light underneath the door. He pressed his ear to the door but didn't hear a thing except somebody moving around a lot. He leaned back on a floorboard that creaked and the movement stopped.

"Did you hear that?" Leila's voice.

"Hear what?" A man's voice. Grover felt his chest tighten as he realized who the man was.

"Sounded like someone at the door," Leila said. "Should I go check on the kids?"

"I didn't hear anything. This old house makes all kinds of noises."

"I thought I heard someone," she said.

"You want me to check?"

There was a long silence in which Grover wasn't sure if someone was coming to the door. He didn't dare move for fear of stepping on the creaky board again.

"I'm not sure about this," Leila said.

"Neither am I," he said.

Grover couldn't pry himself from the door.

"Isn't it too soon?" she said. "For you, I mean."

There was a pause.

"It's just been so long," she said.

Another pause.

"Let's stop talking," he said.

Grover tiptoed to his room and quietly shut the door. He lay in bed, trying to think. His father had been in the room with Leila, and there were noises that seemed to involve both of them. He'd heard similar noises come from his parents' bedroom when his mother was alive, noises he'd known to stay away from. His father shouldn't be making those noises with anyone but their mother. Except of course their mother wasn't here.

Then he remembered. He'd asked Emma Lee to the Christmas Waltz and she'd said yes. Unbelievable. "Unbelievable," he said aloud. He yawned, thinking how back in October he'd hardly noticed this girl who had moved into his neighborhood. He yawned again and, thinking of Emma Lee, rode his exhaustion out beyond the worried world, leaving it far far behind.

CHAPTER FIFTEEN
SHE'S IN THERE

G rover woke to Biscuit standing on his chest. The little dog was crying and making noises he'd never heard him make. Grover sat up and Biscuit jumped off the bed and ran toward the hallway.

"Now what?" Grover yawned.

Clay's eyes opened.

Biscuit stood in the doorway whining.

Clay closed his eyes and in a sleepy voice said, "He's your dog but I'm thinking he might need to do his business."

Grover checked his watch. Three o'clock. Groggy and cold, he pulled on his pants, put on his bedroom slippers and walked through the chilly house. The guest room door was open. From the moonlight coming in through the window, he could see that only Leila was sleeping in there.

With Biscuit still crying, Grover opened the front door to let him out. Biscuit didn't go off the porch, though. The little dog just stood there making those noises.

He started to pick the dog up to carry him out in the yard when he glanced across the street. Bright yellow and red swirls of light framed the Roundtrees' window. A Van Gogh of flames.

"Emma Lee." He ran toward the Roundtrees' house, screaming, "Emma Lee! Emma Lee!" He kept slipping in his bedroom shoes, and finally fell hard on his knees in the street, getting a mouthful of dirt and snow. He ran up on the porch and opened the front door. Smoke poured out. Grover coughed and his eyes stung. "Emma Lee! Are you in there?!" he shouted. All he heard was the fire crackling. As he started in, Merlin streaked out, disappearing off the porch. Covering his mouth with his pajama sleeve, Grover hurried into the house but had to back out because the smoke was so thick. He coughed and wiped his stinging eyes.

He paused at the door, watching the smoke pour out. She might've gone back to his house and was fast asleep in Sudie's room. He started to back down off the porch, when a voice inside him said, *She's in there.*

He stepped back onto the porch and paused in the doorway. A fireman who'd visited Mrs. Caswell's class had told them that smoke rises and that the best way to get out of a fire was to stay low and crawl. Maybe it was the best way to go into a fire too. He dropped to all fours and found he could breathe and see a little better. He crawled in the direction of the glow—the doorway of the front room.

"Emma Lee!" he croaked as he coughed and blinked his eyes.

When he reached the doorway to the front room, he saw that the couch and some of the furniture was on fire, and flames were creeping up the walls. The weavings. Somehow they'd caught. Emma Lee lay sprawled in the middle, her blanket half covering her. The candle had fallen from the windowsill and was on its side on the floor.

"Emma Lee," he said as he crawled up to her.

She didn't move. He turned her over. Her face was the color of ashes and her lips blue.

"Oh, no," he said. He stood up and immediately couldn't breathe. He felt dizzy. His throat ached with the smoke and he coughed, trying to hold his breath. He took her underneath her arms and dragged her across the floor in the direction of the door. But he slammed into the door frame, hit his back hard and dropped her. He had to bend over and feel around for her in the smoke that was getting thicker. He tried picking her up, but was so dizzy he couldn't tell which way to go. He collapsed onto the floor beside her and was getting back up when a firm hand gripped his arm and helped him stand. The smoke was too thick for him to make out who it was. But together Grover and whoever it was dragged Emma Lee out of the room, down the hall and out onto the porch. Then, before Grover could turn his head, the person had stepped off the porch and disappeared. Grover dragged Emma Lee out into the snow, pretty far from the house. Clearing a place for her on the front walk with his foot, he laid her down. His head spinning, he fell to his knees coughing. He knelt there for some time, trying to breathe, but whenever he did, his lungs burned like somehow the fire had gotten down inside him.

"Emma Lee!!" In her nightgown, Leila sank down on her knees in front of her daughter. "Oh Lord! Please, Lord!" She leaned over, pulled her daughter's head back and breathed into Emma Lee's mouth. Emma Lee's chest rose.

"Grover?" His father was in his pants and T-shirt. He squatted down beside Grover, brushing hair out of his face. "Are you okay?"

Grover nodded, not looking at his father. He'd felt a tinge of anger at his father's touch. "I'm okay," he croaked and coughed. The burning in his lungs had let up a little.

They watched Leila breathe into Emma Lee, wait for her daughter's chest to go down and then breathe into her again. His father yelled back to Clay and Sudie, who were making their way across the street toward them. "Call 911."

Sudie started to turn around and run back into the house.

"Already called 'em, Sudie," Jessie said, coming up to Grover and his father.

"Breathe, sweetheart, breathe!" Leila watched her daughter's chest fall. "Come on!"

His father helped Grover to his feet. Jessie stood with them, watching Leila frantically work over her daughter. Clay came up beside them, his face pale, and said under his breath, "Oh, Sis." Grover's father put his arm around Clay and pulled the boy against him. Sudie came and stood next to Grover, clutching her little silver cylinder like she was calling on a higher power.

Years passed. Leila worked over Emma Lee and worked over her. "Come on!" she'd say. "Come on, Emma Lee!" She yelled louder. The longer Emma Lee didn't breathe, the angrier Leila became. Just when it seemed to Grover like Emma Lee was gone in the way his mother was gone, there was a cough. Her eyelids fluttered. She coughed again, gasped for air and opened her eyes. The color came back into her face and her lips.

"Oh, thank you, Lord!" her mother cried out. "Thank You, dear God!" She cradled her daughter's head in her lap and rocked in the snow, as Emma Lee coughed and coughed. "Oh sweet sweet Jesus, thank You!"

A woman who lived down the street stepped out of a semicircle of neighbors and handed them a blanket. With Emma Lee wrapped in the blanket, Grover's father carried her off the cold walk and sat her on the curb where another neighbor had laid out more blankets. The whole time Emma Lee coughed and wheezed.

A loud pop, the sound of glass breaking. The front window of the house had shattered and the fire leapt up, the flames reaching up the side of the house.

"Oh, Jessie," Leila said, looking back, "your house!"

Not even glancing at the house, Jessie wrapped another blanket around Emma Lee.

Two fire trucks followed by an ambulance rumbled up the street, their red lights flashing against the houses and their snow chains ringing on the pavement. The sound of the chains weirdly reminded Grover of sleigh bells.

The EMTs put an oxygen mask on Emma Lee, then carried her to the ambulance and began checking her over with Leila beside her. One of the firemen walked Grover to beside a fire truck and began checking him over.

"How you feeling?" he asked, looking into Grover's eyes with a light.

"My throat hurts."

"The smoke does that," the fireman said. "It does a whole lot worse if it has time." He put a blood pressure cuff around Grover's arm. He nodded toward the ambulance. "The EMTs say you saved that girl's life. Said if she'd been in there much longer that'd a been all she wrote."

They heard a crash and turned to see a couple of firemen knock out the rest of the front window. They aimed a fire hose through the window, blasting the front room. A couple of other firemen went in through the front door with another hose. To Grover's astonishment, the fire was out in minutes. It had seemed so huge when he was in the house, like it would take hours, even days to put out.

Before long, the ambulance pulled away with Emma Lee, Leila riding with her. They wanted to keep Emma Lee at the hospital overnight to keep an eye on her. Leila hugged Clay and said she'd call first thing tomorrow.

"We'll look after Clay," Grover's father had said.

Back at the house, Jessie settled Clay into Grover's sleeping bag while Grover collapsed onto the couch in the living room, feeling dirty and gritty and reeking of smoke, but too exhausted to do anything about it. In a little while Grover's father came and led Grover to the bathroom, where he'd lit a candle. Grover was startled when he saw his flickering reflection in the bathroom mirror. His face was so smudged with soot he didn't recognize himself.

His father helped him out of his pajamas, then turned on the shower. "The water's still warm," he said, testing it with his hand, "even though the power's been out a while now." He helped Grover into the shower. But when he saw Grover could barely move, he took a washrag, soaped it up and gently washed his face, his arms, his back and his legs. Grover remembered when he was a little boy and his father had often bathed him at night after supper.

"Somebody helped me," Grover said, stepping out of the shower.

"Helped you?" His father dried him with a towel.

"Somebody helped me drag Emma Lee out, but I couldn't see them in all the smoke."

"You need to get some sleep." His father led him back to his room, where Clay was already asleep again, and helped him into bed. His father sat on the edge of his bed for a while, watching him. "I'm sorry, honey," his father said after a while, then he leaned over and kissed his forehead. "I should've been there."

CHAPTER SIXTEEN

A MESSAGE FROM GOD

"Class, a little later this morning we'll walk to the Wolfe house," said Mrs. Caswell. "Let's review what we've learned this week. When was Wolfe born?"

"Oh, oh!" Ashley's hand shot up. She waved desperately like a survivor in a life raft, trying to get the attention of a high-flying airplane.

"Grover," Mrs. Caswell said.

"October 3, 1900," Grover said, knowing the date as well as his own birthday. Ever since Emma Lee had left, Mrs. Caswell had called on him more. He couldn't get used to the empty desk at his back. Whenever he went off in his head during class, he expected Emma Lee to poke him in the shoulder and whisper in that Mitchell County accent of hers, "Earth to Grover. Earth to Grover."

Emma Lee had returned from the hospital the day after the fire. She'd been okay except that she was exhausted, had a mean headache and her throat still hurt. She'd slept the whole first day she got back. The Roundtrees were staying at Jessie's. Most of the fire damage to his rental house had been to the front room, but the smoke and water damage made it impossible to live there. Jessie had insisted they stay with him until he could get the house repaired.

The same day Emma Lee returned from the hospital, Leila had come over to Grover's house. Grover'd answered the door, and the first thing Leila did was hug him a long time. She smelled of hospital. When she let him go, she wiped her eyes and said, "Thank you." Her face was pale and drawn. She had big circles under her eyes. He wondered if she'd slept at all since the fire. "We'll never forget what you did," she said.

The way she'd said it unsettled him. What Mrs. Caswell called the past tense had crept in there, as if Leila was already looking back at him from someplace else.

"I had help pulling her out of the house," Grover said.

Leila nodded. "Your daddy told me about that." She smiled knowingly.

"You know who it was?" he asked.

"The Lord Jesus was watching out for you and my Emma Lee." She kissed his cheek. "Come visit Emma Lee tomorrow."

That evening their father and Leila had gone for a long walk. Grover watched through the front window as they walked away up the street toward Riverside. When they came back half an hour later, they didn't look happy. They hugged in the middle of the street, reminding him of airport hugs.

Grover hurried back to his room, sat down at his desk and

opened his sketchbook, looking at his latest drawings. He started sketching on a new idea for a weaving and was so caught up in it that he was surprised when his father knocked on the open door to his room.

"The Roundtrees are moving back to Mitchell County."

"Because of the fire?" Grover asked, feeling the bottom drop out of his stomach.

"There's more to it," his father said.

Grover looked out the window.

"She's put in for a weekend job at St. Joseph's, which won't come through till January. Until then she'll commute from Roan to the hospital. When it does come through, she'll work three twelve-hour shifts and rent a room close to the hospital and go home to Roan Mountain on her days off."

"It's because of what happened in the guest room," Grover said, unable to keep the anger out of his voice.

His father stepped into Grover's room and shut the door behind him. "How did you know about that?"

"I heard y'all," Grover's voice shook. "I didn't mean to. It was hard not to hear."

His father sat on Grover's bed. "Irresponsible and selfish."

"I *said* I didn't mean to—"

"I'm talking about me," he said. "I was selfish to let that happen."

"But what does that have to do with them moving back?"

"She thinks that what happened to Emma Lee happened because she and I . . ." His father sighed. "And maybe it did."

"It happened because Merlin knocked the candle over," Grover said. The fire department had determined that the fire had started when the candle had fallen over. The part about Merlin was everybody's best guess. The cat hadn't been seen since the fire.

"Leila thinks it was a warning from God. She thinks He's telling her she needs to move back to Roan Mountain."

"She told me she thought Jesus was the one who helped me carry Emma Lee," Grover said. "So does she think God almost burned us up so He could save us?"

"Religion is a big part of the Roundtrees' lives." His father sighed again. "I didn't understand quite how big."

"Who do you think helped me pull Emma Lee out of the house?" Grover asked. "It wasn't Jesus."

His father looked at him like he was debating whether to say something. "I don't know," he said, "but I do know that I'm sorry about what happened between me and Leila. When you get a little older, you might understand."

"I know all about that!" Grover said impatiently. "We had sex ed last February. They put the boys in one room and the girls in the other, gave us pamphlets and asked if we had any questions. Mama filled me in on what wasn't in the pamphlet since you were at a meeting in Raleigh."

"I'm sorry I've been such a lousy father."

"That's okay," Grover said.

"And I'm sorry about . . . the guest room. I know your mother hasn't been gone that long. . . ."

"I don't really care about that," Grover snapped. "Not that it made me feel good that my father was in the guest bedroom with the neighbor."

"You sound pretty mad to me," his father said.

"That's not what I'm mad about," Grover said. "Not the main thing anyway."

His father got a knowing look on his face. "You don't want your buddy to move away. Listen, Clay can visit anytime. Maybe for a few weeks this summer."

"It's not *just* Clay," Grover said under his breath.

"Ah," his father said and that was all he said.

Grover rubbed his forehead and looked out the darkening window. "Can't you tell them not to move away?"

"I did," his father said. "She said she'd prayed about it a long time."

"She really thinks what happened to Emma Lee was a message from God?"

"Leila believes it's a sin for people to sleep together before they get married."

"A sin?"

"And that God was punishing Leila for her sin," his father said.

"Why would God take y'all's mistake out on Emma Lee?"

"Leila figures that God knows the worst thing that could happen to a parent would be for something to happen to their child." His father looked at him. "I would've never forgiven myself if something had happened to you when you went in after Emma Lee."

"What kind of God would kill the child to teach the parent?" Grover asked.

Grover and his father sat on his bed for a while. Grover wondered why the Roundtrees, especially Emma Lee, had become so important to him. They'd only been here a couple of months. It wasn't like he knew Emma Lee the way he'd known Sam—since they were little kids.

"They're moving on Tuesday," his father said.

"Why so soon?"

"She doesn't want to impose on Jessie."

"They could impose on us," Grover said.

"Staying here would be about the last thing Leila would consider."

"She blames you for the fire?"

"She blames the situation."

"The situation?"

"Me and her. Such as it is, was."

Grover didn't say anything. His father was trusting him, confiding in him. Even though it felt very strange to hear about a woman other than his mother, he also thought maybe he was getting to know his father in a different way.

‡ ‡ ‡

Mrs. Caswell led the class downtown. When they passed Reader's Corner, Grover tapped on the window and waved at Byron. Several girls gathered around the window, looking at Tom, who squinted up from his usual place among the books. They passed Videolife. Grover didn't pause with the other kids to look at the big poster of *Fantastic Mr. Fox*.

Grover'd been the one to answer the phone the night Videolife had called to tell them *Fantastic Mr. Fox* was in. When he'd hung up, he said, "Mama, that was Videolife. They said *Fantastic—*" His mother had clamped her hand over his mouth and nodded in the direction of Sudie, who sat on the couch doing her homework. She had put her finger to her lips and waved him into the kitchen. "When you get home from school tomorrow," she whispered, "could you ride your bike down to Videolife to pick it up? I want to surprise her." Sudie had missed the movie when it had come to the theaters because she'd had the flu, and she was dying to see it.

As Grover's class neared the Wolfe house, he thought how his father's mood had improved, the reason being the same reason that Grover's class was headed to the Old Kentucky Home. In spite of all his father's doubts, it looked like *A Thomas Wolfe Christmas* might work. Little Bit had hand-delivered pamphlets to all the schools and sent press releases to the newspapers and the radio stations and the TV stations. Schools from as far away as Charlotte and Raleigh shipped busloads to visit the house. In the couple of weeks since Thanksgiving, the house had already had more visitors than the rest of the year combined, and school and church groups had made reservations all the way up to Christmas. County commissioners were beginning to back off plans to downsize the staff, and Delbert Lunsford had been silent at the latest commissioners' meetings.

As his class crossed over the bridge into town, Grover paused and watched a tractor trailer of Christmas trees rumble beneath. Probably from Mitchell County. He'd gone over to talk to Emma Lee at Jessie's on Saturday after she'd come back from the hospital. Grover'd walked into the den, which was warm from the big fire Jessie had going in the fireplace. He found Emma Lee curled up in a big stuffed chair, asleep, a copy of *Jane Eyre* open on her lap. Her hair fell across the back of the couch, a long black shiny sheet. Grover started to tiptoe out.

"Don't go." She stretched and yawned.

"I didn't mean to wake you," Grover said.

She sat up, patting the chair beside her and he sat. "The doctor says I can go back to school tomorrow."

Grover nodded, feeling unable to look her in the eye all of a sudden.

"They tell me I wouldn't be here if it wasn't for you," she said.

"I had help," Grover said.

"Mama told me."

"It wasn't Jesus," Grover said.

"Who do you think it was?"

"I don't know, but whoever it was has a firm grip." Grover went over to the fire, poking at it with the iron poker, sending sparks up the chimney.

"What is it, Grover? You look serious."

"You know the other night when you said 'Thank you for everything'?" He sighed. "The way you said it felt like you were saying good-bye. And it made me wonder."

"Wonder what?" she said, sitting up on the edge of her chair.

He looked toward the fire crackling in the fireplace. "If maybe that candle didn't fall by itself. If *someone* might've helped it fall."

"Someone did," she said. "Merlin."

Grover rubbed his forehead. "You said the only chance you had of seeing your father was up in Heaven and I was wondering if maybe you decided to . . ."

"Are you kidding?" she asked. "Daddy'd give me down the road if I showed up in Heaven having done something as bone-headed as burn myself up."

Feeling a wave of relief, Grover sat back in the chair.

"Besides," she said, "I promised I'd go with you to the Christmas Waltz." Then her face fell. "Except I guess that can't happen now."

"Do *you* want to move back?" he asked.

"I miss Nanna, but to tell you the truth, I was getting used to it here. I like Asheville. I like Claxton. I like Mrs. Caswell. I like Mira and all the kids at school. It's even getting so I don't mind Ashley and them." She paused. "And I like Jessie and your daddy and Sudie and . . ." She looked at him, her eyes shining.

"My father says your mother thinks the fire was a warning."

"Us moving back doesn't have a thing in the world to do with God," Emma Lee said. "Mama's afraid of how much she likes your daddy. She's afraid something might happen between them."

Something already has, Grover thought.

"It's been hard for Mama to get over Daddy," Emma Lee said.

"But he was mean to her," Grover said.

"He was hateful to her in the end. He didn't mean to be hateful. The war did that to him. Still, if somebody slaps you around long enough, it's hard to work up a lot of sympathy for him. I think him being the way he was at the end made it hard for her to get over him. She loved him but she hated him too. So when he died, she couldn't just flat-out miss him. The more you miss somebody, the quicker you get over them."

They looked toward the fire. Grover thought about his mother, about how he hadn't visited her grave lately. How his mind had been on other things. Was it because he'd missed her so much when she first died that he didn't think about her quite as much? Maybe a person could only do so much missing.

‡   ‡   ‡

"Let's spit on a car." Sam had come up beside Grover on the overpass as their class walked toward the Wolfe house. Sam checked to see that Mrs. Caswell wasn't looking, leaned over the rail and spit. The white drop flew through the air and hit a windshield. "Bull's-eye." Grover didn't smile.

"You have to get over her," Sam said.

"You don't get over that kind of thing real quick," Grover snapped.

"I'm not talking about *that*," Sam said.

"Gentlemen!" Mrs. Caswell called and they hurried to catch up.

"Emma Lee isn't the only fish in the sea," Sam said. "What about asking Mira to the Christmas Waltz?"

"I'm not asking anybody else to go anywhere," Grover said as his class wound through the parking lot of the Wolfe house. There must've been twenty school buses—from Winston-Salem, Charlotte, Raleigh, Chattanooga, Knoxville, Greenville, Columbia and even Charleston. Grover saw a cat disappear around the corner of the Wolfe house that looked a lot like Merlin and was about to go after it, when Matthew came walking from the other direction. There was something different about him but Grover wasn't sure what. Matthew's glasses. He was wearing wire-rims instead of the heavy black-framed glasses he always wore. Otherwise, he looked the same. Same green Army coat, same backpack, same distracted look in his eyes. He didn't seem to notice Grover among the long line of students.

"Welcome!" Grover's father stood at the top of the steps, wearing, of all things, a Santa hat. "Welcome to *A Thomas Wolfe Christmas*!" his father said, waving Grover's class in. The house was crawling with schoolchildren. Orderly, well-behaved lines of them. Little Bit wouldn't have it any other way. His father had said at supper last night that the attendance numbers were so high that it would probably support funding for the next year.

Toward the end of the tour, when his father had taken Grover's class down to the kitchen to the woodstove where Julia Wolfe had made meals for her boarders, he told them something Grover had never heard before. His father said Wolfe had been hated by some of the people of Asheville for the way he'd depicted them in *Look Homeward, Angel*. But when it became a best seller, some of the townspeople he hadn't written about were upset for not being included.

"Wolfe couldn't win for losing," his father said, looking more animated than Grover had seen him in a long time. It occurred to Grover that the Wolfe house was probably as important to his father as the Bamboo Forest was to him.

At the end of the tour, Grover's class ended up back in the main room of the house, where Little Bit and her staff served cider and cookies. Grover had never seen the house so packed. Crowds made him lonely.

Grover went off by himself and read the exhibits, taking his time, and paying attention to Wolfe's life in a way he never had before. Emma Lee would've approved. Just a few days after the fire, he and Sudie had come home from school to find a U-Haul driven by Leila's long-haired brother, and the Roundtrees' old van driven by Leila, pulling out of their driveway. After they were out of sight, Grover couldn't stand to do anything but go over to the Bamboo Forest, clear away what was left of the snow from the tapestry and work alone until the sun set. And having forgotten his flashlights, he worked on into the dark, like a blind man, weaving things together by nothing but feel.

Chapter Seventeen

Up into the Mountains

The tires squealed around the sharp curves as their father whipped the car back and forth up Highway 19. With every mile they drove, the road grew windier and the mountainsides inched closer. Grover was sure he could roll down his window and touch the striations in the rock. The road opened up to empty fields and pastures with cows that stood on hills in a way that made them look like two legs were shorter than the others.

It was Saturday morning and their father had announced that they were going to get a Christmas tree. Sudie and Grover had assumed, with their mother no longer alive, that they'd buy their tree at the Asheville Farmers Market. They'd been surprised that they'd stopped to pick up Jessie just to drive over to the Farmers Market. They'd been even more surprised when their father aimed the car north, up Interstate 26 toward Mitchell County.

Grover and Sudie had been excited when they realized

where their father was taking them. But the farther they drove, the quieter everyone had gotten. Until, at one point, Grover looked over and saw Sudie wasn't smiling anymore. Up front their father and Jessie had stopped talking. Maybe this trip wasn't such a good idea.

They had left I-26 and now drove down into a brown rolling valley and passed through a collection of drugstores, fast-food places, convenience stores and grocery stores that made up the edge of Burnsville. They left all that behind and headed east toward Spruce Pine. Grover noticed orderly rows of miniature green triangles that seemed to march over the wintry brown mountainsides.

"They call the Fraser fir the Cadillac of Christmas trees," Jessie said, looking up at the mountainsides. "Christmas tree farming is backbreaking work in the summers—trimming, keeping the weeds down and doing all that while making sure you don't step on a snake."

"Do the snakes ever get up into the trees?" Grover asked.

"They're mostly hibernating in the ground by the time they cut the trees, but one warm winter there was an article in the *Asheville Citizen-Times* about a family finding a copperhead curled up among the presents on Christmas morning."

Sudie just stared out the window.

Grover pressed his hand against the window. It was always colder up here.

"There!" Sudie slapped the window, pointing at a hand-painted sign.

GUDGER'S CHRISTMAS TREES
Two Miles Ahead on the Left
(You pick. We cut.)

They pulled into the long drive that led up to a little brick ranch house above a steep hillside of Christmas trees. When they reached the top and got out of the car, they were met by a young man, maybe twenty years old, who sat on a four-wheeler.

"Where's Mr. Gudger?" their father asked.

"Pappap died in August," the young man said, then spit off to the side. "Had a good life. Most people had no idea the man was ninety-two years old."

"Ninety-two?" their father said. Grover remembered how Mr. Gudger scrambled around the hillsides, cutting trees or climbing onto cars, tying trees.

"When you find one," the young man said, "give a holler." There was a quiet friendliness in the way he talked that reminded Grover of Mr. Gudger.

As the four of them walked down into the fir trees, Sudie frowned and said in a shaky voice, "That's sad about Mr. Gudger."

They heard a chain saw start up on the other side of the hill.

"Mr. Gudger had a good life," Sudie said, the frown fading. She said it like enough was enough, and she'd decided not to feel sad about Mr. Gudger. The four of them walked down the hillside, wandering off between the trees. After a while Grover heard Sudie call, "This is it!"

He found her standing in front of a tremendous, bushy tree.

"Lord have mercy," Jessie said, coming up to them.

"Y'all can't be serious," their father said. He walked around the tree. "I'm not even sure that'll fit in the house."

Sudie took Grover's arm. "We like it."

Their father looked at Jessie. "Can you talk some sense into these two?"

"Y'all do have high ceilings, and if need be I can trim the bottom with my chain saw."

"Thank you, Daddy," Sudie said, hugging their father.

"Thanks a lot," their father said to Jessie.

"We better check it for copperheads, though," Sudie said.

"Too cold of a winter for 'em," Jessie said.

The tree was so big it covered up the four-wheeler. From where Grover and Sudie stood, it looked like the tree was rolling up the hill under its own power. The grandson spent another half hour tying the tree to their car. "You don't want this baby rolling off on the highway."

While Mr. Gudger's grandson secured it to the car, Mrs. Gudger invited them into her kitchen for hot chocolate and homemade cookies. She had them sit at her table while she served them. Grover worried she'd say something about their mother not being there, but, even after all these years of them coming here, it didn't seem she remembered them exactly.

While they sipped their hot chocolate, Jessie started telling a story about working at a Christmas tree farm and coming across a moonshine still. Their father went over to Mrs. Gudger, who stood at the stove, and told her he was sorry to hear about her husband.

"Married sixty-seven years," she said, stirring a pot of hot chocolate. "Losing Henry took the fun out of it." Then she lowered her voice. "But you, you're a young fellow and need to get right back on that horse."

"Ma'am?" their father said.

"I read about your wife in the paper last spring," the old woman said. "I'm real sorry." Then she said, "But those kids need a mama."

Their father looked shaken when he came back to the table, but Sudie was caught up in Jessie's story.

"The moonshiner gave me two quarts of moonshine to keep quiet," Jessie said.

"Did you drink it?" Sudie asked.

Jessie looked at their father. "Me and your parents."

"I've never had such a headache," their father said.

"I was sick for two days," Jessie said.

"It didn't faze Caroline," their father added.

"She sure could hold her liquor," Jessie said.

When they left, Mrs. Gudger came from behind the stove and gave Grover and Sudie big hugs, and Grover knew she'd remembered them down to their very core.

"You come back next year," she said. "I plan to be around a while longer. Figure I'd let Henry fend for himself up in Paradise. Man can't even scramble an egg. He'll appreciate me all over again when I do finally show."

‡   ‡   ‡

"Aren't we headed the wrong way?" Sudie asked.

They'd turned east toward Spruce Pine rather than west back toward Asheville.

"I thought we'd have lunch at that little diner," their father said.

Their father drove slow. Even on its side the tree added four feet of height to the car. Jessie said it was a good thing it wasn't a windy day or it'd blow the car right over. A long line of cars and trucks had bunched up behind them, stretching as far back as they could see.

On the edge of Spruce Pine, they passed a turnoff and a sign said Spruce Pine Hospital. "Isn't that where Leila used to work?" their father asked Jessie.

Their father kept his eye on the hospital as they passed. Grover wondered if Leila being up here had played a part in him deciding to come up here to get a tree. Maybe this trip hadn't been as much for Sudie and him as he'd thought.

They passed the one grocery store in town, crossing over an old stone bridge that looked to Grover like something Druids might have built.

"That's the Toe River," Jessie said as they crossed the bridge. "Named after an Indian princess who drowned. They say she was fleeing her angry father."

"Why was her father so mad?" Sudie asked.

"She had a boyfriend he wasn't all that crazy about," Jessie said.

Their father drove them around downtown Spruce Pine. A couple of blocks of old rock-faced buildings. Baker's Motel and Restaurant, a motel with a blinking vacancy sign. Spruce Pine had two main streets, and because it was situated on the side of a mountain, one street, the one that ran beside the railroad tracks, was a lot lower than the other. The street signs said Spruce Street and Locust Street, but Jessie said people called them Upper Street and Lower Street.

They passed a few clothing shops, a rock and gem shop, a drugstore, a music store and a Hallmark Cards store. It wasn't downtown Asheville but even so, there were a good many people walking around. Several of them stopped and watched when they drove by.

"Seems the Sequoia we have strapped to our roof is attracting some attention," their father said.

At the Upper Street Café, they all ordered BLTs and iced tea, except Jessie got coffee. Every time the waitress, a girl Grover guessed to be in high school, opened her mouth she sounded like Emma Lee.

"Can I bring you anything else?" she'd asked when they were done. She put the check beside their father's plate and as she turned she winked at Grover. He was still blushing when they got out to the car.

"That's some tree," a boy said, who was standing outside a women's clothing store, holding the leash of a black furry dog. "My mama's in there, shopping." The boy sounded exactly like Clay. Everybody up here sounded like a Roundtree.

Sudie bent down and petted the dog.

"The vet says he's part chow and part anybody's guess," the boy said.

"Do you know Clay Roundtree?" Sudie asked.

"Me and Clay were in the same grade at Bakersville Elementary till he moved. Good soccer player. They just moved back. Reckon he'll be starting back to school. They live up on the Roan with Mrs. Sparks."

Back in the car, their father began to veer back over the stone bridge that led to the highway, but the light turned red. Grover looked at his father staring up at the traffic light. "Wonder how the Roundtrees are doing?" Grover said, looking out his window.

"Me too," Sudie said.

"Bakersville isn't far," Jessie said. "And the Roan is just beyond it."

"If y'all want to visit them that bad," their father said, trying to sound casual, "we have a little time." The light turned green, and instead of going over the bridge, he turned right onto a road with a sign that said *Hwy 226* and another sign that said *Bakersville nine miles*.

‡　　‡　　‡

Bakersville was smaller and lonelier than Spruce Pine.

"There's one problem," their father said as they passed an old building Jessie said used to be the courthouse. "We don't know where they live."

"They live on Roan Mountain," Sudie said.

"The Roan is a very big mountain," Jessie said.

"Clay said they live exactly eight miles from his school," Sudie said.

"Where's Bakersville Elementary?" Grover asked.

Their father drove a little bit farther through town.

"There." Sudie pointed to a low brick building on the side of a hill.

His father pushed the odometer. They drove through Bakersville and started up Roan Mountain. Neat cabins and well-kept trailers were set back from the road. The higher they drove, the fewer houses they saw and the more they passed through dark sections of evergreen trees—spruce and fir and hemlock— shading patches of snow. Grover couldn't help thinking that if he lived up here there'd be no shortage of limbs to weave. In the shadowed sides of the mountain, icicles clung to the rocks.

As the road steepened, the car's engine whined, also the wind picked up and the Christmas tree shifted on the roof. "Maybe this wasn't such a great idea," their father said. He pulled off to the side of the road and Jessie got out, tugging on the twine and checking the knots.

"That boy must've been an Eagle Scout," Jessie said, getting back in the car. "I don't think I've ever seen such sturdy knots."

The car climbed on up the mountain, the engine whining louder.

"Clay said Roan Mountain is the second-highest mountain east of the Mississippi," Sudie said.

"The vegetation is similar to Canada's," Jessie said, looking at the plants and trees along the roadside. Just as the odometer read eight miles, a dirt road appeared.

"Turn down there," Sudie said.

"You sure?" their father asked.

They bumped along the dirt road for about a quarter of a mile, their father's eyes going to the roof of the car. Finally they pulled in front of a small cabin with smoke curling out of its chimney. The cabin sat on the edge of a big meadow with wisps of clouds and a few stunted pine and spruce trees that looked like the bonsai trees Grover'd seen on a class trip to the North Carolina Arboretum.

"This is it," Sudie said.

"How do you know?" their father asked.

"I don't see their van," Grover said. All they saw was a green rusted Subaru parked in a shed around the side of the house. This cabin looked too small to hold Leila and Emma Lee and Clay too.

"We better turn around," their father said. "Some old boy might shoot us for trespassing." His father had started backing out when a golden retriever and a black lab tore around from the back of the house, barking fiercely, and circling the car.

"No, wait!" Sudie said. "Those are their grandmother's dogs Clay told me about. Benjamin and Midnight." Sudie started to get out.

"Hold on," their father said. "Those dogs look like they mean business."

Before he could stop her, Sudie was out of the car and calling to the dogs.

"Sudie," their father said, jumping out of the car.

The dogs came up wagging their whole hind ends. Sudie bent down, petting them. They licked her face. "They're sweethearts," Sudie said as Grover and Jessie got out too.

As Grover petted the dogs, he realized how much colder it was up here. The air was lighter up here and richer somehow. Occasionally there'd be a break in the clouds. They could see that the cabin was perched on the side of the mountain. They could see valleys and waves of mountains in the distance.

"Leave those folks alone." A woman stood in the cabin doorway, talking to the dogs. She was dark and tall and had long black hair like Emma Lee except hers was pulled back in braids. She wore a flannel shirt, blue jeans and hiking boots. Grover didn't remember Emma Lee mentioning an aunt.

"Mrs. Sparks?" their father said.

"Yes?" she said.

This was Emma Lee's grandmother? Whenever Emma Lee or Clay had talked about their fierce mountain grandma, Grover'd pictured some toothless hag who walked around with a shotgun over her shoulder and a wad of tobacco bulging in her cheek. This woman was the youngest, prettiest grandmother Grover'd ever met. She could've been Leila's older sister.

"We're the Johnstons," their father said.

"You live across from my daughter," she said, walking down to them.

"And I'm Jessie," he said, stepping up and shaking her hand.

"I know," Mrs. Sparks said.

"I'm sorry for descending on you like this," their father said. "We just happened to be up this way."

"Just happened to be in the middle of nowhere?" Mrs. Sparks didn't smile. She did smile when she saw the tree tied on their car. The tree covered up the whole roof of the car. Some limbs had come loose and hung down the sides. A Christmas tree on wheels.

"We went to Mr. Gudger's tree farm," Sudie said. "It's where we always go."

"Henry Gudger passed this summer," Mrs. Sparks said, "but Irene'll keep the farm running. That grandson of hers is a hard worker." It hadn't occurred to Grover that the Gudgers might actually know the Roundtrees.

She turned to Grover. "You're the boy who saved my granddaughter's life."

Grover looked at the ground. "I just happened to be there."

"Just happened to pull my granddaughter from a burning house. Just happened to drive a good fifteen miles out of the way. You Johnstons are big on just happening." Mrs. Sparks looked at their father. "Leila and them have gone over to Elizabethton to visit a sick cousin. Not sure when they'll be back."

"Elizabethton?" Grover asked.

"That's in Tennessee," Jessie said.

"We're only a mile from the Tennessee border," Mrs. Sparks said. "Roan straddles both states."

Grover felt his heart sink, and from the look on their father's face, Grover guessed his heart had sunk too.

"Come in and have some tea."

"No, thanks," their father said, "but please tell them we came by."

"You went nearly an hour out of your way," she said. "The least you can do is let me give you some tea."

"We better get on down the mountain," their father said. "No telling how long it might take us with that tree." He sounded defeated.

"They'll be sorry they missed you," Mrs. Sparks said.

They started back to the car.

"Could I see your weavings?" Grover asked Mrs. Sparks, who was halfway up her walk.

"Why, sure," she said.

"Maybe another time," their father said to Grover.

"When?" Grover asked. "When will we ever be up here again?"

"Maybe this spring?" their father said.

"We'll never come back here," Grover said, "and you know it!" Grover was surprised at his anger.

"I'd like to see her weavings too," Sudie said.

"Me too," Jessie said.

Their father sighed. "We should only stay a few minutes."

The front room was toasty from the woodstove that roared in one corner.

"I'll put the kettle on," Mrs. Sparks said.

"Don't bother," their father said.

"It's no bother," she said, disappearing into the kitchen.

Bookshelves sagging with books crowded the walls. Emma Lee had said her grandmother drove the county bookmobile. Woven mountain scenes occupied wall space that wasn't taken up by bookshelves, like the weavings Grover'd seen in the Roundtrees' house. Mountain scenes: sheep grazing in a meadow; a man holding the reins of a mule plowing his field; a dark-haired girl, who looked a lot like Emma Lee, milking a cow; two boys, one who looked like Clay, fishing in a stream. Woven scenes hung everywhere. They looked like paintings from a distance, but the closer you got to them, the more you saw the individual strands.

Their father was more interested in her books. "She's got a first edition of *Look Homeward, Angel*. And another one of *You Can't Go Home Again*."

"You run the Wolfe house," said Mrs. Sparks, coming in from the kitchen.

"He's the *executive* director," Sudie said.

A gust of wind whistled down the chimney, making a fluttering noise in the stove.

"Where's this one?" Jessie pointed to a weaving of a little cemetery overlooking a long view of the valley below and the mountains beyond.

"I can take you to see it after we have tea."

"Do we have time?" Jessie glanced toward their father.

"Sure." Their father didn't look up from what he said was a rare biography of Wolfe.

The house seemed bigger inside but even so, it would be cramped for four people. There was this front room, and then as far as Grover could tell, there were three small bedrooms, and the kitchen in the back. One bedroom had bunk beds. He saw a couple of soccer balls and piles of books. Clay and Emma Lee must've shared this room. There was a bedroom that must've been Leila's and another that must've been Mrs. Sparks's. Next to this cabin, Jessie's rental house was a mansion.

"Emma Lee tells me you're quite the artist," Mrs. Sparks said.

"I just mess around," Grover said.

"Emma Lee says she's never seen anything like your tapestries," she said. "You and I both know she doesn't say anything she doesn't mean." Mrs. Sparks sat him at the big loom that was halfway done with what looked like a scene of a garden. She showed him how to slide the shuttlecock through and how to push on the pedal that pushed the yarn into place. It made a satisfying clicking sound.

"How do you know what the scene is?" he asked. "Do you draw it first?"

"I've been doing it so long I work from the pictures in my head."

After they drank their mugs of hot tea, Mrs. Sparks took them, with the dogs running ahead, along a worn path that led into woods, a dim, dripping forest of evergreens. With its ferns and moss, much of it encased in ice, and with its little animal paths running all through it, the place reminded Grover of enchanted woods where gnomes or hobbits might live. The forest held little clouds that they passed through. Sometimes they even lost sight of each other. After a few minutes they came into a large open area and on the far side, between clouds floating by, they saw the cemetery, the wet headstones gleaming. Grover remembered Clay saying that he'd looked after it. They walked among the headstones. They came to one whiter than the others.

"That's their daddy," Mrs. Sparks said, coming up beside Grover. "He was a good father and a good husband." She paused. "Before the war." She showed them older headstones that included her husband's, Emma Lee's grandfather. "I'll be buried here too one day. You can't beat the view."

When they got back to the cabin, their father said they should leave.

"They'll be so sorry they missed you," Mrs. Sparks said.

"We wish they'd move back," Sudie said.

"Sudie," their father said.

Mrs. Sparks put her arm around Sudie. "I like a girl who speaks her mind." Then she said, "To tell you the truth, I wish they'd move back too. Don't get me wrong, I love them to death, but we're in the middle of nowhere up here." She looked at their father and Jessie. "The kids feel isolated. They both like Claxton. They love living in Asheville. Honestly, I was starting to enjoy having my house back. I'd lived alone for fifteen years before they moved in, and I've never gotten used to having so much family underfoot."

"Tell them to move back," Sudie said.

"I tried," she said, "but their mama was shook up by Emma Lee nearly dying in that fire. She thinks it was a message from God."

"And you don't?" Jessie asked.

"I think she's afraid," Mrs. Sparks said.

"Afraid of God?" Sudie asked.

"Afraid of being happy again," she said, not looking at their father.

There was an awkward moment, when nobody said anything.

"We better get going," their father said.

"One second," she said. "Grover, come with me."

He looked at his father, who motioned him to follow her. "Jessie and I will be checking the Christmas tree," his father said.

Mrs. Sparks led him back into the front room and disappeared into the kitchen. In a minute she came out with a long cylindrical package wrapped in brown paper and tied with twine. "A small token for *just happening* to crawl on your hands and knees into a burning house and *just happening* to carry my sweet Emma Lee to safety."

"Thank you," he said, making sure to look her in the eye.

"Your mama must've been one remarkable woman to have such a boy as you." Her eyes seemed to glisten. He was halfway down the path when she called to him from the door. "Grover?"

"Yes, ma'am?"

"The world needs our art whether it knows it or not!"

He ran to the car and climbed in. As they pulled away, they waved at Mrs. Sparks standing in the doorway. The dogs chased their car down the dirt road. As their father started down the mountain, Grover looked at the wrapped package, turning it over and over.

"Well, don't just sit there," Sudie said. "Open the thing!"

Grover carefully untied the twine. One of her weavings. He unrolled it across the backseat and into Sudie's lap. The weaving that Jessie had pointed out—of the cemetery and the mountains beyond.

"Oh, Grover," Sudie said, gently stroking the fabric. "She gave you the best one."

When they got home, Jessie cut off a few inches of the tree with his chain saw so it would stand in their living room. He helped them get it up in the stand, then said he had to go home and check on Tippy.

Their father put on the lights like he always had, with Sudie checking the strands for any bulbs that needed replacing. When their father brought down the big box of ornaments from the attic, Sudie's face darkened and her eyes got all shiny. Grover knew what she was thinking. Their mother had always been in charge of putting on the ornaments. Sudie was reaching to hang a gingerbread man ornament on a limb, when her shoulders slumped and her face crumbled. Their father was busy replacing a bulb. Grover nudged him.

"Sweetheart." Their father sat Sudie beside him on the couch.

"It's not the same, Daddy," Sudie said, rubbing her red eyes with the heels of her hands. "It's just not the same."

"I know," their father said.

Grover agreed with Sudie. It wasn't the same. Hadn't been the same since that April afternoon. If only they'd somehow known what was coming, they might've paid closer attention to the time they had left with their mother.

"We don't have to decorate it now," their father said. "If y'all would rather wait."

"Don't be ridiculous," Sudie said, sniffling. It was something their mother would've said.

Grover and his father exchanged glances as they watched Sudie push herself up off the couch and carefully hang the gingerbread man on the tree. She dug around in the box of ornaments until she pulled out a long small box. She opened it and slowly unwrapped the paper until she arrived at a clear glass teardrop. Grover and Sudie had gone in together and bought it from an artist at the Grove Arcade for their mother Christmas before last. She'd said it was her favorite ornament. Sudie started to hang it on the tree but then paused and her lip trembled.

"Here," she said, taking Grover's hand and placing the teardrop gently in it. "Hang it somewhere high," she said, looking at him with clear eyes. "Where everybody can see it."

Chapter Eighteen

It Wasn't Jesus

Ever since the woman had stabbed the For Sale sign into the Bamboo Forest, Grover had thrown himself into his weavings in a way he'd never done. He spent every spare moment in the Bamboo Forest, weaving harder and faster. Whenever he wasn't in school he was in the Bamboo Forest, cutting, tying and weaving. When he was at school, he filled notebook after notebook with sketches. He hung the weaving Mrs. Sparks gave him on his bedroom wall, and at night fell asleep looking at it, touching it. He dreamed of leaves and limbs weaving themselves. He'd wake wide-eyed late in the night, pull on his clothes and his coat, tiptoe through the house and sneak out to the Bamboo Forest, where he'd work for an hour or two, then slip back into the house before anyone knew.

Grover wasn't sure what had come over him. Maybe it had to do with the Roundtrees moving. Maybe it had to do with this being the first Christmas without their mother. Maybe it had to do with knowing that the Bamboo Forest wouldn't be around much longer. Or maybe it had to do with keeping sadness at the edges. He didn't know, and he didn't have time to figure it out. The ideas for tapestries came so fast that he could hardly keep up with them. His tapestries had gotten so big they needed more support. Instead of tying them in place, he began weaving his limbs between the living bamboo shoots. It kept the big weavings from toppling over and caving in on themselves. He did this more and more, weaving in his collected limbs between the standing bamboo.

He liked the look and the feel of the more brittle cut limbs woven between the flexible living shoots. Up was living, across was dead. He couldn't move these tapestries since they were rooted in the ground, so when he finished one, he'd simply leave it and move on to the next. He cut a spiral hallway into the Bamboo Forest, like photographs he'd seen of the Guggenheim Museum in New York and wove tapestries all along the hallway.

Sudie kept him supplied with limbs. All he had to do was reach into the pile she was always stocking and choose the perfect limb. On the weekend when he wove all day, she brought him lunch. On those nights their father stayed late at the Wolfe house, she carried his supper out to him, while he worked by flashlights.

Their father had become so busy with the Thomas Wolfe Christmas that Grover and Sudie hardly saw him. For a little while their father had said that *A Thomas Wolfe Christmas* was an overwhelming success but lately he'd just been saying that it was overwhelming. He stopped making breakfasts for them. Often he was cranky, like he'd been in the old days when the Wolfe house was empty of visitors. Judging from his father's behavior, Grover guessed that success and failure had a lot in common.

Their father was too preoccupied to notice Grover's grades had slipped. Grover'd been working so hard in the Bamboo Forest that when he was at school he could hardly keep his eyes open. Often he'd lay his head on his desk, and the next thing he knew, Mrs. Caswell would be calling his name, and he'd jerk his head up. At recess, he'd fall asleep working his Rubik's cube. Sam or Mira would wake him when the bell sounded. One day, Miss Snyder woke him and asked him to come back to her office.

"Mrs. Caswell will wonder where I am," he said, sitting in a chair in her office.

"She's the one who asked me to talk to you," Miss Snyder said. "She says you've been falling asleep in class."

"I've been a little tired lately," he said, trying to stifle a yawn.

"Your schoolwork has suffered. Is something going on at home?"

"No," Grover said.

"You answered that mighty fast."

"Our father has been busy at the Wolfe house." He hoped this would be enough to satisfy her counselor's curiosity.

"Are you sure there's nothing else?"

"Nothing." Grover didn't want to tell her about the streak of tapestries he was working on. As exhausted as he'd been lately, he felt more like himself. When he was hard at work in the Bamboo Forest, he became connected to something solid and true. Something he could count on. Something that would not go away.

One afternoon, Grover had been putting the finishing touches on the last weaving—his biggest yet. He was tired but happy. He'd finished a whole hallway of tapestries. He'd woven in the very last pine limb of the last tapestry and was standing back, studying it, when Sudie came running through the bamboo.

"That lady," she said, out of breath. "She's back."

Grover and Sudie crept to the edge of the Bamboo Forest and watched the woman haul five For Sale signs out of her trunk and stab each into the ground. They waited till she'd driven off before they walked over to the signs. Grover'd never seen a realtor put out more than one sign. Every driver who passed would notice and sooner or later someone would buy it.

"I hate those signs," Sudie said.

"Remember what Daddy said," Grover said.

"I know, I know," Sudie said. "If we pull them up we might get him in trouble."

A cold wind blew and the signs made a little singing noise.

"They're so many of them," Grover said.

"Maybe we could pull up just one," Sudie said.

"I don't know," Grover said. "I have a funny feeling about this." He looked up and down the street but he didn't see a soul. "It's too quiet."

Sudie ran up to one of the signs and was straining to pull it up. As she slid it out of the ground a man streaked from around the far side of the Bamboo Forest. Sudie dropped the sign and ran back up the path that led to the studio. The man followed her, and Grover ran up behind him. Sudie had reached the studio when the man grabbed her coat. Grover shoved the man hard, and when he did, the man lost his grip on Sudie's coat, but then he whirled around and grabbed Grover's arm tightly. "Now I've caught you." Grover recognized the voice before he recognized the face. He tried pulling away but Lunsford's grip was strong.

"Grover!" Sudie had stopped when she saw Mr. Lunsford had hold of him.

"Go get Jessie," Grover said. "And take Biscuit with you."

Sudie scooped up the dog and ran hard through the bamboo.

"What is this all back here?" Holding Grover's arm, Lunsford looked around at the tapestries and the lean-to and the piles of limbs. He glanced at a couple of Grover's tapestries. "Hard to believe your father would come to me hat in hand just so you could make these silly things. This is child's play."

Grover tried to pull away.

"Speaking of your daddy," Mr. Lunsford said, "let's see if he's home yet." He walked Grover out of the Bamboo Forest and headed up the street.

"He's not home," Grover said, seeing his father's car wasn't in the driveway.

"We'll wait," Mr. Lunsford said, keeping a grip on Grover's arm. He seemed to be taking in the overgrown grass and the uncut bushes. "Son, you ought to spend your time doing something helpful for your daddy like yard work instead of messing around in that bamboo."

Their father's car turned in the driveway. Grover's heart sank. He would be furious that Lunsford had caught them pulling up signs. Their father had barely stopped when he was out of the car, marching toward them, looking as angry as that night he'd torn up Grover's studio.

"I caught your boy pulling up my signs," Mr. Lunsford said.

"How dare you!" his father growled.

"I'm sorry, Daddy—" Grover started.

"How dare you lay a hand on my son," their father said. "Let go of him."

"But I caught him red-handed, pulling up my signs," Mr. Lunsford said, sounding a little less sure of himself.

"Let go." Their father stepped up to Mr. Lunsford.

Mr. Lunsford frowned at their father for a minute, then let go of Grover's arm.

"Him and that little daughter of yours were pulling up my For Sale signs."

"Sudie didn't have anything to do with it, Daddy," Grover said.

"Honest to God," said Mr. Lunsford, "what is all that mess your boy's making back in there in the bamboo? If what he's doing back there is art, then I'm Pablo—"

His father grabbed Mr. Lunsford by the collar. "Don't ever talk about my kids. They're good kids. My boy is a fine artist and anybody who says otherwise answers to me."

Jessie came trotting up. "Let him go, Walt."

His jaw working, their father stared at Mr. Lunsford like he was making up his mind. Then he let him go. Mr. Lunsford hurried down the driveway, looking behind him and tugging on his collar. When he was at the bottom of the driveway and a safe distance, he said, "You've done it now, Johnston. You've gone and done it now."

They watched Mr. Lunsford hurry up the street. They saw him pick up the one For Sale sign and stab it angrily into the ground next to the others. He climbed into his shiny new Audi and drove back to the bottom of the driveway, rolling his window down.

"I'll be having that canebrake leveled," he yelled. "It's an eyesore. Come to think of it, that's probably why the property isn't selling."

They watched him drive off.

Grover still couldn't believe their father had grabbed Mr. Lunsford like that. "I'm sorry if I got you into trouble," Grover said.

"I was the one who pulled up the sign," Sudie said.

Their father looked at Jessie. "Any openings for an assistant landscaper?"

"I think you're jumping the gun," Jessie said.

"Lunsford has been waiting years for an excuse to get rid of me."

"He won't cut down the Bamboo Forest," Sudie said. "Will he?"

Their father glanced at his watch. "I need to get back. We have five busloads of church ladies coming in." He looked up at Grover and Sudie. "Will y'all be okay a little while longer this evening?"

"They can come to my place and do their homework," Jessie said. "And I'll feed them too. So stay as late as you need."

He nodded at Jessie. "And thanks for calling me."

So that's why their father had shown up out of the blue.

"I'll try not to be too late," their father said, starting to get into his car. He looked at Grover. "Don't go over to the Bamboo Forest again this evening."

"But . . . ," Grover began.

"I said don't go over there!" his father snapped. Then in a quieter voice he said, "At least not anymore today. It is his property." Their father backed out of the drive.

"I left my toolbox," Grover said to Jessie.

"I'll go with you," Jessie said as they watched their father drive away.

Jessie and Grover and Sudie walked back to the Bamboo Forest, pausing on the street to make sure no one was around. Jessie shook his head at the line of For Sale signs.

"Let's do this quick. We don't want Lunsford catching us."

"Will he get Daddy fired?" Sudie asked.

"Your father has a lot of friends in this town," Jessie said.

Grover couldn't get over what his father had just done. Not only had he stood up for him and Sudie, he'd defended his weavings. Grover had gone across his studio to pick up his toolbox when he saw Jessie standing in front of a couple of the big tapestries. They were as tall as Jessie. "Lord have mercy," he said. "These are incredible. You did these?"

"Sudie helped," he said.

"You haven't seen anything," Sudie said, motioning toward the hallway.

"Sudie," Grover said. They hadn't shown anyone the hallway.

"It's Jessie," Sudie said, holding her hands out. "We have to show Jessie."

Grover didn't know why he felt shy about showing these new weavings. He'd worked on them so hard and thought they were his best yet. Maybe that's why he felt shy about showing them. Maybe they were terrible.

Sudie moved aside a little gate Grover'd made to hide the entrance. She led Jessie down the hallway, showing him the dozen tapestries Grover had woven. Tapestries on both sides glimmered and pulsed with colors. Jessie didn't say a word.

Grover picked up his toolbox and followed them. He'd been so busy making the tapestries that he hadn't had the time to see them. He didn't particularly like looking at things he'd finished. He always saw mistakes, something he could've done better. He'd figured out that what mattered wasn't the thing made, what mattered was the making.

The hallway came out on the side closest to Grover's house.

"Has your father seen these?" Jessie asked.

"No," Grover said.

"People need to see them," Jessie said.

"You heard Mr. Lunsford," Grover said. "He's having the bamboo cut down."

"We can move them to your yard," Jessie said. "And set up an exhibit."

"They can't be moved," Sudie said.

"We weaved them into the bamboo," Grover said.

A car passed by. "We better get out of here," Jessie said.

They walked out of the cane, passing the For Sale signs lined up along the road's edge. As they walked up the street, Grover looked over at the rental house. The workmen had left for the day. Not a single light shined from inside. Before the Roundtrees had moved in, Grover had hardly noticed that house. Renters had come and gone. Since the Roundtrees had moved out, he'd catch himself looking for Clay kicking the soccer ball against the house or Emma Lee reading on the front steps or Leila pulling into the drive after a long day at the hospital.

Sudie and Grover walked up to the rental with Jessie to see what the workmen had done today, but as they cut across the yard, Sudie picked up something out of the grass, right by the front steps. "Look," she said, holding it out to Grover as Jessie went on inside.

As Grover took it, he realized it was a pair of mangled and muddy black-framed glasses. They must've been there a good while and been trampled on more than a few times. As he turned them over, he had a flash of Matthew with new wire-rim glasses.

That night Grover went out to the kitchen and found his father at the table, drinking a glass of milk and eating a plateful of Oreos while reading the paper. He looked up from the paper and held out the plate of cookies but Grover shook his head.

"Turning down Oreos? Are you ill?" He smiled a tired smile. Grover set the mangled glasses on the kitchen table in front of his father, who picked them up and put his finger through the hole where a lens was missing. "I'd say these have seen better days."

"Sudie found them off the porch of the rental house," Grover said.

"Really? Maybe one of the workmen's?"

"I'm pretty sure they're Matthew's," Grover said.

"Really?" His father bit into another cookie, then took a drink of milk.

"Matthew, you know, Jessie's assistant? I think he must've been the person who helped me get Emma Lee out of the house that night."

His father nodded.

"You don't seem surprised," Grover said.

"I'd already guessed," he said. "I was fairly sure he'd been watching over you and Sudie."

"Watching over us?"

"Ever since that night I wrecked your workshop and the next morning found the weaving hanging back up and the toolbox back where it had been, I had a suspicion."

"Why would he do that?"

His father sighed and looked up at him. "Matthew was the driver."

"The driver?"

"Of the car that hit your mother."

The force of this news shoved Grover down in a chair and sent his heart racing. Strange as it might seem, he'd never given much thought about who'd been driving the car. The image that had camped out in his mind was of his mother following Biscuit out into the road. He heard the screech of brakes and there it always stopped, the moment frozen, car and driver just out of the frame.

"Matthew was devastated," his father said.

"It wasn't his fault," Grover said, feeling almost numb. "Everybody said it wasn't the driver's fault."

"Even so, I imagine that's not something you get over easily."

"Why didn't you tell me?"

"You and Sudie had been through enough without having to bring it all back up," he said. "Jessie asked me if I minded if he hired him. He thought it might help him. I told him that was fine as long Matthew didn't bother y'all or try to talk to you. I figured he'd be finished up with school and gone soon enough."

"But you said he's been watching over us?" Grover said.

"That's my guess," he said.

"Why didn't you do anything? It's creepy."

"What was there to do? I couldn't prove anything. Besides, I knew he was basically a good guy, a little on the strange side, but a good guy, and I thought it might help his recovery."

"*His* recovery?" Grover said, feeling a surge of anger. "It was *our* mother he hit."

"And she would've been worried about him," his father said.

Grover thought back to the mysterious straightenings of his workshop and of his mother's grave. He remembered the day he and Sudie had fought with the guy who wanted the realtor's phone number off the sign, how his car began to mysteriously roll away. He remembered the firm hand on his shoulder, guiding him through the smoke, helping him carry Emma Lee to safety. Who knew what all Matthew had done for them in the past couple of months? Yet gratitude wasn't among the feelings that trailed him back to his room.

He lay in bed unable to sleep and looked out at the rustling bamboo. In the back of his mind, he had believed that his mother's spirit had been watching over them, and that at least some of these happenings might've been her doing. How foolish he'd been. He felt cheated, tricked and, in a way, as if he'd lost his mother all over again.

CHAPTER NINETEEN
GROVER'S WALTZ

*D*ead, *dead, dead is what I am,* thought Grover as he walked to the Wolfe house. His father had called Claxton and asked that he come straight to his office after school *without* Sudie. For the rest of the school day Grover'd wondered why his father wanted him to come alone. The only explanation could've been that he'd found out about Grover's slipping grades. But if he was in trouble, part of him didn't care. Ever since he'd learned about who was behind the mysterious happenings in the Bamboo Forest, nothing seemed to matter as much.

His father met Grover at the door of the Wolfe house, put his arm on his shoulder, looked him in the eyes and said, "It's time." He started walking Grover along downtown streets.

After they'd walked a couple of blocks Grover finally screwed up enough courage to ask where they were going.

"To buy you a coat."

"A coat?"

"For the Christmas Waltz."

He was surprised his father had remembered the waltz, which was tomorrow. He himself had all but forgotten. Still, every sixth grader had to attend. Although he wasn't a big fan of shopping, shopping for clothes with his father had always been less painful. His father would take him to *a* store, let him try on a few clothes and then buy whatever Grover liked. There was no driving around to five different stores and trying on every shirt or pair of pants or shirts or shoes in his size in the city of Asheville. There were no female hands fluttering over him, tugging his pants, straightening his collar, pushing the hair back out of his face. There were no frowning salesladies. Grover missed many things about his mother but shopping with her was not one of them.

Grover and his father walked the few blocks to Berkowitz's, a men's store where his father had always bought clothes, but this was the first time Grover had gone there to buy clothes for himself. It made him feel like he was entering a kind of club. The bell rang when they walked in, and Mr. Berkowitz came out of a back room. Bald with wild bushy eyebrows and a yellow tape measure always hanging around his neck, Mr. Berkowitz had been in business downtown for almost fifty years. What impressed Grover most about Mr. Berkowitz was that he drew his own ads that ran in the *Asheville Citizen-Times*. He sketched coats, shirts, ties and pants.

"Grover's going to the Christmas Waltz," his father said.

"Ah, the Christmas Waltz," said Mr. Berkowitz, looking over

his glasses at Grover. "Are you taking a girl?" Mr. Berkowitz pronounced *girl* like "goyel."

Grover shook his head, his face on fire.

"And he needs a coat," his father said.

"Ah, a jacket," Mr. Berkowitz said. "Where I'm from it's a jacket. Down here it's a coat. Either way, Grover, we'll find a nice one that'll have the girls lining up." Without asking Grover's size or even lifting the tape measure from around his neck, Mr. Berkowitz ran his fingers along the rack, slipped a coat off its hanger and held it out for Grover to try on. A gray tweed coat. Grover's father sometimes wore tweed. Grover pushed his arms through the silky lining of the sleeves, then Mr. Berkowitz buttoned the buttons, and Grover stood in front of the mirror with his father and Mr. Berkowitz behind him, all three looking at the coat. It fit.

"You're a wizard," his father said to Mr. Berkowitz.

"When the boy is ready for the jacket," said Mr. Berkowitz, "the jacket is ready for the boy." Mr. Berkowitz tugged on the sleeves, patted the shoulders and then said, "What do you tink, Grover?"

"I like it," he said.

"He sounds surprised," Mr. Berkowitz said, turning to his father.

He *was* surprised. Looking at his reflection in the mirror, he appeared different. Bigger. Older. More solid. The coat itself, the form of it, the weight of it along his back, across his shoulders and down his arms, made him feel stronger and more grown up.

Mr. Berkowitz had him try on pants that went with the coat

and pinned the cuffs. He picked out a shirt and a tie that would go with the coat. He promised he'd have the pants ready by tomorrow.

His father carried a bag with Grover's shirt and tie, and Grover carried the coat, which came with a nice plastic protector with a zipper on it. They rode the bus home. Grover hung the coat on the handhold above his seat, and watched it sway with every turn the driver made. He looked at his watch. The whole thing had taken half an hour.

"Why did Mama always take so long to shop?" he asked his father.

"To women," his father said, "it's not the clothes as much as it is the process of shopping for them."

"I don't get it," Grover said.

"Case in point." His father raised his finger, like he'd been waiting for this question. "When your mother and I were about to marry, we drove to a mall to shop for a dress for the reception. The first store, she tried on a red silk dress that looked stunning. I assumed we could buy it and leave." His father looked at him. "I was woefully undereducated in the ways of women."

"You didn't buy the dress?"

"Your mother insisted that we look at every other store in the mall. She must've tried on close to a hundred dresses. None came close to that first dress, and she knew none would. She continued trying on dress after dress. Ten stores and five hours later we returned to the first store, exhausted. Or at least I was. Only then was she ready to buy the red dress."

"Why did you have to go through all that?" Grover asked.

"That's what I asked her."

"What did she say?"

"She said it would have been too easy."

"You mean if she had bought the dress when she first tried it on, she wouldn't have liked it as much?"

"Exactly. The worth of that dress increased with every other dress she tried on."

"But she ended up buying the same dress," Grover said.

"Oh, but it *wasn't* the same dress," his father said.

"It wasn't?"

"Not to your mother. To her way of thinking, by trying on all the other dresses, she transformed *a* dress into *the* dress." His father's voice cracked a little. "And I have to admit, she was right. It was *the* dress. She was stunning." His father was quiet for a moment. He put his hand on Grover's knee. "I wish you could've seen her."

‡   ‡   ‡

Grover stood in a clump of sixth-grade boys, who tugged on their ties, glanced uncertainly across the gym at a clump of girls and then out toward No Man's Land. Daniel and Sarah, a girl in Miss Shook's class, along with two or three other brave couples, waltzed around the gym floor. The glaring overhead gym lights had been dimmed, and lamps with warm yellow shades had been set up around the edge. Christmas lights crisscrossed the ceiling. Mr. Godleski, a second-grade teacher, had his bluegrass band, Buncombe Turnpike, set up on the stage. A short fat man played fiddle, a horse-faced man played the electric piano, and Mr. Godleski stood next to them, plucking his bass fiddle. All three wore coats and ties.

At one end of the gym, a large table had been set up with cookies, cakes and brownies PTO parents had made. Next to that table, Miss Snyder in a black, tight-fitting dress stood behind the punch bowl, ladling punch into cups.

"Miss Snyder is hot," Sam said, coming up to Grover. "And why aren't you dancing?"

"Why aren't you?"

"You know why."

"Ashley doesn't own you."

"I know that," Sam said. "But I'm not sure she knows that." Then he said, "Look who's coming."

Mira crossed the gym floor, wearing a long white dress, a pearl necklace and pearl earrings. She looked to Grover like some African princess.

"Hi, Grover," Mira said. "Hey, Sam."

Grover wanted to say something about Mira's dress but was in a kind of trance just looking at her.

"You look nice," Sam said.

"Thanks," Mira said. She turned to Grover. "I love your coat."

"It's tweed," Grover said, putting his hands in the coat pockets.

Mira nodded, then crossed her arms and looked out at Daniel and Sarah dancing.

Sam gave Grover a nudge and nodded toward Mira.

"They sure are good dancers," Mira said.

Sam nudged Grover again.

"Mira?" Grover said hoarsely. "Want to dance?"

"I thought you'd never ask." She reached for Grover's hand and led him onto the dance floor.

"The only thing is," Grover said, "I don't know how."

"Grover Johnston," Mira said, putting her hands on her hips. "Don't tell me that after all those lessons, you don't know how." For the past two months, Mrs. Brown had devoted ten minutes of every gym class to practice waltzing. Since the classes were divided into boys and girls, boys had to waltz with boys and girls with girls.

"Listen to the music," Mira said. "Let's stand here and count for a minute. One, two, three. One, two, three. Count with me."

"One, two, three," Grover began. "One, two, three." He glanced back at the clump of boys watching and saw Ashley lead Sam onto the dance floor.

Mira placed Grover's hand on the small of her back and took his other hand and they began to move around the room. "One, two, three," Mira kept saying. "One two three." They danced stiffly and stepped on each other's toes.

"I think we're taking too big of steps," Grover said, remembering Mrs. Brown saying something about that. They started taking smaller steps and as soon as they did, they began dancing better. Grover kept getting off the beat. Mira would stop them, make him count with her again, and then they'd start again.

"We're supposed to look into each other's eyes," Mira said.

"We'll run into people," Grover said.

"Mrs. Brown says if you look into the girl's eyes, you'll always know where you're going. Trust me."

He looked her in the eyes, and, as soon as he did, they ran right into a couple.

"Let's try again," Mira said.

They ran into another couple.

"I don't think you're really looking into my eyes," she said.

This time he kept his eyes on hers, and it was the strangest thing, but it was just like she said. As they circled around the room, Grover could sense where they were going, yet he never looked away from her soft brown eyes. With each time around the gym, Grover felt they were getting the hang of it. They were going faster and dancing smoother. He tried to glance around the room, and as soon as he took his eyes off Mira's, they ran into Ashley and Sam.

"Watch where you're going." Ashley frowned.

"*We* ran into *them*," Sam said to Ashley.

"I'm sorry," Ashley said to Mira. "Sam is such a terrible dancer."

"Me?" Sam said. Before he could say anything else, Ashley waltzed him away.

Mira and Grover circled the gym a couple more times. When it was over, and they walked off to the side, Mira said, "You're a good dancer."

They stood there a moment, smiling at each other.

As Mr. Godleski's band started into another song, Tim Buchanan asked Mira to dance. Off they went spinning across the dance floor with the growing crowd of waltzers. Mrs. Dillingham moved through the crowd like a shark through a school of fish, keeping an eye out for misbehavior.

Someone tapped Grover on the shoulder. He turned around and standing there was this beautiful girl who looked vaguely familiar.

"Hey, Grover."

"Emma Lee? Is that you?" She had her hair up and wore some old-fashioned-looking dangly earrings with purple stones that caught the light. She still had her coat on.

"You already forget me, Grover?"

"It's just your hair and all is so . . ."

"Is so what?"

"How'd you get here?"

"Mama. She and Clay went Christmas shopping downtown." She laid her hand on his sleeve. "I like your coat. You and Mira waltzed nice together."

"The trick is to look into the person's eyes," Grover said. His and Emma Lee's eyes met for a second. Then they turned back, watching the waltzers. Grover guessed most of the boys had discovered by now that dancing with girls was a lot better than dancing with sweaty boys in gym class. When the waltz was over, Ashley and Sam stopped right beside Grover and Emma Lee, as if Ashley had planned it that way.

"Hey, Emma Lee," Sam said. "You made it! You look great!"

Ashley narrowed her eyes at Sam, then turned to Emma Lee. "How nice of you to come," she said, like this was her house. "I love your hair up like that. Shows off your bone structure." Grover couldn't tell if Ashley meant it. From the way Emma Lee kept her eye on Ashley, Grover knew Emma Lee couldn't tell either.

"Love the earrings too," Ashley said, stepping up and slightly lifting one of them to see it better. "Are they costume?"

Emma Lee took a step back. "They're my Nanna's and they're real amethysts," she said, touching them protectively.

"Aren't you burning up in that coat?" Ashley asked Emma Lee. "We'd like to see your dress."

Emma Lee looked at the floor. "It's just an old dress my Nanna gave me."

"I'd *love* to see it," Ashley said. "I love vintage."

"Leave her alone, Ashley," Sam said.

"I want to see her dress is all," Ashley said. "Is that so terrible?"

"If she doesn't want to take her coat off," Sam said, "that's her business. Come on, let's waltz."

"But . . ." Ashley began.

"I said let's waltz!" Sam said in the firmest tone Grover'd heard him use. Even Ashley looked surprised. As the music started, he pulled Ashley onto the dance floor.

Emma Lee glared as they moved off into the crowd of dancers.

"Don't pay her any attention," Grover said. "She's jealous."

"Of what, Grover?" Emma Lee's face flushed angrily. "Some redneck mountain girl who wears her grandma's old dress to the school dance?"

"She's jealous of the smartest, prettiest girl at the Isaac Claxton Elementary Christmas Waltz." Grover rubbed his forehead. "I can't believe I just said that."

"You didn't mean it?" Emma Lee asked, her mouth still set angrily.

"Oh, I meant it," Grover said.

She studied him, then slowly smiled.

"Want to dance?" Grover asked.

"Okay," she said. She hesitated as she started to unbutton her coat.

"You can dance with your coat on," Grover said, "if you want."

"It is hot as Hades," she said, finishing unbuttoning her coat. "Would you help me off with this?"

Grover took her coat, draped it over one of the folding chairs against the wall.

She wore a wine-colored velvet dress that shimmered in the low light. Grover'd never known that a dress could be deep, but that's what it was. It had a reddish luster the color of glowing coals. And the way Emma Lee had her hair up, her dark cheeks, her neck and the curve of her chest, all somehow picked up the luster of the dress, making her look lit from within. There was a word for being lit from within. They'd studied it earlier in the year. But he couldn't remember it. All he knew was that the dress fit her in a way that made her more curved, like she'd grown ten years in the couple of weeks she'd been away.

Heads already turned. Grover and Emma Lee walked out onto the dance floor. Grover took her hand, and then put his other hand on the small of her back, like Mira had shown him. His hand sank into the soft velvet, and he could feel the hardness of her backbone beneath the tips of his fingers. He looked her in the eye.

"Daddy used to waltz with me when I was a little girl," she said. "He used to put on this old song called 'The Tennessee Waltz,' and he'd waltz me around the front room with me standing on the tops of his feet. All I had to do was hang on."

Grover began counting out loud to the music. "One, two, three. One, two, three. One, two, three." Then they started, waltzing stiff at first. They stopped in the middle of the dance floor.

"I'm sorry," Emma Lee said. "Daddy used to do all the work, I guess."

"Look me in the eye." Grover counted again and then they stepped off. They went slower than he and Mira had but it wasn't long before the stiffness gave way to a floating feeling. The longer they danced, the more Grover could guide them around couples without looking away from her. It was strange how that worked. By looking deep into someone's eyes, he could see the world around him.

The more they danced, the more Grover forgot the dancers on the dance floor, the musicians on stage, the parents and teachers serving food and drinks. As they circled and swayed, Grover felt alone with Emma Lee. They danced their way into a stillness Grover'd never known before.

It wasn't till the waltz was over, and he looked around, that he realized people had stopped dancing to watch them. He saw Ashley and Sam on the edge of the crowd. Sam grinned. Ashley looked miserable. They'd hardly walked off the dance floor when Emma Lee was mobbed. It was Daniel Pevoe who she went back out onto the dance floor with.

Grover made his way through the crowd to the punch bowl.

"Emma Lee looks absolutely beautiful," Miss Snyder said, ladling punch into a cup and handing it to him. "You two make a handsome couple, Grover."

Grover couldn't get near Emma Lee for the rest of the first half of the dance. At the break Emma Lee came up, grabbed his hand and started to lead him out through the gym door but stopped when Mrs. Dillingham came up.

"Emma Lee," she said. "So good to see you! How's school up in Bakersville?"

Emma Lee shrugged. "I miss Claxton."

"Well, you're welcome anytime," she said, then she turned to Grover. "I had no idea you were such a Fred Astaire, Grover."

When Mrs. Dillingham disappeared into the crowd, Emma Lee motioned Grover to follow her through the gym door and into the lobby. Checking to make sure no one saw them, they passed the one-room infirmary, Miss Snyder's office and Mrs. Dillingham's office. They hurried past the cafeteria, where they heard teachers and volunteer mothers preparing trays of food. They walked quickly up to the second floor, and then to the third. Their footsteps echoed down the hallway. They had the whole third floor to themselves.

"I don't think we're supposed to be up here," Grover whispered.

Emma Lee tried Mrs. Caswell's door and found it unlocked.

"What are we doing?" Grover asked.

She opened the door and went inside and, after a minute, he followed her. She turned on the lights, and they walked up and down the rows of empty desks. Emma Lee sat in her old desk, and he sat in his. The radiators knocked and hissed.

"Claxton feels different at night." Emma Lee walked to the front of the room, tracing her finger across Mrs. Caswell's desk. Heavy footsteps came down the hall.

Grover turned off the lights, and they crouched by the door, peeking through the window that looked out onto the hall. The footsteps were getting louder. Emma Lee pulled Grover down beside her, and they both crouched underneath the window, praying it wasn't Mrs. Caswell. The footsteps passed, and they peeked through the window to see the back of Miss Shook. They heard her stomp into her classroom next door, rummage around, and then come back out and walk past them again. She carried a stapler. They crouched at the door until they couldn't hear her footsteps anymore.

"We ought to get out of here before somebody catches us," he said.

Emma Lee had walked over to the row of windows that looked outside. "Nobody else will come," she said. "Look."

He got up and, glancing back toward the door, walked over to her. Out the window, they could see downtown laid out before them—the glowing streetlights, the warm squares of window light from apartments, stores and restaurants, and the winking Christmas lights the city had wound around and up into the trees.

"It's like there's light coming up from underneath the city," Grover said, "leaking out from all the windows. It looks . . ."

". . . incandescent," Emma Lee said.

That was the word, Grover thought. *Incandescent* was the word he'd been trying to think of when he'd been thinking of how Emma Lee looked tonight in her dress.

"Who's Fred Astaire?" Grover asked.

"A famous dancer," Emma Lee said. "He's in old movies my grandmother likes."

They heard Mr. Godleski's band start up somewhere down below.

"We better go," Grover said.

"Just a minute more." Emma Lee reached for his hand and turned back to the window. He stood there looking down on a place he'd lived all his life but, until tonight, had never really seen.

‡   ‡   ‡

Emma Lee was mobbed by boys. Grover watched her waltz away with Morgan King, a stout, red-faced boy who could beat anybody in the hundred-yard dash. When the waltz was over, Grover climbed the steps to the stage and found Mr. Godleski tuning his bass.

"Mr. Godleski, can your band play 'The Tennessee Waltz'?" he asked.

Mr. Godleski looked at the other men tuning their instruments. "What do you think, boys?"

"If I can remember how it goes," said the bald fat man who played the fiddle. He scratched his head.

"Yeah, if we can remember how it goes," said the long-faced piano player, who stroked his chin. They were fighting off smiles.

"We'll save it for the last," Mr. Godleski said. "That'll be a good one to go out on."

"If we can remember how it goes," said the fiddle player.

The three men laughed as Grover headed back down.

For the rest of the evening, Grover couldn't get near Emma Lee for everybody wanting to dance with her. Mira tapped his shoulder, smiling.

"You've caught on quick," Mira said as they waltzed around the room.

"Dancing with girls is better than dancing with Chris Norris or Bill Parks."

She threw back her head and laughed. When she did, he glimpsed the pink of her tongue and the red of her throat and it made something stir below. A stiffness that he'd been feeling more often. Luckily the waltzing helped it go back down.

Grover waltzed with a couple of other girls, but mostly he stood by the punch bowl, watching Emma Lee waltz. Sam came up to him.

"How'd you get away from Ashley?" Grover asked.

"Told her I was going to the bathroom," he said, looking over his shoulder.

"Why don't you dance with somebody else?" Grover asked.

"I don't feel like it," Sam said.

"You like Ashley," Grover said accusingly.

"What if I do?"

"She is pretty," Grover said. "When you subtract her personality."

Sam saw Ashley coming toward him and darted off toward the boys' bathroom. After a couple more waltzes, Mr. Godleski stepped up to the microphone. "Ladies and gentlemen, we'll wind up the eighty-ninth Isaac Claxton Christmas Waltz with a special request."

Grover made his way across the crowded gym floor in the direction of Emma Lee. The band played the melody a couple of times through and then Mr. Godleski stepped up to the microphone and started singing in his high, nasally voice.

Grover needn't have worried about Mr. Godleski knowing the words. He sang it like he'd sang it hundreds of times before, like the words were part of him. It was a song about someone remembering the night of a dance when he lost his girlfriend to an old friend he'd introduced her to. As Mr. Godleski sang, Grover imagined Emma Lee as a little girl riding her father's feet, squealing and laughing, while he danced her around the grandmother's cabin. Then he thought how neither father nor daughter could've known what was coming to change everything. Even good memories had a sadness to them, because they were memories.

After Mr. Godleski had sung the song through one time, he

stepped back from the microphone and rejoined the band as they played through the melody again. Grover dodged through the dancing couples but didn't see Emma Lee anywhere. He was running out of time. The song would be over before he could get to her. Someone tapped him on the shoulder. Emma Lee held out her arms and they began to waltz. As they danced around the gym floor, Grover saw her eyes were glistening.

"Thank you," she said.

They danced around the gym floor, having to go much slower with all the couples crowding the floor. Mr. Godleski stepped up to the microphone and sang the song again. This time, he sang it a little slower, a little sadder, and Grover thought it was one of the most beautiful songs he'd ever heard. As Mr. Godleski sang the words, *Now I know just how much I have lost*, Grover looked into Emma Lee's eyes, thinking about this girl who, after the Christmas Waltz, would be gone. But the dancing didn't let him stay in his head. The weight of Emma Lee in his arms as they circled the floor, the press of her back against his hand, the warmth of her other hand in his, all kept him firmly in the gym. Moving across the crowded floor, Grover felt more with her than he'd ever felt.

"What wonderful music." Mrs. Dillingham had climbed on stage and was speaking into the microphone. "Please join me in giving Buncombe Turnpike a hand." The gym thundered with applause and whistles as Mr. Godleski and the other men bowed.

Grover and Emma Lee stood looking at each other. Then they started out of the gym together and into the lobby, where parents were waiting to pick up their kids.

"Doesn't Sis look like a movie star?" Clay said, coming up.

"There they are." Leila gave Grover a hug. "Don't you look handsome?"

"How's the Bamboo Forest?" Clay asked. "Any new weavings?"

"A few," Grover said.

"A few?" Sudie'd walked in with their father. "He's made a whole hallway."

Sudie and Clay moved off by themselves, talking a mile a minute.

Their father talked to several parents in the crowd and then made his way over to them. Their father stopped smiling when he saw Leila, and Leila did the same.

"I didn't know y'all were coming," their father said to Leila.

"Emma Lee promised Grover," Leila said.

"It's good to see you," their father said to Leila.

"Sorry we missed y'all when you came up to Roan Mountain," she said.

"We were already up that way getting a tree," his father said.

"You'll have to bring the kids up again," Leila said. "Maybe they could spend a night with us." Leila looked at their father, then looked away. "Well, I guess we better get on back up the mountain."

"Right," his father said.

"Could we go for hot chocolate?" Clay asked.

"I've got to get up pretty early tomorrow," Leila said.

"Come on, Mama," Clay said. "Can't we visit a little bit?"

"I'm not even sure where we could get hot chocolate this time of night," their father said.

"Bean Streets," Sudie said.

"What do you think, Leila?" their father asked.

Leila glanced at Clay and Emma Lee, then looked back at their father. "Oh, I guess it wouldn't hurt to get back a little later."

"Yes," Clay said.

"But we can't stay long," she said.

They started out the front door but Emma Lee stopped. "My coat."

"I'll get it." Grover trotted back into the gym. Most of the kids were gone. Miss Snyder, Mrs. Dillingham and a couple of teachers were carrying food and punch back to the kitchen. Mr. Godleski and his band were packing up. Grover found Emma Lee's coat draped over the same chair he'd put it on. He was heading back when he spotted Sam leaning against the wall.

"Where's Ashley?" Grover asked.

Sam nodded toward the girls' restroom. "She went in there with a couple of her friends. What all do girls do in the restroom anyway?"

Grover shrugged.

"I can't believe Emma Lee came all the way down from Bakersville to dance with you," Sam said. "I saw you dance with Mira a couple of times too. You danced with the two prettiest girls in the whole place." Sam nodded at the coat in Grover's hands. "That's Emma Lee's, isn't it?"

"We're going to Bean Streets with her family," Grover said.

Sam put his hand on Grover's shoulder. "When it comes to advice about girls, next time *I'm* coming to *you*."

They heard girls' voices coming out of the bathroom.

"Uh-oh," Sam said.

"See you later," Grover said.

"Have fun for the both of us," Sam called after him.

Just before the gym door closed after him, Grover heard Ashley say, "What was *that* supposed to mean, Sam? Don't you have fun with me? You *better* have fun with me...."

Bean Streets was so crowded that after they got their hot chocolates they had to wait for tables to clear. A good many people were dressed up like they'd been to a concert or a play. Some Claxton kids from the Christmas Waltz were there with their parents. Then there were the usual hippie-ish tattooed dreadlocked quasi street people, whose dogs, tied up outside, pawed at the window.

Grover couldn't walk into Bean Streets anymore without checking for Matthew. In fact he couldn't go by Riverside or ride the bus downtown or even walk down his street without checking for him. He hadn't seen him once since the night his father had told him Matthew had been the driver. It made him wonder if somehow Matthew knew he knew and was avoiding him.

"Why don't the kids sit there," their father said to Leila, as a table of four women got up to leave. "We can sit over there." He pointed to a table for two by the window.

So Grover, Sudie, Emma Lee and Clay sat at their own table. Grover and Emma Lee ended up sitting in such a way that they could see their father and Leila across the room from them. Sudie and Clay sat with their backs to their parents. The four of them talked for a while, but then Grover began watching his father and Leila, even though they were too far away to hear what they were saying. For a long time his father and Leila hadn't talked at all. They mostly looked out the window and sipped on their hot chocolate.

"We miss y'all," Sudie said. "The neighborhood isn't the same."

"Nothing against Bakersville," Clay said. "Just feels kind of on the slow side after living in Asheville. Doesn't it, Sis?"

Emma Lee nodded but was also keeping an eye on Leila and their father, who talked some now but didn't smile.

"I'm a city boy at heart," Clay said, looking around at all the people in Bean Streets.

Grover and Emma Lee glanced at each other. Something was being decided in the conversation between their parents. Leila's eyes had reddened and their father looked down, tracing his finger around his cup. The more he watched them not talking, not smiling, not offering the least glimmer of hope, the angrier Grover felt.

"Mr. Lunsford says he's cutting down the Bamboo Forest," Sudie said.

"He can't do that," Clay said.

"Daddy says it's his land and he can do what he wants to with it."

"Grover," Emma Lee said.

Grover looked away from their parents and tried to focus on Emma Lee.

"You didn't tell me about Mr. Lunsford," Emma Lee said.

"What's there to tell?" Grover said, trying to hold back the anger in his words.

"I'm your friend," Emma Lee said.

"So?" Grover said, feeling his face heat up.

"I'd want to know something like that," she said.

"It's the end of everything, okay?!" Grover said, hearing himself shout. "It's the end of everything and there's nothing you or anybody else can do about it!"

Bean Streets grew quiet, except for a couple of the street people who laughed about something. Grover ran out the front door and started down Biltmore Avenue, hands thrust deep in his coat pockets.

"Grover!" his father called. Grover heard footsteps come up beside him. Then he felt a hand on his shoulder, stopping him. "What in the world was that all about?" his father said, catching his breath.

Grover shook his head and started walking again. His father followed after him, walking along beside him. "Did Emma Lee say something? Or Clay?"

"I don't want to talk about it," Grover said.

"Was it something I did?" his father asked.

Grover stopped. "I don't know what it is. All I know is that for a little while tonight everything was okay. In fact, everything was really good, and then all of the sudden everything wasn't. And talking about it won't help!" Grover said, and started walking again. "Talking about things just makes them worse."

His father walked with Grover, but didn't say anything else. As they walked through downtown, Grover was vaguely aware of the brightly colored lights outlining buildings and hanging in storefronts. Christmas decorations made him feel left out.

"Daddy," Grover said, "if you like Leila, then do something about it."

They walked along for a little bit.

"Isn't it too soon?" their father asked.

"It'll always be too soon," Grover said.

"Won't it be strange for you and Sudie?" their father asked.

"Of course," Grover said.

After they'd walked three or four blocks, Grover began to calm down. He remembered his sister. "Where's Sudie?"

"The Roundtrees were going to drop her by Jessie's on their way back up the mountain," he said.

Grover felt foolish for ending the evening the way he had. The Roundtrees had gone back up the mountain, probably for good, and he hadn't even said good-bye. By the time Grover and his father walked across downtown, Grover felt too tired to be upset. His father must've sensed the change, because when they turned a corner and found a city bus idling there with the door open, his father put his hand on Grover's shoulder and said, "How about we ride the rest of the way home?"

Cold and tired, Grover nodded, and together they climbed into the light and the warmth of the bus. They were the only passengers.

His father dropped change into the change counter. Grover

always liked the sound of the coins tinkling against the glass. They sat a couple of seats behind the driver, a gray-haired man. The driver closed the door and pulled out into traffic.

After a while the bus driver looked up at them in his rearview mirror and said, "How y'all tonight?"

"Better," his father said, "now that we're on your bus and out of the cold." He patted Grover's knee.

"I know that's right," the bus driver said.

Grover yawned.

"Grover," his father said, "I want you to know that you don't ever have to take care of me. At least till it's time for the old folks home."

"Okay, Daddy," he said. As if all the night's events suddenly caught up with him, Grover felt exhausted. The bus rounded a corner, leaning him against his father. But even when the bus straightened out, he let his head stay on his father's shoulder.

Chapter Twenty

Bad News

Saturday, Grover spent all all morning in his workshop, remembering his father's warning to check for Mr. Lunsford's car. As usual, Sudie had come with him and was a lookout. Mr. Lunsford hadn't returned to the Bamboo Forest, at least as far as Grover could tell. Jessie, who'd come down a couple of times to walk through the hallway again, said Mr. Lunsford had always been a little afraid of their father.

Grover had continued to work hard, knowing it was only a matter of time—weeks or even days before Mr. Lunsford had the Bamboo Forest leveled. He felt like the man in "The Pit and the Pendulum," a story that Mrs. Caswell had had them read. The blade lowering, getting closer and closer. He could almost hear it. Wanting to make the most of the time he had left, he'd been working on his biggest weaving yet. Twelve feet wide and seven feet tall. The size of a small billboard. He'd had to a haul a stepladder into the Bamboo Forest to be able to weave in limbs high enough.

At lunchtime Sudie brought him a peanut butter and honey sandwich so he could keep working. After lunch Grover had just gotten started back working on the big weaving when Sudie called to him. "Someone's coming."

Grover started down the ladder.

"Never mind," Sudie called. "It's just Jessie."

Grover climbed back up the ladder.

"But he's bringing some people with him," Sudie called.

Grover jumped down off the ladder and ran to where Sudie sat on a rock, looking through their father's birding binoculars.

"You're never going to believe this!" She handed him the binoculars and when he finally focused on the group, he saw that Jessie was leading Mrs. Caswell, Miss Snyder and Mrs. Dillingham straight to the Bamboo Forest.

"Why's he bringing them?!" Grover whispered.

Sudie was already racing out of the Bamboo Forest to meet them. She ran up and gave Miss Snyder a hug.

Grover ran back to the workshop, packed up his tools, then, grabbing up his toolbox, started to make a run for it, but when he turned around, Jessie and the three women were there, looking at the big half-finished weaving behind him.

"Oh my Lord," Mrs. Caswell said, walking up to it and lightly touching it.

"Goodness," Miss Snyder said, looking at Grover and then back at the weaving.

"Astonishing," Mrs. Dillingham said.

"I brought these ladies over to get a look at your work," Jessie said.

Grover nodded but didn't really understand.

"Sudie," Jessie said, "why don't you show them Grover's gallery?"

"Sure," Sudie said. "This way." She showed them the entrance to the hallway, and the three women disappeared down the passageway with Sudie. Grover could hear them oohing and ahhing as they went deeper into the gallery. At one point he heard Mrs. Dillingham exclaim, "Miraculous!"

"I'm sorry to surprise you like this," Jessie said in a low voice to Grover. "I figured you wouldn't let me bring them if I told you ahead of time."

"Why?" Grover asked, feeling angry.

"People need to know what you're doing back here," Jessie said.

"But why'd you bring *them*?" Grover whispered. These were the last people on earth he'd ever want back here. His teacher. His counselor. His principal. And it wasn't even a school day.

"For one thing, I do their yards, and I've been telling them about your weavings for a while, and with Lunsford about to do away with the place . . ."

A flock of crows passed overhead, making a loud racket and settling on the far edge of the bamboo.

"You know when he's cutting it down?" Grover asked.

Jessie sighed. "I ran into a fellow yesterday walking around the edge of the Bamboo Forest. He told me Lunsford had hired him to clear this all out."

"Did he say when?" Grover asked, his heart feeling suddenly hollow.

Jessie looked at the ground. "Day after tomorrow."

"Monday?" Grover sat down on the big stump in the center of his workshop.

"I asked him if he'd mind giving me a call as soon as he was sure what time of day he'd be clearing it." Jessie sat down next to Grover.

After a little while, the women emerged with Sudie from the hallway. They surrounded him.

"What you've done here is remarkable," Mrs. Dillingham said.

"I'd heard about your weavings," Miss Snyder said, "but I'd had no idea."

"This is important work, Grover," Mrs. Caswell said. "People need to see this."

"Indeed," said Mrs. Dillingham.

Grover only half heard the women as he sat on the stump, looking around at the Bamboo Forest. Monday it would be gone. As the women left, Jessie said he'd go with them, that he needed to get back to work. Sudie followed them out, then returned in a minute and found Grover still sitting on the stump.

"I'm not working anymore," he said.

"You mean today?"

"Ever."

"Why not?"

"They're cutting it down on Monday."

"Oh," she said, sitting down on the stump beside him. They were quiet for a little while. Finally, Sudie said, "You need to finish this one." She nodded at the giant half-done weaving.

"What does it matter, Sudie?" he snapped. "I've been working on these weavings for weeks, and I've been working in the Bamboo Forest nearly all my life, and it's all going to be gone in a couple of days."

"You have the rest of today and tomorrow," she said. "Finish it."

He pushed himself up off the stump. "I have to go someplace," he said.

"Can I come?"

"No."

"Come on, Biscuit," she said, sounding hurt. "*Sesame Street*'s on." She stomped out of the Bamboo Forest.

Grover waited to be sure Sudie was gone, then headed up the street and turned in at Riverside. He hadn't visited his mother's grave in a while. The tapestries he'd made for her had all but fallen apart. The leaves and limbs had mostly disintegrated. Mainly what was left were the sturdy bamboo grids, tapestry skeletons. Grover sat down on a little wall and faced her headstone. He'd been thinking a lot lately about a night just a few days before she'd died.

It had been a Friday night. Their father had had to stay late at the Wolfe house and Sudie was spending the night up the street at Grace's. Grover and his mother had eaten supper and Grover was headed out the door. "I'm going up the street," he'd said. Sam had a new video game he wanted to show him.

"I was thinking we might play a game," his mother said.

"Like what?"

"Anything but Candy Land." Candy Land was the main game little kids wanted to play in her office.

"I told Sam I'd come up after supper," he said.

"How about checkers?" she asked. "Or Monopoly?"

"That takes so long."

"Scrabble?"

"I'm terrible at Scrabble."

"What about chess? Let's play chess. Come on, Grover, I play games all day but I never get to really try." She started to get the chess set out of the game cabinet.

"I told Sam I'd come up," Grover said. What he didn't say was that Sam had been telling him about his new Minesweeper video game all week. The other thing was that lately Grover'd found his parents more and more boring. The idea of playing a game with his mother on a Friday night when he could be up the street with his friend made him feel trapped.

Grover had walked up the street to Sam's that evening, glad to be out of the house and headed toward his friend's. If only he'd known, he would've played every single game in that cabinet with her. He thought about his father. He thought about Sudie. Even Jessie. What if something happened to one of them? What wasn't he doing with them now that he would regret later? Life, he was beginning to understand, was one long last chance.

‡   ‡   ‡

Grover was walking out of the cemetery when he saw Matthew raking up around some very old headstones in the Jewish section. At the sight of him, Grover felt a bolt of anger streak through him. He charged over to him.

"I know about you," Grover said.

Matthew stopped raking, pushed his glasses back on his nose and leaned on the rake as if he'd been expecting Grover.

"I know about you looking after Mama's grave," Grover said. "About you repairing my workshop. About you helping me get Emma Lee out of the burning house." With each thing he listed Grover heard himself become angrier. "And I know why."

Matthew looked at him calmly.

"My father told me you were the driver," Grover said. "He said it wasn't your fault."

"He didn't tell you everything," Matthew said matter-of-factly.

"Everything?"

Using the rake, Matthew picked up a handful of leaves and twigs, putting them into the wheelbarrow he'd been filling. "I had been answering my cell phone."

"What are you talking about?"

"I glanced down at my phone to see who was calling, and when I looked back, your mother was right there in front of the car." He motioned as if looking through the windshield at her.

Grover felt ambushed by this news. All he'd ever heard from his father, his friends, even the article that had run in the paper, was that the driver, who the paper had not named, wasn't at fault.

"I can't help thinking if I hadn't taken my eyes off the road . . ."

"Did you tell the police?" Grover asked, his throat tightening.

"I told the police. I told your father. I told anybody who would listen. They all said the same thing—that I would've hit her anyway. They all said no one could've stopped in time."

"You told my father?" Grover asked.

"He wouldn't press charges." Matthew sounded as if he'd wanted his father to press charges.

"You looked down at your cell phone?"

"I did."

"And then your car hit my mother."

"Yes."

Disturbed by something, a flock of crows erupted from a nearby tree, cawing loudly as they settled into a hemlock halfway across the cemetery.

"I haven't driven since the accident," Matthew said, "and will never own another cell phone as long as I live."

"Why tell me this?" Grover asked.

"I knew you wouldn't be afraid."

"Afraid?"

"The way I see it," Matthew said, putting another handful of leaves in the wheelbarrow, "my only chance of moving on is to tell the person who is likely to hate me the most." He glanced at Grover.

Grover just stood there, taking in the cemetery. The

headstones and monuments came into such sharp focus it almost hurt to look at them. And there it was, the something else that had been weaving itself into his feelings since the day of the accident, almost without him knowing.

"I'm to blame." Grover heard himself say it but he no more understood his words than if a stranger had spoken them.

"For what?" Matthew asked.

Grover felt a wall give way inside himself. "If I had gone to get the movie at Videolife like she'd asked, she wouldn't have gone on that walk," he said. "She wouldn't have been on Charlotte Street with the dog in the first place." This un-thought had been lying unspoken, hidden inside himself like a copperhead curled up in a Christmas tree.

A police car pulled into the gates, its blue lights silently swirling, and for a nanosecond Grover thought they'd come for him. But then came a hearse and a few solemn cars, their headlights shining. A funeral procession. Usually the lines of cars were much longer. The line for his mother's funeral had been too long to fit into the cemetery. People had had to park throughout the neighborhood.

"You don't have to do this," Matthew said as he watched the line of cars wind along the far side of the cemetery and disappear over a hill.

"Do what?" Grover asked.

"Try to make me feel better."

"Why would I care how you feel?!" Grover snapped. "You killed our mother!"

Matthew's eyes widened and it appeared to Grover that he almost smiled.

"I've about finished up here." The way Matthew looked around Riverside, Grover thought he meant he'd finished up at the cemetery. "I graduated," he said. "I'll be heading out in a couple of days."

"Good," Grover said, feeling confused and angry and something else he didn't have a name for. Having remembered one person's feelings he did care about, Grover began to trot up the little road. He happened to glance back and saw that Matthew had set his rake down and taken out a little notebook. He was bent beside a couple of headstones, scribbling away as if the dead were dictating to him.

‡   ‡   ‡

Sudie was sitting on the couch with Biscuit beside her, watching *Nova*, when Grover walked in and turned off the TV.

"Hey! I was watching that," Sudie said, clearly still mad.

"I have to finish that big weaving and I need your help."

"You were snotty," she said, staring at the dark TV screen. "You've been snotty a lot lately." Frowning, she pet Biscuit.

"I'm sorry," he said, sitting down on the couch beside her. "It's just that with the Bamboo Forest about to be—"

"Listen, just because you're not happy doesn't give you the right to make other people unhappy," she said, looking up at him. "I don't need help being sad." Her eyes reddened.

"But I need help finishing the big weaving."

She stared at the blank TV screen.

"Please," he said, petting Biscuit. "I can't finish it without you."

She glanced at him, then, pushing herself up from the couch, said, "I'm not doing this for you."

They worked in the Bamboo Forest till dark. Sudie got his flashlights and set them up, and they worked till their father, who'd had a big group of Rotarians he'd had to take through the Wolfe house, had come home late. He'd heard from Jessie that the Bamboo Forest was going to be cut down on Monday, so he'd brought home a bucket of Kentucky Fried Chicken and had taken it out to the Bamboo Forest so they could keep working.

"Amazing." Their father walked around the huge weaving as he chewed on a drumstick. He gave Grover and Sudie permission to work as late as they wanted.

Grover worked till about ten o'clock that night, and when Sudie yawned a couple of times, he told her to go inside.

She shook her head, yawning again.

Seeing that his sister could barely keep her eyes open, Grover looked at the weaving. Amazingly, it was nearly done. He could easily finish it tomorrow.

"Let's both go in," he said, cutting off his flashlights and gathering up his tools.

Sunday morning, Grover was up early. Sudie had told him to wake her, but when he tried, she moaned and turned over, so he left her. She'd worked so hard last night he knew she needed the extra sleep. As he walked out to his workshop in the early morning cold, he realized he needed a little alone time with the Bamboo Forest. As he began to work, he became aware that ever since his encounter with Matthew yesterday he'd felt a little better, as if a weight he hadn't even known he carried had been, if not removed, at least lightened.

Grover'd been working about an hour when he heard someone crash through the bamboo. Probably Sudie. She'd be mad that he hadn't woken her, but he'd let her do some of the last limbs and she'd calm down. Sam appeared at the edge of his workshop. He couldn't remember the last time Sam had come by.

"That's a huge one, Grover," Sam said, gently placing his hand on the weaving. "My dad told me that they're cutting this place down tomorrow."

Grover shrugged and turned back to his work. "I should've outgrown it by now."

Sam sat on the stump for a while, not talking, just watching Grover work. Finally he said, "I'd forgot how much I like this place." He watched Grover work a while longer, then said he'd see him tomorrow at school. It wasn't long after he left that Sudie came out. She was mad he hadn't woken her, but he let her weave the last couple of limbs and she calmed down. Then suddenly, the weaving was finished.

The two of them sat on the stump, looking at it.

After a while Grover turned to his sister. "Will you pray for the Bamboo Forest?"

"I already have," she said. "You should pray too."

"The only reason I'd be praying is because I'm desperate."

"God likes desperate people to pray," she said.

"How come?"

"Because they mean it."

CHAPTER TWENTY-ONE
VINCENT VAN GROVER

Grover had finished the math test ahead of everybody else and was sketching weavings in his notebook, checking the clock on the wall. Last night Jessie had called and told his father that the man he'd run into in the Bamboo Forest had called and said that he and his crew were cutting it down after lunch.

"But we have school," Grover'd said after his father had hung up with Jessie.

"That's just as well," his father said.

"I want to be there," Grover said.

"Me too," Sudie said.

Missing school was a big deal to his father. So Grover was surprised when he said he'd come get them out of school at noon tomorrow and bring them home in time to watch. That night Grover'd dreamed an army of bulldozers rumbled into the Bamboo Forest, flattened it and then gouged out the ground, tearing the bamboo up by its rhizomes.

He woke very early, dressed and arrived in the Bamboo Forest at the first purplish hint of dawn. He walked along the hallway touching the weavings, stopping in front of the big weaving Sudie had helped him finish last night. He sat on the stump in the middle of his workshop and listened to the wind rattle the bamboo. He'd been coming here since he was barely old enough to walk. He'd probably spent more time in the Bamboo Forest than he'd spent in his own house. At one point he smelled sandalwood, and after a while he heard his father call for him.

"Coming!" he called. Then he placed his hand flat on the stump and said, "Good-bye, old friend." And as he did, the breeze blew and the bamboo gave a long soft rattle, almost like a sigh.

When Grover's father appeared in his classroom doorway with Sudie, Grover felt a pit open in his stomach, like when the nurse at his doctor's office came into the waiting room and announced his name. Grover went back to the cloakroom for his knapsack and his coat. As he was walking out, Mrs. Caswell came over, put her hand on his shoulder and said, "We're with you."

When they got home, they walked up the street to where a couple of big trucks loaded with chain saws and other cutting tools were parked in front of the Bamboo Forest. They'd left Biscuit shut up in the house. The men, who were all Mexican Americans and who wore orange vests, hadn't started. They sat on the curb eating sandwiches and drinking from their thermoses and talking in Spanish. Jessie was there with them, talking to the man who Grover guessed was the boss. He was a big man with huge shoulders and a big belly too. He wasn't Mexican.

"Harold Sluder," Jessie said, "this is Walter Johnston and his daughter, Sudie, and his son, Grover."

"Pleased to meet y'all," the man said, shaking their father's hand. He had kind eyes and a gentle smile. "Sorry about this." He nodded toward the Bamboo Forest. "Looks like you've spent a whole lot of time down there, making it your own."

"A job is a job," their father said. Maybe he was thinking of his own job and whether he would keep it much longer.

Jessie checked his watch and looked toward the street. "Y'all want to walk through one more time?" He turned to the big man. "Mind if they walk through?"

"Go ahead," the man said. "We've waited this long. We can wait a few more minutes. The boys won't argue about a little longer lunch break."

Grover, Sudie and their father had started into the Bamboo Forest when there was a screech out on the street and the slam of a car door.

"Lunsford," their father said under his breath.

"What's going on, Sluder?" Mr. Lunsford said, walking up to the big man. "I said I wanted that bamboo down first thing this morning."

"We didn't finish up the job at your house till midday," he said. "And the boys had to have lunch."

"What are you doing here, Johnston?" Mr. Lunsford said, turning to Grover and Sudie. "We've already been through this."

"The kids wanted to say good-bye," their father said.

"Oh, good grief," said Mr. Lunsford. "The way y'all act

you'd think I'm cutting down the rain forest. It's a scrubby old patch of bamboo like a million other patches of bamboo around this town."

"Kids have been playing here for generations," Jessie said.

Mr. Lunsford turned to Mr. Sluder. "Well, what're you waiting for?"

Mr. Sluder nodded to the men, who got up slowly, putting away their lunch pails.

A chain saw started up and then a couple more. The men headed toward the Bamboo Forest. Jessie kept glancing at his watch and back toward the road. Sudie buried her head in her father's arms. Grover made himself watch as the bamboo fell away from the saw blades like the men were cutting through butter. The bamboo fell around them as they moved deeper into the cane. Grover watched as one of the men discovered the entrance to the hallway of tapestries. The man disappeared down the hallway and his chain saw went silent. The man called out in Spanish to the other workers and waved them over. They all disappeared down the hallway. Grover heard their excited voices but could understand only a few words.

"¡Increíble!"

"¡Milagroso!"

"¡Es muy bonita!"

"What's going on, Sluder?" Mr. Lunsford said. "Why have they stopped?"

Mr. Sluder disappeared into the Bamboo Forest. Grover heard him talking to them in Spanish. Finally, Mr. Sluder ambled back up. "They like what all the boy's done down in there. They're saying it reminds them of some of the weaving from back home. They say he's the real thing."

"Sluder," Lunsford said.

Mr. Sluder nodded curtly. "Yes, sir." He disappeared back into the Bamboo Forest. After a little while Mr. Sluder led the men out of the bamboo, and one by one they started up their chain saws. They cut slower than before, like their hearts weren't in it. Still they were doing it, cutting down the Bamboo Forest, foot by foot, yard by yard. It wouldn't be long before they'd be cutting away the tapestries. They'd cut about twelve feet into the grove when Grover felt the ground rumble beneath him. He turned around expecting to see bulldozers. A long line of school buses pulled up along the road. The buses all said *Isaac Claxton Elementary School* on the sides.

Children streamed off the buses and headed toward the Bamboo Forest.

Mr. Sluder shouted something to the men in Spanish, and the men all turned off their saws as the children poured past them and disappeared into the Bamboo Forest.

"Hold on there," Mr. Lunsford said, standing in front of the children, holding his arm out like a traffic cop. But the kids just flowed past him like a river around a rock.

"We thought it was time for a field trip, Commissioner Lunsford," Mrs. Caswell said, as she and several teachers stepped past Mr. Lunsford. As soon as the children entered the hallway of tapestries, they quieted, like they'd walked into a church. Sudie joined her class, showing them down the hallway like a tour guide. The kids walked along the hallway, gaping at the weavings.

"Whoa!"

"It's like . . . like art or something!"

"Looks like it's part of the bamboo."

"The bamboo grew some art!"

"Who did all these?"

"Sudie's brother."

"Grover did all these?"

"They look kind of like that *Starry Night* guy."

"Van Gogh."

"Vincent van Gogh."

"Vincent van *Grover*!"

Laughter.

"Vincent van Grover!"

"Vincent van Grover!

The Bamboo Forest rang with children's voices chanting "Vincent van Grover, Vincent van Grover, Vincent van Grover." The workers were all standing off to the side, watching and talking among themselves in Spanish.

Hearing Mr. Lunsford speaking angrily, Grover had walked back to where his father and Jessie stood facing the commissioner. "You planned this," Mr. Lunsford said, "didn't you, Johnston? Well, none of it makes a bit of difference. It's still my land and as soon as those kids are out of there . . . "

Grover heard the slam of more car doors. He looked up to see Byron from Reader's Corner getting out of a car, and Little

Bit with several of the Wolfe house tour guides getting out of another. Neighbors from the neighborhood walked from down the street. Grover noticed several store owners from the Grove Arcade and other downtown stores.

"So, Grover, on such an important occasion as your opening, why aren't you wearing your new coat?" It was Mr. Berkowitz. "Impress the girls and give me a little advertising." Grover noticed a glimmer of yellow at the back of the old man's neck. He was wearing his measuring tape underneath his coat.

"Where did all these people come from?" Grover looked at his father, who was looking at Jessie.

"I do a lot of yards," Jessie said, looking a little sheepish. "Oh, look who's here."

Mira's mother, the mayor of Asheville, was walking down the path.

"Oh, good," Mr. Lunsford said, turning to their father. "She can see firsthand the mischief you and your buddy have been up to."

"Mayor, you're just in time," Mr. Lunsford said, taking her by the elbow.

Mira, who'd been down in the Bamboo Forest, ran up to her mother. "Mama, you need to come see what Grover's done down here."

"I've heard, I've heard," the mayor said.

"So then you know that Johnston's kids have been—" Lunsford began.

"Good to see you, Walt." The mayor shook their father's

hand. "I hear the Wolfe house has been revived thanks to the Thomas Wolfe Christmas."

"But, Mayor," Mr. Lunsford interrupted.

"Commissioner Lunsford," the mayor said, taking Mr. Lunsford's hand. "I wanted to come down and personally thank you for your generosity. I just learned of your plans to donate this land to the city."

"Donate?"

"Is that not accurate?" the mayor asked. "I was told—"

"Look!" Daniel Pevoe called out. "Channel Thirteen is here!"

A dressed-up news anchor and a man carrying a camera got out of a van that said *News 13* along the side. They came down the path toward them.

"Hello, Mayor and Commissioner Lunsford, you're just the people I was hoping to see," the newswoman said. "We're here about the land the commissioner is donating for a children's park."

"Children's park?!" Mr. Lunsford said.

"Do you mind if we ask you a few questions?" the woman said.

The cameraman had turned his bright lights on Mr. Lunsford. A crowd of kids and adults gathered to watch. The newswoman turned toward the camera and said, "We're here on Edgemont Road, where a group of children and teachers from Isaac Claxton Elementary as well as people from across Asheville have gathered to celebrate Commissioner Lunsford's donation of his property for a new children's park." She turned to Mr. Lunsford, whose face had gone pale. "Commissioner, why did you decide to donate this valuable piece of property to the city?"

Mr. Lunsford looked at the camera and smiled a weak smile.

"The commissioner is too modest to say it," Jessie said, stepping into the camera light and putting his hand on Commissioner Lunsford's shoulder, "but this whole thing is his idea."

"And who are you, sir?" The woman tilted the microphone in Jessie's direction.

"Jessie Cole," he said. "A fan of Commissioner Lunsford."

A fan? Grover mouthed to his father.

"In his capacity as commissioner Mr. Lunsford had noticed that development was swallowing up empty lots where children once played. So he decided to set an example, and instead of selling this lot, he decided to donate this valuable piece of property as a Christmas gift to the children of the neighborhood."

Different expressions flitted across the commissioner's face— puzzlement then anger then astonishment then resignation.

"A Christmas gift to the city," the newswoman repeated. "We also have on hand Mayor Hodges." The woman motioned for the mayor to step up to the microphone. "Mayor, I have to assume you're excited about the commissioner's donation." The woman held up the microphone to Mira's mother.

"Most certainly," the mayor said. "It is an extraordinary act of generosity and kindness. Clearly, Commissioner Lunsford puts the children of Asheville first."

"Commissioner, do you have anything to say?" The woman held out the microphone.

Grover'd noticed that the commissioner had been smiling bigger and bigger since Jessie had said that about a Christmas gift to the city, as if he was already reading tomorrow's headlines in the *Asheville Citizen-Times*: COMMISSIONER DONATES CHRISTMAS GIFT TO ASHEVILLE'S CHILDREN.

He leaned into the microphone. "I remember when I was a little fella we kids ran around in the woods all day. We didn't need toys. We didn't need video games. We didn't need a thing but our imaginations. Well, there aren't all that many woods left to run around in anymore. So I figured what better way to make use of this land, this valuable land, I might add, than to donate it to Asheville's most treasured resource." He paused and patted the head of a little girl who happened to be standing beside him. "Our children."

"Commissioner," the newswoman asked, "do you envision this as a playground with swings and slides and other playground equipment?"

Mr. Lunsford opened his mouth as if to speak but Jessie stepped up. "The commissioner thought it would be best to leave the land as it is. Kids need some left-alone places. A childlife refuge, you might say."

The commissioner eyed Jessie.

"A childlife refuge?" the newswoman asked, tilting the microphone toward Mr. Lunsford, but Jessie leaned in.

"The commissioner is too humble to admit it but he came up with the idea himself," Jessie said. "In fact, he's going to propose to the commissioners in their next meeting that the city sponsor a Childlife Refuge Program through which landowners can donate undeveloped land to set aside for children to play in and receive a tax write-off."

"What a fascinating concept," the newswoman said. "How on earth did you come up with such an idea, Commissioner?"

Mr. Lunsford looked at Jessie as if he was too stunned to talk. But then he turned to the microphone and said, "It just came to me."

The mayor said a few more things and then the interview was over. As soon as the camera lights went off, the commissioner sort of collapsed like a balloon losing air. He glared at Jessie and seemed about to say something, but then all the people who'd been watching the interview came up to shake the commissioner's hand and pat him on the back and more than one of them said, *You have my vote next year*.

Grover watched as the men with the orange vests loaded their chain saws and Weed Eaters and sling blades back onto their trucks. Grover felt a hand on his shoulder. Mr. Sluder leaned over and said under his breath, "Between you and me, this is one job I don't mind leaving unfinished." He climbed into his pickup truck and pulled away, and the rest of the big trucks followed him.

As Grover watched them drive off, it finally hit him. The Bamboo Forest wasn't going to be cut down. He felt a rush of air and light, like a door had been flung open somewhere inside him, a door that had been closed so tight for so long that he'd forgotten it was there.

Sudie grabbed Grover's hands and was jumping up and down. "I can't believe it!"

Grover couldn't help laughing.

"I'd like to show y'all something," Jessie said to the

newswoman and the cameraman. "Do you have a minute?" Jessie motioned for Sudie and Grover to follow them. Sudie started after them but Grover stayed where he was. It was all he could do to try and comprehend what had just happened. The Bamboo Forest was about to be cut down, then it wasn't. Something was about to be dead, then it wasn't. How could that be? That's when he noticed that Jessie was leading the newswoman in the direction of his weavings.

"Why's he showing her my work?" Grover asked Mira, who happened to be standing beside him.

"Grover," Mira said, "your weavings aren't a secret anymore." She nodded toward the Bamboo Forest, where a long line of children and adults waited to walk through the hallway of tapestries. "Hey, where are you going?"

Feeling too much, Grover walked out of the Bamboo Forest and headed up the street. He passed by the parked school buses and the news van and all the cars lining both sides of the street. Even as he got farther up the street, he could still hear the crowd. It sounded like a huge party being held in the Bamboo Forest. Grover never felt comfortable at parties.

He turned in at the Riverside gates and walked along a path, his hands stuck deep in his coat pockets. What had just happened? Jessie had saved the Bamboo Forest. That was pretty clear. Grover couldn't have been more relieved. But what was the uneasy feel underneath it all?

Instead of heading for his mother's grave, Grover stopped in front of Thomas Wolfe's headstone.

"Feels so strange," Grover said to the writer's headstone. "All this attention."

Grover sat down on the little wall that enclosed the Wolfe family plot. He needed to think. He was of course glad that the men hadn't cut down the Bamboo Forest. Still, something gnawed at him. He didn't mind family and friends looking at his weavings or even his teachers really, but having half of Asheville walk around in the Bamboo Forest looking at his work was unnerving, even kind of painful. Something private that had been between him and the bamboo was not his anymore. His weavings and the world he'd created them in had gotten away from him.

Crows cawed from a nearby hemlock, and a breeze swayed its shaggy limbs. Grover sat there for he wasn't sure how long. After a while, the murmur of the crowd softened. Car doors banged shut out in the street and then the ground shook as buses headed back to Claxton. People were leaving but they were taking something with them. He realized now what Jessie must have known for some time: The only way to save the Bamboo Forest had been to lose it.

‡ ‡ ‡

That night, Grover had trouble sleeping. He kept going over all that had happened in the Bamboo Forest. It was too much, so he slipped out of bed, dressed, grabbed his flashlights and his toolbox, tiptoed through the dark house, opened the door very quietly and headed out to the Bamboo Forest. But as he walked toward it, he noticed light flitting through the bamboo, and for a moment his heart stopped. A fire! He ran, but as he neared the bamboo he realized it wasn't a fire but a flashlight. He slowed and, moving as quietly as he could, stepped into the hallway of tapestries. Light glowed from around the curved hallway. For a moment he didn't recognize the man in a coat, shining a flashlight on a tapestry, was his own father. His father studied the tapestry, then walked up to it and gently ran his hand over it.

His father saw him. He looked almost embarrassed, as if Grover had caught him at something. "What are you doing out here?" his father asked.

"Couldn't sleep," Grover said, walking up beside him. "Thought I might do a little work." He set down his toolbox.

"An eventful day," his father said. He shined the flashlight on the next tapestry. "These weavings of yours are really quite remarkable." His father sounded as if he was seeing them for the first time, and in all the years Grover had been making things, never had he seen his father pay this kind of attention to anything he'd made.

"So much to notice," his father said as they walked along the hallway, looking at each one by his father's flashlight. There was something about seeing them in the dark out here with his father that gave Grover a whole new appreciation of his weavings. Already, they felt like they'd been done by someone else.

"So intricate," his father said, stopping in front of another one. "The more you look, the more you see."

As they came to the end of the hall Grover sighed and looked around him. "I can't believe Jessie was able to save this place."

His father frowned. "Jessie didn't save it. You did."

"Me?" Grover said.

His father pointed the flashlight beam along the hallway of tapestries. "If it wasn't for your artwork, no one would've ever understood the importance of the Bamboo Forest. No one would've understood what can grow out of a place like this."

It hadn't occurred to Grover that he'd played any part in saving the Bamboo Forest. Earlier today, as all the students and teachers and neighbors and friends had filed through this hallway, he'd felt like a bystander, a helpless bystander at that. The idea that his weavings might've helped save this place cast a new light on all the years he'd been coming out here, driven by nothing more than the urge to put things together. Without Grover understanding quite how, his work had taken on a life of its own.

A siren started up in the distance, a dog barked somewhere and the bamboo rustled with the breeze. Standing there with his father, Grover felt he'd moved to the center of something. His mind, which had been racing in so many directions all day, was suddenly still.

His father yawned. "I better hit the hay. You staying out here to work a little?" Grover couldn't help yawning himself and as he did, a welcome wave of exhaustion came over him. "I'll come with you," he said. After all, he reminded himself, the Bamboo Forest will be here tomorrow.

‡ ‡ ‡

The next day, Grover rolled the wheelbarrow to the cemetery to clear off the remnants of the tapestries he'd carried over to their mother's grave these many months. Mostly what was left were the bamboo frames, which seemed to be pretty much intact. He had the idea that he could recycle them and weave in new green leaves in the spring. He'd loaded up the wheelbarrow and was on his way out of the cemetery. But when he passed by the Wolfe plot, he noticed a letter propped against Thomas Wolfe's headstone. Seeing no one around, he picked up the note. It was addressed to *Mr. Thomas Wolfe* and it was sealed. He paused. The notes weren't usually sealed, which made him think it was private and he started to set it back down. But before he knew what he was doing, he tore open the letter. Written in blocked and shaky print, it said,

Dear Mr. Wolfe—Clara, my wife of fifty-two years, died a few weeks ago. She loved your books. She read them and reread them every few years like she was revisiting a close friend. She tried to get me to read them but I was never a big reader. Even so, now that she's gone I've been reading Look Homeward, Angel. *It's slow going but sometimes I'll come across a comment Clara scribbled in the margins, and it'll be like hearing her voice. She's buried nearby. I thought you'd want to know you have an admirer in the neighborhood.*

Gratefully,
Paul Fallon

"Reading someone else's mail?"

Grover whirled around and found Matthew standing there.

"I'd say you have a pretty high startle response," Matthew said, pushing his wire-rim glasses up on his nose.

"I thought you were gone." Grover's heart pounded as he stuck the letter back in the envelope and leaned it against Wolfe's headstone. He felt irritated, even angry. He picked up the wheelbarrow and started walking quickly toward the entrance.

"I came by to tell you something," Matthew said, walking along beside him.

Grover didn't slow down. He didn't want to hear whatever Matthew had to tell him. Every time this guy opened his mouth Grover's world was turned upside down.

"You aren't to blame for what happened to your mother," Matthew said.

Grover stopped the wheelbarrow. "Because you are?"

"No," Matthew said.

"Then who's to blame?"

"I was in the middle of a history exam last week," he said. "One essay question was 'Who was responsible for dropping the atomic bomb on Hiroshima?' At first I thought how could that be an essay question? It was a two-word answer—Harry Truman. But then I got to thinking that the pilots and crew of the *Enola Gay* actually dropped the bomb. Or you could blame Einstein for writing Roosevelt about the possibility of such a bomb in the first place. Or you could blame Oppenheimer or the guys at Oak Ridge. Or you could blame the American people, who didn't want more GIs dying on foreign soil. Or you could even argue that the Japanese brought it on themselves. You could argue that all of humanity dropped that bomb. You could say everybody was to blame. Or . . ." He looked at Grover with his eyebrows raised. ". . . you could say that nobody was to blame."

"I don't see what the atomic bomb has to do with who killed my mother," Grover said.

"When terrible things happen we want to blame somebody, even if that somebody is us. But what if nobody is to blame?"

"Somebody definitely dropped the atom bomb," Grover said.

"Maybe so," Matthew said. "But does that mean they're to blame?"

"I don't know what you're talking about." Grover started pushing the wheelbarrow. A big flock of crows flew over them, veered away to a corner of the cemetery, landing high in a hemlock, making a loud ruckus as if unsettled by something.

Grover and Matthew passed a few family plots, and stopped in front of a new headstone that Matthew nodded to.

CLARA NORTON FALLON
MARCH 10, 1935 – NOVEMBER 29, 2011

The letter writer's wife. She'd died just a few weeks ago.

"What I came to tell you is this," Matthew said. "Sometimes things just happen."

"Maybe you just want to feel better," Grover said.

"Is that a bad thing to want?" Matthew asked.

They walked out the cemetery gates, where a faded gray Honda Civic wagon sat parked. The car was crammed with boxes and clothes and piles of what must've been history books.

"I thought you said you'd stopped driving?" Grover asked.

"Until I figured out that nobody else was going to get me to where I needed to go."

A thought occurred to Grover. "Was this the car that . . . ?" He touched the hood.

Matthew sighed, held his hand out to Grover and said, "So long."

Grover looked at Matthew's hand but couldn't bring himself to shake it.

"I don't blame you," Matthew said, then got in his car and started it, the muffler rattling. He was backing up when all of the sudden Grover ran after him, banging on the driver's-side window. Matthew stopped the car and rolled down his window.

Grover looked at him. "So long."

Matthew pushed his glasses up on his nose and nodded.

Grover watched the car rattle down the street. Even after Matthew had driven out of sight, his words hung in the cold air, taking real form, so that Grover could read them as clearly as if they'd been etched into a headstone. *Sometimes things just happen.*

CHAPTER TWENTY-TWO

BE THAT WAY

It was the last day of school before Christmas holidays. Grover had delivered some reports to the main office for Mrs. Caswell, and on his way back, Miss Snyder waved him into her office and handed him an article she'd cut out of the *Citizen-Times*. "I figured you couldn't have too many copies," she said. "I thought they did a great job."

As part of the big segment about Mr. Lunsford donating the land for the park, the TV people had done a tiny bit on Grover and his weavings. Then the *Citizen-Times* had sent out a reporter and a photographer and run a big two-page article with color pictures. In the past couple of days a lot of people had come by to see his weavings. At first he didn't like being interrupted, but as more people came by, he became kind of used to it. The more people looked at his weavings, the more it felt like the weavings weren't his anymore, like they belonged to everybody who came to see them. What he figured out was that the only weaving that

— 285

really mattered to him was the weaving he was working on at the moment.

"I have something else for you," Miss Snyder said. She went to the wall behind her desk, took down his mother's calendar and handed it to him. He flipped through the pages, looking at Van Gogh's paintings and his mother's neat pencil handwriting.

"How are you doing?" Miss Snyder asked.

"Okay," he said. *The Starry Night* was the picture for December. He always loved that painting; all the circles of light against the dark made it feel alive. "It'll be our first Christmas without her," he was surprised to hear himself say.

Miss Snyder didn't say anything for a little bit. "What will that be like?"

"Hard," Grover said, "at least for Sudie."

He felt her looking at him.

He sighed and said, "Hard for me too."

They talked a while longer and toward the end of their conversation Miss Snyder handed him a little card with her name and cell phone number on it. "If Sudie or you need anything over the holidays or you just want to talk, give me a call."

"Okay," he said, knowing this was something Miss Snyder probably didn't do for most kids. He put the card in his pocket and started to walk out, but then he turned around and, hardly knowing what he was doing, hugged her. Then feeling his face flush, he picked up the calendar and the article and walked quickly down the hall, not turning around when she called him to wish him a merry Christmas.

He walked back toward his classroom in a daze. What was that all about? Since when did he go around hugging counselors? He walked into his classroom and sat down at his desk in a daze.

"Be that way," said a familiar voice. "Don't say a word."

Grover whirled around and for a minute thought he was seeing things, because there, right back in her old desk, was Emma Lee.

‡   ‡   ‡

Grover and Sudie had planned to meet their father at the Wolfe house to celebrate the end of school, and they talked Clay and Emma Lee into coming with them. As they walked up Montford, Clay explained that the Roundtrees were moving back to Asheville. He said that Emma Lee and he and even their grandmother had been saying to their mother that they should move back, and Leila had seemed to be thinking about it. "But after that night when we all went to Bean Streets after the Christmas Waltz, and Mama and your daddy didn't hardly talk, and Grover walked out and your daddy went after him . . ."

"What was that about anyway?" Emma Lee asked Grover. "All of the sudden you just got up and left."

"*Anyhow,*" Clay said, "after that night at Bean Streets, Mama seemed dead set on not moving back. But your daddy started calling."

"He called every night at ten o'clock on the dot," Emma Lee said.

Grover remembered hearing his father on the phone in the kitchen with the door closed. He'd thought he was making work phone calls, although he remembered thinking he was calling people pretty late. He also remembered thinking how his father laughed more than he usually did when he made work calls. But then he'd been laughing more in general, since Mr. Lunsford had stopped threatening to close the Wolfe house.

"At first Mama and your daddy hardly said a word," Clay said. "But your daddy kept calling and each time Mama got off the phone, she seemed a little better. Then one morning last week she said we were moving back."

As they passed Reader's Corner, Byron rapped on the window and waved at them. She pointed to the article she'd taped to the window. There were several photos, including one of Grover and Sudie standing in front of the biggest weaving.

"Hey, we read that," Emma Lee said. "You're famous!" She elbowed Grover.

They'd walked a little farther up Montford, and as they passed Videolife, the clerk with the pointy beard came out. "Your weavings blew my mind," he said to Sudie and Grover. He handed Sudie a little wrapped package. "Merry Christmas."

Sudie being Sudie, she immediately unwrapped it. "*Fantastic Mr. Fox*!"

The sight of the DVD sent Grover's heart racing. Maybe this was the very copy of the movie their mother had been on her way to pick up. The very copy Grover himself should've picked up the day before.

"We don't have any money with us," Grover said to the clerk.

"It's a gift," the clerk said.

"But . . ."

"Please," Sudie said. "Can't we keep it?"

"We over-ordered copies," the clerk said. Then he leaned over and, lowering his voice, said to Grover, "I was working here the day your mother was hit. I was the one who answered the phone when your father called, asking if your mother had come in yet. Your mother and I used to have long talks about movies. She had excellent taste."

"Can I keep the movie?" Sudie asked, studying the back of the DVD case.

Grover looked at the clerk and then back at Sudie, and as he did he heard Matthew's *Sometimes things just happen.* Something lifted in him. "I guess it won't hurt anything," he said.

Sudie hadn't waited for his answer to start tucking the DVD into her knapsack.

When they reached the Wolfe house, Little Bit told them their father had someone in his office and that they could wait in the break room, that she'd bought a brand-new box of powdered doughnuts. The Wolfe house wasn't as busy as it had been the day Grover's class had come. Attendance had gone down with school about to be out. Even so, there were two church groups and several families.

Mr. Lunsford walked in the front door as they headed to the break room.

"Come on," Grover whispered, motioning for them to hurry

up. Just as Grover thought he'd made it into the safety of the break room, someone caught his arm.

"Saw the big spread in the paper," said Mr. Lunsford, like he was impressed. He started talking to Little Bit. Grover couldn't believe Mr. Lunsford was making small talk with her, asking her how her day had been, asking about her family. Grover's father had told him that Mr. Lunsford was a changed man.

Mr. Lunsford had been all over the TV and the newspaper for donating the land for the children's park. The headline in the paper had read GENEROUS COMMISSIONER A MODEL OF CHRISTMAS SPIRIT. The Atlanta and Charlotte papers had run articles about county commissioners passing the Childlife Refuge Program. The Associated Press had even run an article and Mr. Lunsford had been getting calls from all over the country to come speak about the Childlife Refuge Program. Grover's father said Mr. Lunsford had gotten so much attention for being the Generous Commissioner that he had become . . . well . . . generous.

Only after talking with Little Bit a while about her grandchildren did Mr. Lunsford ask if their father was in.

"He has someone with him," Little Bit said. "He has an appointment after this one as well."

"Tell him that Delbert stopped by to see if he needed anything," Mr. Lunsford said, wished Little Bit a nice day and left.

Little Bit shook her head. "I can't get over how much that man's changed."

His father stuck his head out of his office, whispering, "Is he gone?"

"He said to tell you that *Delbert* stopped by," said Little Bit.

"Why were you hiding?" Sudie asked.

"He comes by two or three times a day, asking if he can do anything," their father said. "I'm starting to think I prefer the old Lunsford."

Leila came out from their father's office, wearing her nurse's uniform. She must've come over from St. Joseph's and they'd met for lunch. She looked sort of embarrassed and happy at the same time. The six of them walked over to Bean Streets and ordered hot chocolates, and like the last time, it was crowded and the four kids sat at one table and Leila and their father sat across the room. Unlike the last time, Leila and their father talked and when they weren't talking they were just looking each other in the eyes. Grover was pretty weirded out.

When a family got up from the checkerboard table, Clay and Sudie went over to play, leaving Grover and Emma Lee alone.

"They sure seem different," Grover said.

"You can say that again," Emma Lee said.

"They sure seem—"

"Very funny." Emma Lee sipped her hot chocolate.

"I never thanked you for coming to the Christmas Waltz," Grover said.

"No, you didn't."

"Thank you," he said.

She looked up at him.

"I mean it," he said.

"It was a really nice night," she said. "The nicest night I think I've ever had."

"The kids still talk about your grandmother's dress," Grover said.

Emma Lee's face reddened a little.

Grover's father burst into laughter at something Leila had said.

"It's strange for me too, you know," Emma Lee said, cutting her eyes toward their parents.

Grover didn't know what to say. He felt selfish having not given much thought about how it might be strange for Emma Lee and Clay too.

"Still," Emma Lee said, her face softening. "Your father's a good man."

"I guess so," Grover said.

"No guessing about it," she said. "I know a good man when I see one." Emma Lee looked at Grover.

"Did God tell your mother it was okay to move back?" he asked.

"Mama hasn't brought up God much lately."

Out of the corner of his eye, Grover saw his father lean over and cover Leila's hand with his own for a moment.

"Guess this means we'll have to be just friends," Grover said.

"Were we ever anything else?"

Grover felt his face burning. "Well . . . I guess I just . . ."

Emma Lee laughed, and he knew she was messing with him. But then her face went serious and she leaned toward him and lowering her voice said, "Grover. You and me aren't *just* friends."

"We aren't?"

"Never will be."

"No?"

"We're *good* friends. And no matter what happens . . ." She glanced toward their parents. ". . . we'll stay that way."

‡   ‡   ‡

"Are you going to marry Leila?" Sudie asked, carrying the wreath.

Their father laughed.

It was Christmas Eve afternoon, a clear but warm December day. Their father and Sudie had bought a wreath with a red bow on it at the grocery store, and on their way over to Riverside Cemetery had stopped by and gotten Grover, who had been working in the Bamboo Forest.

"No, sweetheart," their father said, pulling her against him.

"You're not?" Sudie said.

"You sound a little disappointed," he said.

"I like Leila," Sudie said. "I like her a lot."

"What about you, Grover?" their father asked. "Do you like Leila?"

Grover shrugged.

As they walked out of the Bamboo Forest they passed by the big wooden sign the city workmen had installed where the For Sale signs had stood. The sign read

Lunsford Park

A Childlife Refuge

Biscuit walked over to the sign, sniffed around it for a minute, then lifted his leg and peed.

They walked through Riverside and when they reached their mother's grave, Grover moved aside what was left of his old weavings, and then Sudie leaned the wreath against the headstone.

"Why aren't you and Leila getting married?" Sudie asked.

"We're just getting to know each other."

"Did you and Mommy have to get to know each other?" Sudie asked.

Grover rolled his eyes.

"Yes, we did."

"How long did that take?" Sudie asked.

"A couple of years," their father said, looking at the gravestone, his face emptying out.

"A couple of years? Oh, that's forever."

Then their father said, "I want you and Grover to know that if I ever do want to marry someone I would never do it without y'all's permission."

"*Our* permission!" Sudie smiled like she thought this was silly. "Parents are the ones who give permission."

"Not in this case," said their father.

"Would you need us to sign a permission slip?" Sudie grinned.

Grover hadn't been surprised that Sudie had asked if they might get married. Leila and their father had been going for walks every evening after supper, and a couple of times they'd gone out to supper alone. It all made Grover feel pretty unsettled, but he had to admit that his father had seemed happier and more like his old self. Grover kind of understood what his father was feeling. At night whenever Grover went out to the kitchen for a glass of milk and some Oreos or a late-night bowl of cereal, he'd stop by the front window to see the lights on in the Roundtrees' house. Just knowing they were over there made him sleep better.

"Guess we better get back," their father said, glancing at his watch. "I told Jessie we'd come over at six." They were having Christmas Eve dinner at Jessie's, and the Roundtrees were coming too, along with Mrs. Sparks, who'd come down from Bakersville and was spending Christmas with them.

Grover turned to their father, wanting to offer him something. "I'm glad the Roundtrees moved back," he said.

Their father put his hand on Grover's shoulder.

They started to leave but Sudie ran back, leaned down and kissed their mother's headstone. "Merry Christmas, Mama." She squatted there for a minute, but her eyes didn't redden and her lips didn't tremble. Biscuit came up beside her and sat.

"You know that dream I used to have?" Sudie said, standing back up.

"The one where Mama gets in the car with us?" Grover asked.

"Yeah," Sudie said. "I don't have that dream anymore."

"You don't?" Grover asked.

"I didn't know you'd been having a dream about your mother," their father said.

"Just about every night since she died," Sudie said.

"Well, where have I been?"

"Away," Sudie said. "You've been away." She looked at the headstone for a second. "But it's all right," she said, taking Grover's hand. "My brother's been here the whole time."